The Wilful Lady

Here on the boards of the landing was a patch of fresh blood; and dragged away from this a trail or smear through the doorway into the chamber beyond, where there was a sound of dreadful coughing and women's voices. Within were three of them weeping about the lieutenant, one holding a candle and another kneeling by him to support his head; a haggard bitch but handsome at one time and plain to see what she was now. As for the sad fellow himself, it was just as plain. Struck in the back outside the door I concluded, a grievous wound soaking his coat in red on the faded blue, then fallen to the ground to drag himself in here as far as the pallet bed; so to cling there half on it and half on his face, and clutching at the mattress. He was still living; but, if I was any judge, not for long.

Other titles in the Walker British Mystery Series

J.G. JEFFREYS
The Wilful Lady

WALKER AND COMPANY · NEW YORK

First published in the United States of America in 1975 by the
Walker Publishing Company, Inc.

ISBN: 0-8027-3035-3

Library of Congress Catalog Card Number: 75-12190

Printed in the United States of America

10 9 8 7 6 5 4 3 2 1

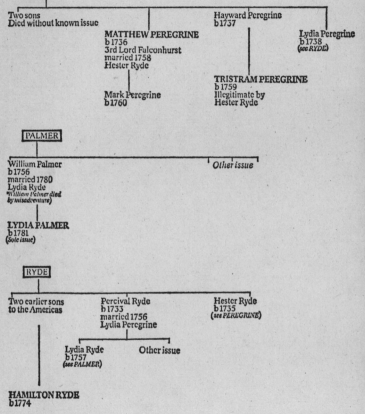

PEREGRINE — LORD FALCONHURST

2nd Lord Falconhurst
Died by suicide

Two sons
Died without known issue

MATTHEW PEREGRINE
b 1736
3rd Lord Falconhurst
married 1758
Hester Ryde

Hayward Peregrine
b 1757

Lydia Peregrine
b 1738
(see RYDE)

TRISTRAM PEREGRINE
b 1759
Illegitimate by
Hester Ryde

Mark Peregrine
b 1760

PALMER

William Palmer
b 1756
married 1780
Lydia Ryde
*William Palmer died
by misadventure)*

Other issue

LYDIA PALMER
b 1781
(Sole issue)

RYDE

Two earlier sons
to the Americas

Percival Ryde
b 1733
married 1756
Lydia Peregrine

Hester Ryde
b 1735
(see PEREGRINE)

Lydia Ryde
b 1757
(see PALMER)

Other issue

HAMILTON RYDE
b 1774

The inter-relations of the PEREGRINE, PALMER and RYDE families
as delineated for Mr Jeremy Sturrock by Mr Ashmole Fossdyck of
the College of Heralds. The persons appearing in this Memoir
are set in bold type.

A simple country maiden, so rosy and so neat,
    With a hey, hey, hey, hey Oh...
She went to church and Sunday school,
And sang this anthem sweet
    There's fire down below.

The parson was a misery so scraggy and so thin
    With a hey, hey, hey, hey Oh...
He said look here you people
If you lead a life of sin,
    There's fire down below.

He took his text from Malachi, and pulled a weary face
    With a hey, hey, hey, hey Oh...
I took my leave and sailed away,
That's how I fell from Grace,
    And there's fire down below.

There's fire in the galley, and in the cabin too,
    With a hey, hey, hey, hey Oh...
There's no fire in the forepeak,
And it's cold on the crew ...
    But there's fire down below.

Adapted from a nineteenth century
sea shanty

CHAPTER ONE

I have been requested by several admirers to relate some account of one of my adventures and mysteries different from the ordinary run of mere bankers or vulgar highwaymen; the first villains being too much with us these days, and the last being as common as horse-flies on every street corner. It is always my wish to combine the best instruction in the Art and Science of Detection with genteel entertainment, to say nothing of such moral and philosophical observations as I let fall freely from time to time, so here then is a particular touching and romantic tale. It concerns an uncommon pretty wench and a just as uncommon gang of villains, an attempt to rob her of her inheritance and her virtue, if nothing worse, and the damnedest, ugliest raw boned Scots physician you ever saw in love.

As I recollect the occasion I was at Hanover Square attending a musical soirée given by Lady Dorothea Dashwood, Lady Dorothea Hookham as was, on the afternoon of Wednesday September 17, 1802. London then was full of fashion and the troubles of war stilled for a while with the Peace of Amiens—but not for long if I was any judge, for though our Jolly Tars had whipped that rascal Bonaparte off the seas and given him a bloody nose or two in Egypt he was already up to his tricks again—and the weather unseasonable hot, sulphurous and still. It was a most polite affair; twenty or thirty ladies and gentlemen seated all ears and a rustle of silks and muslins in Lady Dorothea's drawing-room, and this being an elegant apartment with every evidence of taste and refinement done out after the modern style of Mr Adam.

Our Lady Dorothea is a famous blue stocking and what is worse a female radical Whig with her noddle stuffed full of Frenchy notions of equality and suchlike nonsensicals, and a perfect passion for doing good whether you like it or not; but a virtuous soul other-

9

wise. Along with her duenna or companion Miss Harriet—a sharpish little ancient lady of whom we shall hear again soon—she is forever surrounded by a rabble of philosophers, doctors, encyclopaedists, and penny pinched scribblers who will write you a book about anything for a guinea a week, while I am bidden to her salons now and again as not so long since I rendered her a small service; namely to save a certain gentleman from the troubles he had brought upon himself. This same gentleman she has now trained into a fair to middling husband and even found him a seat in the House of Commons; and about the best place for him. Nor is it true, as some of her vulgar critics say, that she has a face like a horse's arse. Like a horse if you please, but not its hinder parts; and moreover lit with a singular sweet and generous smile.

So you are to see me sitting at ease with the best, and reflecting on my own wits and the Hand of Providence in rising from nothing to this present eminence; a master of the Art and Science of Detection, ornament of the Bow Street Police Force, and one of the two bodyguards to that most kindly gentleman His Majesty King George III, God bless him. My old father was a costermonger, indifferent honest but not a lot in his head, and even at a tender age I soon perceived that your end in the Spittalfields is most likely either by way of the rope or transportation, pox or the cholera and I had no great notion of any of these. I set out to improve myself, learning my letters with a scrivener and lodging with a silk weaver's family, but was flung out of this with a boot up my breech one bitter night for trying also to improve their youngest daughter under the table. A matter they need not have been so nice about as there was nine of 'em to choose from; but it was the Forethought of Providence again for next I turned to the law and took up with a drunken old lawyer's clerk, though a very learned man who taught me much before he at last died of a flux of gin.

By then being a fine sturdy young fellow, as knowing in the wickedness of London as anybody, and as handy with a lively wench as with my fists, I applied for recruitment to the Bow Street Runners—the Robin Redbreasts or Thieftakers first founded by

Mr Henry Fielding—and thus began my rise to fame. A proper man in bed, at board or in a rude encounter; of genteel manner with the ladies, nobility and landed gentry, yet a terror to evil doers; coat and britches cut by Mr Yorke of Piccadilly, pistols by Wogdon, and an informed critic of the drama as I have often discussed its finer points with Mr Sheridan himself—though there is little enough in that for, like the common talk of the Bank of England presently, the poor man is head over his heels in debt.

Along with this other refined company then I am giving my ears, and wishing I could stop 'em, to a lady of majestic amplitude in a chemise gown, cross gartered sandals and Grecian fillet, who is swinging her tits with wind and passion, and pouring out her soul in German; a useful language for the exercise. This being an accomplishment I do not have, the gentleman alongside was kindly pleased to advise me that the song concerned an innocent maiden who got herself with a rising bun in the oven by the old watermill and then, deceived of her lover, heaved herself into the raging flood and was thereupon turned into a bird; of what kind I never made out but to judge by the squawks it should have been a magpie. The applause for this pathetic relation at last hushed, she was followed by Signor Alberto Tomaso, a fellow reputed to put all the drawing-rooms in a swoon, and he set about his fiddle with such a scraping, screeching and wailing of arpeggios, scales, glissandos and contra-puntals as you never heard in your life before.

I'll own I was dumbstruck with it, and when it was all over and he retired through the further genteel rapture, bowing low enough to break in half and flipping the sweat from the ends of his mustachios, my kind gentleman cried, 'By God, sir, what virtuosity; what brio! And a piece so difficult.'

'Difficult indeed, sir,' I agreed with some feeling. 'I wish it had been impossible.'

How the end of that discussion might have turned we shall never know, for on this Mr Masters, Lady Dorothea's butler, presented himself behind me, coughing in my ear, looking not more wall faced than commonly and presenting a salver as if he was afraid what lay on it might give him the pox. 'Your clerk, sir,' he breathed. 'Awaiting in the hall.'

It was a sealed and folded paper, much creased and finger-marked, and in the crabby hand which I recognised as my old friend Captain Isaac Bolton's addressed 'To Jeremy Sturrock Esqre, at the Brown Bear Tavern Drury Lane' to which he had added, 'Or else where he may be found' and 'In all haste and best speed'.

Breaking the seal this is what I discovered. 'Jrmy: Have hauled a wench aboard, her being adrift and half scuppered. The same Mrs Captain Rooke declares to be a lady, though little enough like it but babbling in her fever about 50,000 £ laid in the Consols. Physician McGrath declares same ditto in a contusion of the brain, the which I never heard much of before but say plain she has took a smack on the head. Said physician being an uncommon proper man opines there is mischief about and a beam sea, as likewise sniff a stink of it myself. Whereupon so be the King's Business permits pray favour us your immdte attention at haste and oblige. Yr obdnt friend, Isaac Bolton (Captn. Rtrd.) at The Prospect of Whitby, Wapping.'

'So ho,' I mused, 'and mischief it sounds like.' Yet I was of two minds about it, for this Wapping is a mysterious village on the river beyond the Tower of London, full of vaporous airs, ships, sailors and cut-throats, and a pestilential long journey from Hanover Square. But the claims of friendship are sacred; likewise no man should turn his nose up at any wench who can babble of fifty thousand invested in the Consols. So while my obliging friend was still crying for Signor Tomaso to return and scrape his guts again I gave him a courteous farewell, and made my way through the throng to Lady Dorothea who was also engaged in animated rapture with several other of the gentry.

Miss Harriet was close by; a lady who resembles nothing so much as a sharp little grey parrot, and she gave me a look along the side of her beak and demanded, 'So ye're off are you? Fancy honest rogues better, eh? Begod, I can't blame you, it's enough to curdle your bowels.'

This being by no means an observation you could make to Lady Dorothea I waited until she was at leisure to turn to me and then announced, 'Ma'am, never have I heard such virtuosity. And as for the brio, it'll be the talk of the coffee houses tomorrow. But I fear I must beg your leave.'

Perceiving the paper in my hand, and with her singular kind smile, she asked, 'You're called away, Mr Sturrock? What a vexation for you. We're about to have Madame Résonner with her harp.'

'Ma'am,' I assured her, 'I'm désolé,' this being a word in particular fashion that year, 'but duty's a hard master.'

With Mr Masters holding the door for me I escaped into the hall, this no less elegant than the drawing-room. A black and white tiled floor, white pillars and a domed ceiling, stairs with a scrolled and gilded rail, pictures after the Italian manner and a naked statue or two. A very different matter from the stews of Seven Dials, New Bridge Street, or the Brown Bear in Drury Lane.

Here my lewd and horrible little monster Master Maggsy was studying one of these works of art with indecent attention, and guarded by a watchful footman was announcing, 'God's Pickles, that un's got an arse on her ain't she? I dunno as I never see an arse like that.' But then perceiving my approach he broke off to demand, 'What was they an-imitating in there, was it strangling a cat or slitting a pig? I see a fiddler once at Bartholomew Fair as could imitate anything, even a cock fight if you wanted; he done it with his britches down and you never laugh so much in your life as he used his...'

'Maggsy!' I roared to stop the little rogue in time and preserve Mr Masters' sensibilities. 'When we want your observations on Art we'll ask for 'em.' I flapped Captain Isaac's epistle about his ears. 'Where did you get this, and how long since?'

'Brown Bear,' he answered indifferently, ' 'bout an hour. Little cove as called himself Nicko the Runner on account of carrying messages from the sea captains and suchlike to Lloyd's Coffee House and 'Change, hundred paces walking and hundred paces trotting, would you believe that? And he says it'll be a sixpence for bringing it and I says anybody as gets a sixpence out of you's just as like to see a Jew drop his purse.'

By now Mr Masters was raising his eyes somewhat heavenwards, and taking from him my beaver and cane—this last being a mark of esteem presented to me by His Majesty the King—I drew the wicked child out to the stately portico by his ear, and there desired the flunkey to whistle me a hackney from the carriages lining the railings of the square. Thus in another minute or two we were clattering and creaking through the press of Oxford Street in a damned flea bitten old rattle trap, with our surly dog of a driver flourishing his whip and cursing all the other coachmen as willingly as they cursed him. And here I shall pause to explain this Master Maggsy, or you will wonder what he is and find no answers.

In short he is a kind of urchin which I picked out of a dung heap some three years back, where he was sheltering from a snow storm and no doubt ripe for mischief. Of about fifteen years old, as near as either of us can guess, he knows neither his father nor his mother—and very likely has cause to thank God for it—and his first recollection is of a begging academy kept by one Mrs Bagot. This being a trade whereby a band of three or four children, particular washed and clean for all their rags, are taught to tell a pitiful tale; most often about their poor old aunt or grandmother caring for them to her last penny piece as their own mother is dead and father lost at sea fighting the French, and they are weeping for a few pence to buy her a pinch of tea for her comfort: a plea which never fails with the tender hearted who know no better.

Master Maggsy, however, having an uncommon knowing look even at that tender age as often as not spoiled the game, and seeing that no manner of correction could improve the little villain in the end Mrs Bagot sold him for a crown piece to Mr William Makepeace, the Practical Chimney Sweep. So then he took to chimney climbing and to the other commonplace of that profession; namely slipping out from fireplaces in the ladies' chambers to pilfer whatever trifle he could lay his hands on. But growing tired of singeing his backside, scraping his knees, and the encouragement of Mr Makepeace's stick whenever he failed in his duties, he ran away from his master to end in the King's Head stables at a certain village full of rogues where I was engaged on a matter of highwaymen. As black as the Earl of Hell's fundament, while I was three parts full of mulled claret at the time, I took pity on the rascal, had him doused in the horse trough to cleanse him and thereupon appointed him my clerk, servant, and messenger. As to person he is small and mean, with an uncommon wicked face, a most inordinate love of blood and disaster, and a fund of lewd and ungenteel observations. But I persevere with him and even spend sixpence a week on his education.

Having so whiled away our long journey with the little monster's history—and an extreme exchange of courtesies with our driver when he refused to carry us a step further than the Belle Savage on Ludgate Hill—we have now procured a fresh carriage and are rattling down past the Tower of London and on by Goodwyn, Skinner, and Thornton's famous brewhouse, over a wooden bridge across the dock to Wapping Street. Here we have the warehouses and yards of the merchants and chandlers, the reek of the breweries and whiffs of tea, coffee and spices, tallow, and tar. Through the street ends down to the water such a tangle of masts and ropes and spars as makes it look like a forest, all swaying under a coppery sky and the river glinting like brass in the late afternoon, a bustle of dockers and dark skinned seamen, and a mess of carts, wagons and drays carrying all the merchandise of the world.

Such is the prodigious thirst of Wapping that one dwelling in every twenty-five is a beer house of some sort or another—the most also whore shops, slop shops or chandlers with it—but the three main taverns are The City of Ramsgate against the Old Stairs, The Prospect of Whitby, and The Grapes. Of these the Prospect is much affected by sea captains and agents meeting to eat their dinners and discuss cargoes, bills of lading and similar mysteries, the Ramsgate by ships' mates and suchlike, and the

Grapes by sailors of the commoner sort; and by no means a place to say a word out of turn. All three are on the river and shipping, and each close by stairs to the water; stairs that see some mysterious cargoes carried up and down them on foggy nights. For the rest the village is a warren of secret lanes, docks, rope walks, manufactories and mean lodging houses; but also here and there the pretty little residence of some master mariner retired.

After a further exchange with our fresh charioteer at the Prospect—him offering to take twice the fare I tendered him or fight me for it, me offering to pitch him down the steps into the tide with my boot up his breech—we shouldered through the knot of idlers lounging about the horse trough to the door, and our first encounter with the mischief to come. For here was a piratical looking fellow with an eye patch and a cutlass scar down his cheek, once tanned but now faded to a tallowish colour, a naval frock coat just as faded, and an old-fashioned three cornered hat clapped to the back of his head; and, as Captain Isaac would say, more than half seas awash. 'Heave to,' says he. 'You're hard across my bows, sir.'

'If it comes to that,' I answered, 'you're tacking in the wind yourself.'

'Aye.' He pondered on this. 'Why, so I am. But it ain't every day as I see a prodigy.'

'Well, sir,' I said, good humoured enough, 'a prodigy I may be, but I'm in some haste; and about the King's business. Be so good as to let me pass.'

'The King is it?' he asked, now screwing up his eyes at me. 'Then I could tell the King a word or two. But I won't; be damned if I will. Be damned to the King; and his government.'

I was struck speechless. The government is one thing and any man of good sense may damn it as he pleases, but His Majesty is another matter. It was Frenchy republican talk such as there is all too much about these days, and made no better by Master Maggsy giving a hearty snigger. But the little wretch cried, 'Come up, sailor. You'm as pissed as a tinker's drab; but you want to watch it, Sturrock's a wicked man when he's roused.'

'Wicked is he?' the fool enquired. 'Well then, he ain't the only one.' With that he clapped one hand on my shoulder and broke into a few notes of one of the vulgar sea songs you hear these drunken roisterers bellowing. ' "I says to him Captain and how do ye do? Wayo, blow the man down. Says he none the better for seeing of you, oh gimme some way to blow the man down." '

It might have ended with me losing my patience but for the land-lord then appearing; a stoutish fellow in a red weskit and white apron, smoking a churchwarden pipe, and honest enough no doubt but like most of 'em along the river with his thumbs in many another pie beside veal and ham. 'Come now, lieutenant,' he said, 'you've got a load aboard. Best go along to your lodging now and sleep it off.'

'Lodging be hanged, Nat Comber,' the man retorted. 'I'm in full sail today.' But he sheered off into the bystanders, greeting one or two of them, slapping another on the back, and at last turning away along the street laughing and bursting into his sea shanty again.

'Lieutenant Robert Kemble,' Mr Comber said. 'He's got his troubles, poor man. But he don't often get like this.'

'No more he ain't got that song right neither,' Maggsy announced. 'Not the way I've heard Captain Isaac sing it when he's drunk, and if he don't know the way it goes nobody should.'

'Be damned to your rude ditties,' I announced, turning inside; a fair to middling place with wooden pillars and panelling cut from old ships' timbers, curiosities of stuffed fishes, heathen masks and weapons, high settles and scrubbed tables, and serving men and wenches bustling about their duties. There was much the same business air as many of the City coffee and eating houses; sober broadcloth and blue coats of a more nautical style, two or three gentlemen dressed to the pink of fashion, a murmur of respectable conference and all in vapour of tobacco smoke; well enough known to me, as most of the London taverns are. But Captain Isaac would be found in the upper chamber, where he commonly sits in the great bay window to view the shipping in the Pool through his

spy glass, and requesting the landlord to send up some refreshment
—a pint of the captain's punch, a pint of the best claret for myself,
and the same of small beer for my clerk—I ascended the stairs
with Master Maggsy clattering close after in his dainty way.

Here it was quieter, there being two clerkish fellows muttering
over a bundle of manifests, an elderly gentleman dozing in an
ingle behind *The London Packet*, and the captain himself sitting
with three others. A fine old gaffer, having a fancifully carved
wooden leg and a great white beard, naughty eyes, and a rosy coun-
tenance both baked by the tropic suns and enlivened by the fearsome concoction of rum, juice of limes and a pinch of gunpowder
which he drinks in inordinate quantities; and which he declares
keeps the bowels open, is a specific against scurvy and pox, and
disperses ill humours. Though there is little need of such dispersion
with Captain Isaac, as a more genial, comical rascal you could never
wish to meet. But a most extravagant liar; some of the tales he
tells might make a fiddler's drab blush for modesty.

I observed the others with him. One more ancient mariner, but
somewhat curds and whey, another gentleman wearing a brown
coat with a high collar in the Frenchy style, but otherwise respectable enough, and last a snuffish merchant kind clutching a ledger
like it might have been a bible. They seemed to be sitting in con-
clave on Isaac's matters for the second salt was announcing, 'A
wench is always a scorpion. I've had 'em all; black, brown, yaller
and spotted, and they're all snakes. I rec'lect a Kanaky trot once't
as was like riding a beam sea without steerage way and arse uppards; she'd get her legs about your neck, near enough throttle
you, and then say "You gib me silber, gold, sailor?" Let this'n be,
Isaac. Send her about her business.'

'You got a gut full of misery, Thomas Coggins,' Captain Isaac
observed. 'Arse deep in your own bilge water, you be. I keep telling
you this wench ain't of that sort. And as to your Kanaka trot,
why I had one in Batavia once as could twist herself...' Perceiving
us the old rogue stopped and coughed, gave a sidelong glance at
Master Maggsy who was listening with his snout twitching like a

piglet's, muttered, 'Not in front of the child,' and added, 'Ahoy there, Jer'my; so you've come aboard.'

But before I could get a word in Maggsy declared, 'Wager you can't tell me a lot as I don't know to start with. Not after Mr William Makepeace the Practical Chimney Sweep; God's Tripes, you want to hear some of his rollicksomes. But here's another thing, Capt'n Bolton; how's that song go? "As I was awalking down Winchester Street, a saucy young damsel I happened to meet"?'

'Why, lad, like this,' the captain answered by no means unwilling, for he was near enough doting on the little wretch. He opened his mouth to bellow, '"I says to her, Polly and how do ye do? Wayo, blow the man down. Says she none the better for seeing of you..."'

'God's sake,' I cried, 'that's enough,' adding a sharp touch of my cane to Maggsy to bring the matter home, and continuing, 'Now then, Isaac, I've come a pestilential long journey, and at the expense of two hackneys. And it ain't to hear a Heavenly choir either, so we'll come to your business if you please.'

On that the other old salt cod turned his curds and whey look on me and demanded, 'Be this your Bow Street Runner, Isaac?' He shook his head dolefully. 'Shouldn't have done it, capt'n. Shouldn't have fetched a thieftaker down here. They ain't took kindly to. He's as like to get his throat cut as not.'

I felt my neckcloth growing tight but was interrupted in further observations by a serving wench approaching with our liquor and followed close behind by an uncommon modish gentleman. Boots you could see to shave in, tan pantaloons with never a wrinkle, and a coat of most uncommon cut; yet another with a whiff of the sea about him by the mahogany of his face. A man who knew his own mind, fortyish or so I judged, but still a figure and a fine free stylish air to set the ladies' heads spinning. For the minute all eyes were on him before he asked, 'Your pardon, gentlemen; do I break on private affairs?'

'Not by no means,' Captain Isaac roared, 'lay alongside, and welcome.'

It was like a bit out of one of Mr Sheridan's plays. 'Very civil, sir,' he answered, 'and I'm obliged. But I'm seeking only Mr Dombey Wells.'

At this the snuffish merchant fellow leapt up crying, 'Why, to be sure, sir. You'll be Mr Colville. I had your message lately.' Clutching his ledger the tighter he asked, 'Shall we draw aside, sir?' and snuffled off after Mr Colville to another ingle like a hound scenting a fat hare.

'Business may not be neglected,' the Frenchy collared coat observed. 'Begod no. Not these days. The price of tea's ruinous.' He took a pinch of snuff, offering me the box as if afraid there wouldn't be all that much in it before very long, and lowered his voice. 'Some cursed odd whispers in the City. They say the Bank's none too sound.'

'Very likely, sir,' I said shortly. 'Nobody expects the peace to last long.' I took a draught of my claret and turned to the captain to add, 'Isaac, I'd as soon consider your business in private. There's little we can do here.'

'Aye,' the captain agreed, pushing himself up. 'We'd best haul away. You're bidden to take a glass of wine at Mrs Captain Rooke's, Jer'my.'

'Am I bid too?' the other old mariner demanded.

'Not as I knows of,' the captain replied, 'but you can swing a sounding if you like.'

So with something of a list he stumped off to the stairs with Thomas Coggins rolling behind, and myself bringing up the rear not in the best of tempers. Nor was this improved below by the spectacle of Maggsy snickering and ogling with the serving wench, a pretty pert little bitch with a pair of tits half out of her bodice and a look in her eye to match. But his naughty notions I soon checked with a finger and thumb nipped to his ear, dragging him out protesting to the street, where he complained, 'God's Weskit, I was only adoing as you say, finding out what I could; don't you always say wherever you go get nosing around? Well I was,' he added sulkily. 'And I tell you one thing for certain, that Rosie's a right piece. I reckon there ain't much she don't know and the most part of it ain't reading the lessons of a Sunday morning neither.'

My observation on this was cut short by a singular occurrence. We were then pushing our way through the crowd of idlers, now swollen to a score or more by several carters and draymen stopping to slake their thirsts in the dust and coppery heat of the afternoon. There was a fair noise of talk and rough laughter, but of a sudden somebody spoke to me close and quiet from behind. A strange, lisping voice which said, 'Master Sturrock, sir; tell the old captain to put the wench back where he found her so he won't come to no harm.'

On the instant I swung round demanding, 'Who spoke there? Who said that?'

But there was no answer, only the ring of doltish faces begrimed with dirt and sweat; sailors and workmen, a few urchins, a mulatto with a red bandana about his head and some mere idle villains, all standing silent until one of them laughed and spat. It might have been any of them and I demanded again, 'Who was it, I say? By God, if you lot don't fancy the Law, you'll still have it so long as I'm here.'

'Reg'lar cock bantam, ain't he?' one asked. That raised an ugly sound, half between a growl and a laugh; and another bawled, 'The gen'leman's overheated, let's have'n in the arse trough to cool'n off.'

It was a dramatic situation and looked like turning worse. Nonetheless I kept my ground for such rogues will often hold back if you stand and face 'em; though behind me the cowardly little wretch Maggsy whispered, 'Come out of it. God's Tripes, they'll gut you; you ain't in Drury Lane now.'

Yet retreat I would not, both for my own dignity and the surety that as soon as I turned they would be on me like a pack of starving street dogs, and the affair might have ended in a rude encounter had not old Isaac come stumping back bellowing and cursing. 'Avast there, you poxy sea cooks,' he roared. 'You God damned sons of a stinking Jakarta whore and a lousy Bactrian camel. Bear off, or I'll have your foreskins for it. You know who I am and by God I've keel hauled many better men than you lot.'

It was a rousing address which fetched a more good humoured laugh and even a cheer or two, the more so as Isaac was a rare spectacle with his beard bristling, his face purple with rum and rage, and wooden leg beating a tattoo on the cobbles. Then also came a fresh diversion as on the other side, coming from London, a post chaise clattered up to stop at the tavern door and let first a gentleman and then a lady alight. I saw little of either of them, for both Maggsy and Isaac was admonishing me; a glimpse of a fashionable blue coat and beaver with its back to me, a dust cloak and hood with beneath it dark hair and a face more touched by the sun than is modish. No great matter save that it drew the rabble off.

We turned away in safety, though myself answering the continued chorus of complaint somewhat testily, and within a minute or two more now arrived at Captain Isaac's lodging. A neat and pretty little residence on the water front, and nicely secluded with a timber yard and an old empty warehouse to right and left, opposite a tenting field—which is where they strain and shrink sailcloth and so we get the word tenterhooks—and little to remind you of the meaner sort of tenements save one narrow lane at the corner of the street. It was built by the late Captain Rooke, a master with the East India Company who looked to make a nice retirement but never did as, according to Isaac, he died of yellow fever at sea and was buried in a barrel; whereupon after a decent interval his widow offered a chamber to Captain Isaac. A snug berth and nothing improper in it, neither being of the age or fancy for such matters, except to sit at night over a game of cribbage while Captain Isaac tells his tales of the wonders of the seas; and damned wondrous some of them are.

So coming up a pebble path, with cantankerous Coggins at our heels, Isaac flings open the green porch door and bawls, 'Ahoy there, Mrs Captain!'

It called forth an instant rebuke, for a little maid in pinafore and mop-cap popped up crying, 'Shush, Captain sir, do,' while Mrs Rooke herself appeared at the head of the stairs. A smallish figure of a woman, and now plainly displeased. She whispered, 'Be quiet, Captain Bolton, now. You'll disturb the child with your roaring like a whale.'

Deeply abashed the Captain answered meekly, 'Ask your pardon, Mrs Captain. But here's Mr Sturrock, come to give his advice. Will you let him view the wench, ma'am?'

'D'you think she's some mermaid in a raree show?' the good lady demanded. 'I'll not have you all up here trampling and bellowing. Go and sit yourself in the parlour; and you too, Captain Coggins. I dare say you've come for your supper.'

Some nicer manner was demanded here, and I interposed, 'Ma'am, your servant, as ever. And a privilege once more to see you so goodly. But if I'm to assist I must observe the whole matter, including the *corpus delicti* as the law requires.'

That foxed her, and with Maggsy at my heels I was admitted up into the chamber with such a stream of instructions to go on tiptoe, not to speak above a breath, etc., as you might have thought we were visiting a death watch.

So indeed it looked at first sight. There was one other personage present; a raw boned fellow of about thirty attired in what seemed a patched and faded uniform coat. But I had no eyes for him. They were fastened on the bed itself and the young woman lying there. Now I will own that although of a very fine turn of our noble English language I have little or no poetic graces, and moreover I most fancy a woman of some figure; thus I can find few words to describe the pale beauty which lay there. She seemed little more than a child, her head turned sideways on the pillow and surrounded with cruelly cropped hair of a singular colour of dark auburn; a soft pallor on the cheeks but somewhat flushed, blue shadows on her eyelids and the deeper blue of a dull bruise darkening her left temple. But one thing I noted even in that affecting moment; alive, sleeping, or dead, she had a damned determined line to her jaw.

It was left to Master Maggsy to improve the occasion in his own elegant style. He said, 'God's Weskit; copperknob.'

The rogue went out with a cuff that must have rattled his teeth, flying arse first through the door into the arms of the little servant maid who was standing there. Mrs Rooke was offended afresh, and neither was the physician any better pleased for he observed, 'You've a saucy callant there,' and asked, 'you'll be Sturrock, I presume?'

I perceived that here we were dealing with a Scotsman, and as to that shall say little more. But I shall also confess handsomely—and when handsome Jeremy Sturrock is particular handsome—that a more fighting mad devil than this Dr Ian McGrath when the mood took him I have never found before or since; a man as you could wish no better by your side in a fisticuff mill or worse. Nevertheless not one to take to on the instant; of a dour and disrespectful nature, a remarkable ugly face as it might have been rough chipped out of his own native granite, all elbows, knuckles and knees, and plainly in some poverty for his clothes, although neat and clean and again of a naval cut, were sadly threadbare and his boots cracked.

'Commonly addressed as Mr Sturrock,' I advised him.

'No doubt,' he said. 'Aye. And ye'll find there's a deeper business here than apprehending some common footpad.'

The rude Hibernian might have got a sharp answer had not Isaac then come peeping round the door with his rosy face as if he fancied Mrs Rooke might not see him. He whispered, 'Show Jeremy her legs.'

'You'll do no such thing,' Mrs Rooke burst out. 'I'll not hear of it.'

'There's no harm, mem,' the physician answered. He turned back to the bed, lifted back the covers from its foot, and asked, 'Well now, Mr Sturrock, what d'you make of that?'

Above each ankle, plain and angry, was a red, rubbed scar. I knew what to make of it, for I'd seen such in Newgate often enough. 'D'you take me for a fool, sir?' I demanded. 'Leg irons.'

'Leg irons,' he repeated. 'Aye. We've a fine bonnie devilment here. And if I find the one who put her in 'em I'll break his damned neck with my own hands. Well,' he concluded, 'we can get below. She'll not stir yet awhile.' He turned to cast one long gaze back at the wench, and I was struck with a sudden gleam of light; for begod, here we not only had a Scots physician, but a Scots physician stricken deep in love. There was not a doubt of it. Never before have I seen such a sheeplike look, nor one so mingled with rage.

Wondering greatly at this miracle I followed Isaac stumping down the stairs and into the parlour; an apartment curiously hung with pictures of clipper ships, models, cutlasses, bones and tusks, so that there was scarcely room to move. Here Captain Coggins was already applying himself fervently to a black bottle, and pausing only long enough to make sure that the Widow Rooke was not with us—as she could now be heard scolding the little maid somewhere outside—he announced, 'Mrs Captain Rooke's parsnip. By God it's a drench as might give a dray horse the staggers before it killed him.'

Master Maggsy found that vastly amusing and first silencing him I said, 'Well then, let's proceed. Who is she?'

'Jer'my,' Isaac cried, 'that's what we want you to discover. And you set that bottle down, Thomas Coggins.'

'Can't she tell you herself?' I asked. 'What's stopping her?'

'A contusion of the brain,' the physician answered, and went into a curse so oratorical as to confirm my worst suspicion that at some time he'd been in the Royal Navy.

These medicos are always inventioning some fantastical new disease, and the half of those they've already got they don't know what to do with. I asked, 'What might that mean?'

'I'll tell you plain,' he confessed, 'we know little of it. Save it can end in damn near anything. Aye,' he communed with himself, 'I've seen it once or twice before. Young boys of the weaker sort struck like it after a sea battle.'

'There's little weak about that young woman,' I observed. 'So wait till she wakes up and ask her yourself. That's simple enough.'

'Ye'll not tell how she'll wake. She might be as clear as you or me. Or wandering, mebbe for days or weeks. Forby she could forget everything, even her own name; I've known that happen. I've told you, man, we don't understand the condeetion. Save she's sleeping calm enough now.'

'Begod,' I said, 'here's a fine kettle of herrings. A physician as don't understand and a wench who don't know who she is. Have you set about enquiries yourself?'

'I've been putting questions between this and Limehouse the morn,' he growled.

'Then we'll have the answers to 'em. But first I want the whole tale of how she came here. There's a due order and procedure to the Art and Science of Detection.'

'If you'll give me the wind,' Isaac announced pettishly, 'I'll tell you. 'Twas after our supper the last night,' he continued, 'Mrs Captain Rooke and me was moored here about a leg or two of cribbage. Was black as the Devil's arse outside and very near as hot and I says "Mrs Captain Rooke, there's a typhoon coming up." I recollect once in the China Seas...'

'Nothing like an hurricane I met once't down Florida way,' Captain Coggins broke in.

'Be damned to your hurricane,' Isaac roared and then checked his voice to a windy whisper. 'I was recollecting on this typhoon when of a sudden there was a tapping and banging on the window as we'd got closed against the rats. That old wareh'uss is lousy with 'em and they get saucy at night. Well then, was a little voice crying "Ahoy there, please to let me in, God's sake let me in." Whereupon Mrs Captain cries "Lord help us, here's the Press Gang after some poor soul."'

'Not so,' Coggins argued with a belch. 'Ain't no Press Gang now. They're alaying ships up, not impressing.'

'Blast your timbers,' Isaac exploded like a broadside. 'One more word from you, Thomas Coggins, and I'll have you put ashore,' and after some further silencing went on, 'So Mrs Captain's aflinging back the bolts, for the Press can't enter private property, and

I'm in line astern with a candlestick and a cudgel as I've catched up. And what should fall in but a kind of youngish fellow, little more'n a boy it seemed. Also hard behind five or six of the rogues.'

He broke off into a descriptive opera which set Maggsy jigging for admiration until I said impatiently, 'Come, on with it, Isaac. So they invaded you?'

'Not at first go. One says "Master, we don't mean you no harm, but this here's our business," and I cry "Be off, you ugly dogs." By now the boy's at the foot of the stairs and scuppered, also Mrs Captain herself catching up a stick as she keeps behind the door. The villain says "Master, we're bound to come and fetch her," whereupon I dab the candle in his chaps, and on the instant we've a set to; eight or ten of 'em.'

'Four,' the physician said.

I turned to him. 'You were in it too?'

'By the Maircy of Providence. I was at a lying in. By a further Maircy the woman's husband was lighting me on my way with a lantern, and himself carrying a cudgel. A wise precaution hereabouts.'

'As Dr Samuel Johnson observes of London,' I remarked, '"Prepare for death if here at night you roam, and make your Will before you sup from home." There was an altercation then?'

A sudden grin illumined the physician's face, as it might have been sunlight on his own native crags. 'Man, there was a braw, bonnie fight. Aye. Mrs Rooke bloodied one's nose for him, whiles Captain Isaac just as near took my head off with a cutlass he'd fetched from the parlour. There was knives out too.' He showed a long cut in the shoulder of his coat, now most tidily stitched over, and with some regret finished, 'It didn't last that long after I'd put two of 'em down. The others took to their heels dragging them away. I was for going after but Mrs Rooke called me to see to the little lassie.'

'And she was dressed as a man?'

'Sailor's slops and a shirt and little else,' Isaac answered. 'Mrs

Captain says "Captain Bolton, kindly look the other way." That's how we knowed it was a wench.'

'You can't never be sure,' Maggsy interjected. 'I see a wonder once at Bartholomew Fair. They had it in a cage and let on it was a Frenchy and called it Marie-Pierre, the Man-Woman; that'd got a monstrous great black beard and a pair of bubs like corn sacks. And that ain't the lot neither; it'd got the biggest...'

I fetched him a backhander which steadied his reminiscences and asked, 'Then you put her to bed, and she's never uttered another word since?'

'Oh aye,' the physician replied. 'Several.'

'God's sake,' I cried, 'why didn't you say so? Do I have to extract information like a tooth puller at a bumpkin fairground?'

'You can have 'em for all they are. She was best not fretted with questions, but for most of the night she was in distress and cried continually to drive the rats away. Aye.' He mused on that with a lovesick look in his eye and then added, 'I was of two minds about it but in the end gave her a wee drop of laudanum as I had in my bag. She was calmer on that but then several times spoke the words "Coffin Mill". Once she said clear and loud "It's fifty thousand pounds in the Consols" and then again several times repeated the name "Mary Carson".'

'One time her screeched it out,' Isaac observed. 'Heard it down in the parlour, where I was sitting with my blunderbuss and a bottle of rum.'

On this Captain Coggins, who had been dozing and grunting through the last exchanges, vented a loud snore, woke himself with it, and enquired, 'What's you say? Mary Carson? I knowed a Mary Anne Carson long back. Boston family of ship builders. Damned fast handy ships. Aye and so was the wench; damned fast and handy. This'n you got here ain't Mary Carson, Isaac; that's certain sure.'

But we were preserved from this old barrel of parsnip wine and salt pork's further recollections and Captain Isaac's fresh explosions alike, for on that same instant came such a hammering and rattling at the street door as stopped us all, caused Isaac to very near fall over his wooden leg, and Mrs Rooke to come running from the kitchen and demanding, 'Lord above us, what's this now?'

'That, ma'am,' I announced, 'we shall discover,' and was the first out in the passage but with the doctor close behind and Maggsy, not to be outdone, hard at our heels. With a fresh outburst of banging and a voice crying outside I flung back the door; and there, whatever it was we might have expected, was nothing more than a small urchin jigging for excitement and impatience.

'The doctor,' he screeched, 'where's McGrath?' and then seeing him there bawled, 'Doctor, you'm wanted double damn quick. It's the lootenant, Mr Kemble, got himself knived, and lying there acoughing his blood out.' As a dreadful messenger not even Master Maggsy could have bettered it.

CHAPTER TWO

I will confess that for all the physician's slow Scots deliberation he could move fast and sure enough when occasion called. With a word to silence the boy, another to Mrs Rooke and the two captains now exclaiming behind us, pausing only to catch up his bag, he set off after the urchin with Maggsy and me following at a brisk pace. It was a short but hurried journey, and the lad panted out his tale while we turned away from the mercantile bustle of docks, wharfs, and shipping into the meaner alleys beyond; where rents and tenements and ancient clap boarded hovels leaned close together under the weight of a strange and lowering sky, now with the twilight settling in shadows and candles already lit in the beer houses and chandlers' shops.

This urchin, it seemed, was in some sort attached to the lieutenant by way of doing errands for him and cleaning his boots in exchange for an occasional ha'penny and tales of sea battles. It seemed also that he was near as well known to the physician, who addressed him as Tonks, held him by the arm and questioned him very kindly as we hurried on our way. His account was simple enough. Barely an hour since he had met the lieutenant coming as it appeared from the direction of the Grapes Tavern; the lieutenant being a shade drunk, in great good humour and laughing to himself. He had then tossed Tonks a few coppers, told him to fetch his supper, and announced that he'd soon be off to sea again now and would take Tonks with him. Whereupon the boy had run off to the tripe shop in the next court, remained there only so long as several idle women were served, and then returned to the lieutenant's lodging all agog to hear this news of going to sea; when he discovered the bloody scene which I shall soon describe for you, and set up a yell of 'Murder!'

By now we had entered a place of somewhat better tenements though still mean enough, where a knot of the idle inquisitive was gathered like flies about one doorway and raising the outcry of their kind at any sudden death or calamity. 'Now then,' the physician said, 'be off,' and it was a measure of his authority which I did not fail to note that they fell back on the instant, as did others crowded on the darkening stairs inside. Pushing up them to the sound of women's wailing from above, cursing the rough steps, we came to a landing where there was a glimmer of candlelight from an open door and a spectacle which caused Master Maggsy to whisper, 'God's Tripes, there's a bleedin' mess for you.'

Here on the boards of the landing was a patch of fresh blood; and dragged away from this a trail or smear through the doorway into the chamber beyond, where there was a sound of dreadful coughing and women's voices. Within were three of them weeping about the lieutenant, one holding a candle and another kneeling by him to support his head; a haggard bitch but handsome at one time and plain to see what she was now. As for the sad fellow himself, it was just as plain. Struck in the back outside the door I concluded, a grievous wound soaking his coat in red on the faded blue, then fallen to the ground to drag himself in here as far as the pallet bed; so to cling there half on it and half on his face, and clutching at the mattress. He was still living; but, if I was any judge, not for long.

As was proper the physician took command; and, as I shall again confess, quick and sure with it. 'Ye've not moved him?' he demanded, and added, 'Away then. But bring me more lights, and after wait on the stairs; I might want ye.'

The urchin now starting to blubber as McGrath went on one knee beside the helpless figure I ordered Master Maggsy, 'Have him out; you know what else,' and brought the candle closer myself but it was all too plain there was no help for the man.

The physician shook his head at me and observed, 'You've got yourself a mischief this time, Kemble. D'ye ken you're done for if I turn you over?'

A painful grin twisted the man's lips but he got out, 'Spoke like a true ship's surgeon.'

'Be easy, lad,' McGrath said with a rough kindness. 'But you've not much time; so tell us if you can. Who was it?'

'Damned if I know. Turned to see him scuttling down the stairs, and half dark. Couldn't tell.' He coughed once more, a mess of froth and blood, and tried to thrust himself up. 'God's Teeth, McGrath, I wouldn't ha' split on him. I never would.'

With an arm under him McGrath eased him down, repeating, 'Be easy, I say. Take your time; but tell us.'

'Mr Midshipman...' he started. But that brought on another fit of coughing; and then the last catch of breath which told its own tale.

The physician straightened up and stood looking down on him. 'Aye,' he said. 'Well that's the end of it.'

'It's a poor epitaph,' I observed. 'But to stab a man when he's drunk's the pink of villainy; we might none of us be safe. And why in such a damnation hurry?' I reflected on that and at last asked, 'What d'you know of him?'

'It's verra simple. Another fine bonnie hero whiles he's fighting for the King, but left aside to rot when there's no more use for him.'

'Doctor McGrath,' I told him, 'you sound like a damned radical Whig to me. I've little time for such talk and less patience. So let's have it short and plain.'

For an instant I thought the man would strike me, as plainly he'd an uncommon ready temper. But he said instead, 'As short as you like. Age of forty-six or seven and in the Navy since a boy. Served in the West Indies Station, as he once told me, and then with Nelson commanding *Agamemnon* under Hood in the Mediterranean. Was with Nelson's squadron under Jervis at Cape St Vincent in '97. The poor devil was badly wounded there and laid off as unfit for further service. Aye. He was getting old to be a mere lieutenant still. And that's the end of it. Save that his one notion was to get back to sea again.'

'And it seems that he thought he might; little more than an hour ago.' I mused on that and asked, 'How did he go with the people here? They're a rough lot.'

'He was well enough liked. Even considered something of a fine fellow. I doubt you'll find they had much to do with this.'

'I doubt it myself,' I agreed. 'It goes deeper than a mere neighbourly difference. Nonetheless I'll thank you to question 'em for me, doctor; I fancy they'll answer you freer than they might me.' One of the cardinal principles in the Art and Science of Detection is never to do the work yourself if you can find others better suited to do it for you. 'For the rest,' I finished, 'I'll ask you to notify the Parish Constable and Coroner's Officers and the mortuary men. It'll save my time and he'll be none too fresh soon if he's left lying here in this heat.'

He bit off some fresh retort as on this one of the women returned bringing fresh candles and snivelling like a fountain, while yet more stood crowding and peering at the doorway. These again the physician drove away, desiring only two of them to come in to lay out and cover the poor fellow decently on his bed, and while they were about this melancholy duty I turned myself to survey the apartment.

There was not much of it, but all clean and neat and of a ship-shape tidiness. Beneath the window a table and plain chairs, behind a hanging curtain a threadbare shirt or two, britches, and a pair of patched boots; and against the other wall a sea chest having the lieutenant's name lettered on it. I neither expected nor gleaned anything from these poor remnants and at last opened the chest; and here again was evidence of a man who still hoped for better days to return. A wig and cocked hat, a shirt, trousers, and a uniform coat for best, all much worn but folded closely in newsprint to keep the moth away; a nautical book or two and navigational guides, a sextant, documents and commissions. And at the bottom a little bundle of letters. These I took to the candles to read while the physician watched me until growing somewhat impatient I said, 'Doctor McGrath, the sooner you ask questions the less likely people are to forget,' when he too went out leaving me thankfully alone.

I shall give some part of these letters, observing only that Lieutenant Kemble was a man who never had any luck in his life.

Here is the first, written in a childish hand, much miswritten and scratched out, and addressed from Tottenham, July 1771, to Mr Midshipman Kemble, aboard *Avenger*, West Indies Station. It said, 'Dere, derest Robert: Such News! The littel spaniul you presented me last summer has now surprized us with her Own Family. 4 derest puppies and you may depend upon it I shall name the derest of them Robert ... But also alas I fere such other news. The *Odius Tirant* Miss Fitton has discovered my most secrit and precius jurnal, wherein I have writ of our attachment. This carried to Mama, and Mama very stern and wise. Derest Robert why are Mamas always so wise? ... I have writ this in *Stricktist Secricy* and intrust it to Tristram Peregrine whos ship is now commissioned and sails to join the West Indies Squadron in Aug. Tristram is my *devoted slave*, tho *very young* and I think *wicked* and Mama will not bear me to speak of him, but swears to deliver it safe in your own hands, tho he knows not when ... So I avow myself *ever* your faithful Georgiana.'

There were three more over the next several years, and this is the fifth, seemingly with the outer sheet lost and most like about the end of 1775, for it started '...Papa says the war with the American Colonials will not be much and little for the Navy to do. We have met with a most personable Ltnt Charles Motley, who agrees on this and tells us also that the only *sure* way to advancement is by friends and influence in the Right Quarters. Therefore, dear Robert, you should seek to find such friends, as I am sure your valour would make easy ... Papa much plaged with the gout and has carried us away to Bath: such a profusion of routs, balls, soirées and subscription entertainments as you never saw. Mama is much taken by Ltnt Motley, as much by his maners as by being heir to a Baronetcy and considers he is sure to go far: tho I consider a little elderly...'

There was another, urging him now for his own sake to seek powerful friends, and here is the last; but one year later, and the tale tells itself. 'Dear Mr Kemble; I am constrained to write thus formally to you as Mama says this is correct though I fear you may desire I had other news for you. To be very simple I am to marry Ltnt Sir Charles Motley this July next. Dearest Robert I am so very sorry and do not know what to write, but Papa says Mature Considerations bring Assured Lives, so I hope for your happiness and advancement and pray always that you will account me your dear friend, Georgiana Woodforde.'

I read them all through again, pondering over them while the dusk settled outside with that chamber as silent as the tomb save for whispering still behind the door, and be damned I was thankful when Maggsy came bursting in followed hard by the physician looking as black as thunder. Then I stowed them away in my tail pocket, for I had a notion that before long I might make some use of those letters; this I fancied already was a mystery whose beginnings lay in the past and, as I ever advise the ladies, a few words in writing are worth a bellyful of wind. 'Well, sir,' I addressed McGrath, 'have you discovered anything?'

The answer was short and simple; he had not. True there was one tale of a monstrous negro with a knife a yard long between his teeth and another of a little misshapen dwarf chattering like an ape, but such fantastics are a commonplace of the meaner population. None of them had seen or heard anything untoward and with ships of all the world in the river strangers were less noticed than your next door neighbours. Nor did any of them know of the lieutenant's family save some talk of a brother; a clerk in Bombay. The physician could add only one thing. He said, 'For what it comes to, Meg swears that when she ran first to Kemble's aid he muttered something about a Captain Blackbird.'

'Captain Blackbird?' I repeated. 'What the devil does that mean? Be hanged, this affair's as full of half said words as a herring is of bones. And who's Meg? Did you question her close?'

'Close enough. There's no more she can tell us. She's a whore, but had a fondness for Kemble; I fancy she obliged him now and again. She declares if she finds the one who did this she'll have his eyes out with her own finger nails.'

'A savage bitch,' I observed and turned next to Maggsy.

'Same and likewise,' he announced. 'Nothing. Tonks sticks to the tale as he told, swears he never see nobody afollowing the corpuss, and I reckon that's true enough as I offered to fight him for it but he couldn't tell no more. Nor there ain't no sight nor smell of the knife neither; I'd admire to have a knife as'd done a murder, all in blood, and I looked most particular.'

'Then there's little more to do here. Save only have you ever heard of Lieutenant Sir Charles Motley?' I asked the physician.

The fellow was dumbfounded. 'God's sake, what's he got to do with it? Captain Sir Charles Motley; and no doubt Rear-Admiral if the fighting starts again. You're flying high, my man.'

'It's no matter,' I told him. 'And I've still questions for you concerning the wench.'

He was all of a prickle again. 'I'll thank you to speak of her with more respect. But d'ye think her business has any part of this?'

'Am I a crystal gazer?' I demanded. 'We don't know; not yet. But I'm bound to warn you that if it ain't I count this affair the more important. I mean to hang the rascal responsible for that; and whoever she might be your pretty little mystery can tell you for herself when she wakes up. Now let's be out of here; the place is starting to stink and it'll be full of flies soon.'

'Aye,' he muttered. 'There's a beer house a step away.' Going to the door he called, 'Mrs Nabbs, I want you and one of the men to keep watch here. You'll find me at Kettle's, and mind you send to fetch me when the constable or the mortuary men come.'

So we pushed our way down through the thickening crowd on the stairs and for my part not sorry to get out to the court, though the air there was pressing down upon us from the low sky, but not yet so dark as it had seemed from that tenement. Once emerged the physician announced, 'Aye; Mrs Nabbs'll charge 'em a ha'penny apiece to view the body.'

'Begod,' I said, not unamused, 'you've got a sharp eye for profit in Wapping.'

'Losh, man,' he retorted, 'use your senses. The woman's husband's away at sea and God knows whether she'll ever see him again. And she's lost a lodger in Kemble. She's bound to make a copper or two as best she can.'

By this time we were at the beer house, a miserable place but very likely better than some of them; in short, the front room of one of these tenements with its door open on the court, a rude bench around the walls, sawdust on the floor, and barrels on their trestles at the far end. Save for a squint eyed old harridan presiding over these the place was empty as there was better entertainment to be had a few doors away, but she managed to crack a smile for the physician and it seemed that here too his writ ran better than the King's law. I observed that Maggsy, who has his own superstitions, crossed his fingers at her but Dr McGrath said, 'Now, Mother Kettle, we'll have a pint each of your strong ale, but then take yourself off; we've private business to talk about.'

It was Pichard's beer, a brew which I find uneasy on the stomach and uncommon fartacious; I noted also that our dour Scotsman left me to pay for the stuff but I magnanimously allowed this to go, waiting only for the old crone to shuffle off before dragging up a rickety stool and staring, 'Now, Dr McGrath, we've little time. That wench is what we see of a plan miscarried, and the rogues concerned will stop at nothing to set it right for one simple reason. A few words from her will stretch their necks for 'em.'

'You've little need to tell me what I can see for myself,' he observed. 'And I'll thank you again to mind your manners about her.'

A smaller man would have lost his patience with the fellow, and even I was near enough to it. But I asked, 'How long might it be before she can talk?'

'I don't know. We dinna ken which way this contusion will take her. But I'll tell ye this much. In no caircumstances will I have her questioned and fretted before she's fine and ready for it. In no caircumstances whatever.'

'D'you understand the wench's danger?' I demanded. 'I've told you, she's as good as a rope necklace to some rogue or rogues.'

'I understand it well enough,' he retorted. 'As I understand the danger of driving her clean out of her wits. Would you see the puir wee lassie in Bedlam? We must stand close by and be prepaired to fight. Aye,' he growled, 'and by God I will. Tonight'll see the worst of it.'

'You're making a Covent Garden Opera of the matter,' I said, 'but let it pass. Can you tell me this much? The fetter scars upon her ankles. I'd set 'em at some three to four days old. Is that your reckoning?'

'Near enough,' he agreed cautiously. 'Four or five.'

'So that puts it about last Saturday she was taken; and held since then, most likely aboard a ship. By God, this is pestilential beer. Now then, Dr McGrath, here's an oddity that sticks in my gullet like a fishbone. You may know that by long custom and advertisement in the *Bow Street Gazette* all gentlemen of standing are requested and required to send immediate messages at fastest to the Bow Street magistrate when they hear of any crime, felony, or misdemeanour. I'd say abducting and kidnapping this young woman was one of those if not all three. Yet nothing had been heard of it at the Bow Street Office even this morning, as I was there myself; five days after. So what does that mean?'

Maggsy stopped guzzling and took his snout out of the pot. 'Somebody don't know or don't want to know, and most like don't want to; I reckon anybody'd notice if Copperknob was about, they wouldn't say of a sudden "Why, God's Weskit, where's Copperknob got to? I don't recollect seeing her since Saturday." '

'In his genteel way he's got the sense of it,' I said. 'Yet it's out of all sense to suppose that of an entire household, family and servants, one or more would not report the matter. Anybody who can talk of fifty thousand in the Consols is a person of some consequence. As to that I've certain notions, but they can wait for a bit.

For now, Dr McGrath,' I concluded, 'a little before that boy came to fetch us to Lieutenant Kemble you was saying you'd made certain enquiries about Limehouse yourself.'

'Aye,' he agreed. 'The object, ye'll understand, was to discover folk who might have seen her. I had little good of it save for a single wherryman, the name of Joseph Binns by Limehouse Hole Stairs. It seems he saw the lassie come ashore.'

'God's Teeth,' I exclaimed, 'and you've kept it to yourself till now? If you're as careful with your money as you are with your words, Dr McGrath, you'll die a rich man.'

'And if you don't mind your manners, Mr Sturrock, you and me might well come to blows before we've done,' the physician observed darkly. 'You'll conseeder that I've had verra little chance to tell you.'

'I'll admire to see that,' Maggsy announced, 'I reckon you and him might have a rare mill, but you want to watch it, as he's a damnation dirty fighter when he starts.'

McGrath turned on him a look which silenced the monster as well as I could have done and continued, 'This Binns was at work on his boat under the stairs, which are constructed of open timber so you can see through 'em, but not much. It was a little before darkening, at which time he obsairved two boys, as he thought, pull in with a ship's gig. They'd come from downstream and across the river. One of them, and I've no doubt it was the lassie, got out on the instant and passed out of his sight. But he heard her tell the other, "No, Henry, you must please do as I ask. You are a strong boy and very brave and you'll be there by the morning. Remember to say that I have gone first to Mr Moxon, and they must please enquire quickly for Geoffrey at Coffin Mill." Upon that Binns heard the lassie's feet running up the stairs, while the first boy turned the boat and pulled away downstream like the devil was at his tail.'

'Commonly these ship's boats have a name on 'em,' I said. 'Did your wherryman see it?'

'Binns canna read, and was not all that concairned. He did not recognise the boat, nor will he swear to the precise words of the lassie. But I'm satisfied that's the sense of them.'

'Then could he describe the boy?'

'Little better. Sixteenish, seventeen he thought mebbe, but dressed like the lassie. Sailor's trousers and shirt and short blue jacket with brass buttons. Like a fancy captain's rig, he said.'

'And what's a fancy captain?'

'Some of them affect to put their cabin crews in a kind of uniform; cabin boy or mebbe a clerk or servant. It's commonplace enough. You see it often in the Navy.'

'The Navy again,' I mused. 'But I can't fancy that. Even allowing for naval officers being what they are I can't fancy 'em abducting this wench and holding her in leg irons.' The physician made a Scottish rumbling in his throat, but I went on, 'She was dressed like the boy, sailor's trousers and shirt and short blue jacket, yet when she fetched up at the Widow Rooke's it was only sailor's trousers and shirt; as we have that good woman's concern for her modesty. And I don't wonder; what some of these young ladies get up to these days takes your breath away. But somewhere in Limehouse or Wapping there's a blue jacket lost with brass buttons. I'd like to have that. It might tell us the name of the ship; and that's the heart of your mystery.'

The physician was somewhat flushed about the neck, but I did not expect him to take a seizure at his age. With a certain malice he said, 'If it's been found it's most likely in a slop shop by now. There are dozens if not scores of 'em. You might search for a month.'

'We'll not try,' I told him. 'The girl was in leg irons and she couldn't have got out by herself. Somebody had to unlock 'em and that other boy's the most likely. It's Master Henry we must find.' Maggsy perceived his own fate in this and opened his ugly mouth to protest but I went on, 'And here we've Coffin Mill once more. Seemingly down river and a damned long pull if he was not to get there till morning. D'you know of any such place?'

'He'd wait for the tide. And if I knew of it I'd be away there

40

myself. But you've dozens of creeks and close about thirty miles between London and the sea.'

'Be damned,' I reflected, 'we've a fine mess of names too. Geoffrey, Mr Moxon, Mary Carson and Captain Blackbird. And save for one of 'em I'd say again wait until your wench can tell them all for herself. But note that "Blackbirding" is a seaman's term for the slaving trade, and leg irons are an adjunct of slave ships.'

'Then you do propose that the murder of Kemble has a part with the lassie?' he demanded.

'We can't tell,' I replied with some impatience. 'That's a mere observation yet. In the Art and Science of Detection it's a prime error to run ahead of your evidence, though we're bound to consider it. This woman now, Meg; are you certain of it that's all she had of Kemble? No more than the words "Captain Blackbird"?'

'So she persists. She said he was muttering more but she could not make it out. There was one word which sounded like "resistible".'

'God's sake,' I requested, 'let's have no more conundrums. We've got a bellyful of 'em for a start. Now then, do you know of any woman named Mary Carson in this pestilential place?'

He fell to coughing and grumphing in his throat. 'Not Mary Carson as preecise. There's a Mary Larsen in Ropemakers Yard. She's a whore mistress. Man,' he burst out, 'I'll swear the lassie cried "Mary Carson" plain enough.'

I reflected on that and at last said, 'It won't do. To be sure there's some such stink about this business. It's regular traffic in country wenches but they go willing, poor sluts, hoping for the joys of London; there's no need of leg irons with 'em. Nor this one ain't the kind to waste on a common sailor's knocking shop. She's more like Piccadilly.'

Once again I feared the physician was either going to take a seizure or attack me, but high words were saved by one of the women from the tenement then appearing, and screaming that the constable and mortuary men had come. He calmed himself on the thought of his professional affairs, but still turned a confounded ugly look on me and observed, 'You've the courtesies of the lower deck, Mr Sturrock. But what d'ye propose now then?'

'Courtesies enough,' I retorted. 'There's no harm in plain words. I propose you shall ask the girl short and simple what her tale is. But if you won't, then put it about that she's out of her wits and can't talk and very likely never will again. That might hold these rogues off for a time, but if it don't they're bound to try and quieten her for good. You'll do well to keep a close watch by her at night.'

Seemingly bereft of words our good physician went off and I continued to Maggsy: 'Now, you little monster, I'm more concerned with Lieutenant Kemble, so for a special treat you shall have the mystery of our red headed lady all to yourself. And you'll start by going first to find this Joseph Binns at Limehouse Hole Stairs, and then on to look for the other boy. We want any word you can hear of him.'

'Not likely,' he said flatly. 'To hell with Limehouse Hole Stairs. It's as dark as the inside of a sow's belly now, and if there's some cove aroaring round along of a nine inch knife I don't fancy getting my tripes tickled with it. Let it wait till the morning.'

I cannot put up with rebellion. 'Recollect where your bread and butter comes from, Master Maggsy, and reflect where you'll end if I cast you off.' Yet a little flattery also goes a long way with the young and I added, 'I never thought to hear you confess that you're no match for poor rogues. You know as well as I do you can move as silent and unseen as a cat in the dark. Moreover,' I finished, 'you shall take sixpence to spend as you like on bread and cheese and beer. We'll set off by way of Captain Isaac's to have the latest intelligence.'

So with him cursing and complaining beside me we hastened back through the dark lanes and alleys in the sulphurous air; still with not a breath of wind stirring, the ships hanging sullen on a molten tide in the river, and dimly perceived figures going about their own business—no doubt unlawful—in the penumbra of the close buildings. It was very near as bad as the stews of Seven Dials

where even Providence holds His Nose, and there was fresh drama-
tics at the captain's lodging. He was at the gate stumping on his
wooden leg for excitement; but, thank God, the other old salt pork
was not to be seen. 'Jer'my,' he cried, 'where's Dr Ian?'

'Why,' I said, 'looking to the business of one corpse that he
ain't despatched himself. Is all safe here?'

'The wench's woke up,' he answered, 'and Mrs Captain Rooke
clucking like a hen with chickens for the doctor.'

'Is she clear or addled?' I demanded.

'Dunno for sure,' the old gentleman answered. 'Pretty fair so
Mrs Captain says, but not to be fretted. What's the news about
Lieutenant Kemble. Is he bad?'

'He'll never be worse.' I told the tale shortly, at the same time
giving Master Maggsy a light tap with my cane to start him on his
way, for the unwilling wretch seemed disposed to linger. Then cutting off Isaac's explanations I added, 'We'll have some plain talk
now without McGrath's damned medical obfuscations.'

'You'd best not,' he started, but before he could stump after me
I was already mounting the stairs, set on having a quick and simple
end to one mystery at the least. Nevertheless at the chamber door I
put on my most genteel manner, scratched on it like any footman,
and entered with my hat in the crook of my arm. But for all my
pains the Widow Rooke was not overjoyed to see me, and with an air
halfway between that of a laying out and a lying in, she whispered, 'I'd as soon it was Dr Ian, Mr Sturrock.'

A sour welcome considering all my trouble, but I made my best
Frenchified bow at the bed; and a most pathetic and affecting sight
it was, like the romance of some lady novelist. Our wench was lying
half propped up, pale still but with a bit more colour now, and that
mop of coppery bronze hair not unbecoming for all its immodest
cut; and then opening a pair of very pretty violet eyes which gave
even me a singular start. It was no wonder the poor physician was
struck between wind and water and damned near foundering. But
I said, 'Your servant, ma'm. And I hope I see you well.'

'Pretty well, I thank you,' she answered. 'I have a pesty headache.' Her eyes strayed past me, turning about the chamber, while I stood observing her, reflecting again that by the look of that chin when she was in her right mind it would be a particular mind of her own. Then, her eyes coming back to me, she continued, 'I am something in a daze. Who are you, sir?'

'Sturrock, ma'am,' I told her. 'Of Bow Street Police Office.'

The eyes closed for a minute and then opened their violet at me once more. 'Bow Street Police Office? What is that?'

Be damned, I was not a little touched myself, but for all Mrs Rooke protesting and rustling behind me I was bound to try to get some sense out of her before that doting physician jumped up like a Jack-of-the-Box. 'It's of no matter. Only tell us who you are, ma'am. Where's your family? They should be asking after you. Your father; or brothers? Or husband maybe?'

She seemed to ponder on that, frowning over it, whispered something so soft it was no more than a breath, and then shook her head and closed her eyes yet again; while Mrs Rooke plucked at my sleeve saying, 'I'll not have this, Mr Sturrock. Dr Ian says she's not to be fretted.'

'There's one man been fretted worse,' I told her, 'and I mean to know why. Now, ma'am,' I went on, 'but one simple question and I'll trouble you no more. I have my headaches myself and a touch of the livers now and again; but they're commonly from Madeira laid on top of port. I'll ask no more than to shake or nod your head. Have you ever heard of one Captain Blackbird?'

But I had no answer to it, or not a plain one, for she said, 'Please; let him leave me be,' turned her head to one side and, be hanged, went clean off in a swoon.

I was nonplussed; the more so as Mrs Rooke turned on me hissing like a swan with cygnets, flapping me away, thrusting me from the chamber and there using such a variety of observations as I hope never to hear from a lady again; if she'd picked 'em up from her late husband he must have been a brisk man in a strong wind at sea. A predicament not improved by discovering Captain Isaac stumping his wooden leg and clasping his belly in laughter.

'I knowed it,' he announced. 'I told you so, Jer'my. She ain't a woman to be crossed. Belay now,' he continued in answer to several pronouncements of my own. 'Come and smoke a pipe on the after deck. I've got a bag of prime Latakia as a captain brings me from Smyrna.'

So I suffered myself to be led out to a pretty neat little enclosure at the back of the house, where there was even a few fanciful rose bushes, a lantern and a flag staff, a seat to survey the river, and a flight of private steps down to the water. Here among clouds of fragrance—though not a tobacco I commonly take to as being somewhat too scented for my taste—I let some of the wind spill out of my sails, as old Isaac put it, while I pondered on several curious matters in this mystery.

'Flat calm,' Isaac observed. 'Ain't never a ship moved this last six watches.' Calm indeed it was for with a brassy moon now coming up the masts rose before us scarcely swaying, fading in brush strokes in a dim haze, the sails of such as had them set hanging as limp as cotton, and the only movement the reflections of ships' lamps rippling in the river, and a line of distant twinkling torches and flares on the further bank. 'I recollect we was once laid up like this twenty-two days in the Bay of Bengal,' the captain continued. 'The water like molten lead about us and the sky like a copper platter set atop of our mast heads. Aye, and the sharks cutting great swathes of sea fire around us as they was waiting for the corpusses that had died of thirst and fever to be tossed overboard.'

'A flat calm,' I mused. 'And if our rogues are quartered on a ship they can't move.'

'They could tow her. Though they'd not get little more'n steerage way. I recollect once,' Isaac started again, 'we towed the old *Susannah and Jane* for three days and nights. Cutters port'n starboard and crew spell and spell about at the oars. Be blasted, we could see the wind but couldn't catch it. And the more the poor swabs pulled the thirstier they come. Was very near a mutiny save for...'

'A fine tale, Isaac,' I said. 'But have you thought Mary Carson

45

might be the name of a ship? And lying somewhere down river.'

He was put out by having his opera spoiled and agreed pettishly. 'Might be. That old fool Coggins declares it is. Swears he knowed of her when he was on the Americas trade five or six years back, and Boston built. But I wouldn't give a sea cook's fart for a word he says, and less when he's drunk. Anyways, I ain't never heard of her and, God bless you, there's hundreds of ships between this and Greenwich.'

'I want you to find out,' I told him. 'Tomorrow, Isaac. And if it is we've one mystery done with. Or perhaps two.' I reflected on one useful thing that physician had said and then asked, 'How's the tide, Isaac?'

'Why, scuttle and sink me, you hop from one tit to another like a flea on a doxy,' he complained. Nevertheless he stumped away to stand regarding the river as all these ancient mariners must ever do before they give a simple answer. 'Just on running up,' he announced, returning. 'Be full flood close on four o'clock the morning and then turn to ebb.'

'And if you was leading an expedition,' I asked, 'as it might be from down river, how would you use it?'

That put him in a chuckling good humour once more at the thought of a fresh recollection. 'A cutting out party? Did I never tell you of that occasion in the Sunda Sea? All them damnation islands, scores of 'em; and the fuzzies'd got my fust mate trussed up on account of him trying to show one of their women Christian charity. So I calls a boat's crew away...'

I cut him short yet again. 'It's the London River we're concerned with. How would you use the tide?'

'Why it's plain and simple enough. Come up on the last of the flood, see about my business, and go back on the ebb. I'm damned if I see what tack you're on now, Jer'my. And there's another matter,' he continued, puffing smoke from his pipe like a manufactory, 'I'd as soon you didn't go aheaving across his hawse all the time with Dr Ian. He's a rare good messmate. An uncommon ship's surgeon as was, but got dismissed the Navy by way of disagree-

ment with his captain over too much flogging, and don't have two
pennies to his name now. For all that there's never a kindness nor
attention he'll deny a soul, and I'll not see him put down. Not me
nor Mrs Captain.' He vented another blast from his pipe. 'So we'll
come to an understanding.'

'That's as may be,' I answered, 'but he entertains some pestilential Whiggish notions. Moreover he's a hindrance in this matter of
the wench.'

'Is he so?' the fellow himself demanded from behind me. 'And
what are you then?' He had come unseen from the house, with a
face once more as black as thunder and yet most curiously suf-
fused with red; indeed I was about to advise him to consider his
health when he burst out, 'By God, you dab footed dotterel, you
damnation lubberly Drury Lane thieftaker, I've a great good mind
to break your bluidy neck for you.'

'Pray, sir, moderate your manner,' I replied, 'else I shall be
obliged to toss you in the river. What's upset you now?'

'What's upset me?' he demanded on a strangled note and falling
into his own uncouth tongue, 'Laird of Heaven hear the mon.
What's upset me, ye skelpie? What but you might have druv the
lassie into Bedlam.'

'Sir,' I retorted, 'you're an indifferent fanciful physician yourself,
obfuscating the world with your whimsical notions. I'll tell you
that wench'll cozen you before she's done.'

On that he started at me like a baited bull, and there might
well have been a mischief and bloodshed had not old Isaac bravely
interposed his wooden leg between us and cried, 'Avast there. Spill
your wind, Dr Ian. And you, Jer'my, haul off.'

I drew back agreeing, 'Haul off it is, Isaac, and haul off I will.'

'What?' demanded the physician on a fresh belch of the bag-
pipes, now seemingly wanting his fish both fried and boiled. 'You
canna do that, man. You're an officer of the Law and you're bound
to investeegate a felony.'

'And so I shall,' I replied, 'but in my own fashion. As to the
young lady, I'll advise you to keep a close guard on her tonight.

And for the rest pray tell my clerk that he'll discover me at The Prospect of Whitby.' I felt a pang of pity for Isaac in his astonishment, but settling my beaver more firmly and taking up my cane I turned out through the wicket gate to the passage beside the house leaving them both dumbfounded. An unkindness to a good and innocent old gentleman you may fancy; but to be plain I had my own plans, and this short and sharp tiff suited them very well without need of further explanations.

CHAPTER THREE

At the Prospect there was a fairish crowd in the downstairs common-room, a haze of tobacco smoke in the lamplight, serving men and wenches still bustling, and a rumble of conversation; but respectable and sober as befitted the place. I noted Landlord Comber in close talk with Mr Colville and several more gentlemen but did not approach them, pretty certain that before long they would come to me. Taking one of the settles I called for a pint of claret from that pert plump and lustful little baggage—noting as Master Maggsy had claimed that her mind was on other matters than Sunday School hymns—and within a minute Mr Comber came carrying it to me followed close by the others.

'God's sake, Mr Sturrock,' he started. 'What's this we hear of poor Kemble?'

Then followed volley and broadside of questions which I answered one way and another with all eyes upon me until becoming tired of it I finished, 'Well there it is. A mystery and like to remain one. It could have been a quarrel over some doxy or trot; though they ain't commonly stabbed in the back in such cases. Or it might be he was engaged about some smuggling enterprise. I hear there's a lot of it up and down the river now the French ports are open again.'

I fancied the landlord turned a thought towards a chamber pot look about his chaps on that, but Mr Colville said, 'I don't see how a man can engage in smuggling short of a ship.'

'That's very true,' I agreed. 'You knew the lieutenant then, sir?'

'I'd heard the tale of his ill luck, and thought to enquire to find him a berth. Not much. No more than Second Mate, but the blue water again. Well, there's an end of that now.' He added, 'Gentlemen, shall we set about our hand of whist?' and then as three of them trooped off to the stairs turned back to me and said, 'Join us

49

later if you've a mind, Mr Sturrock. I've a proposal for you concerning Kemble.'

So I was left alone with the landlord and asked, 'Can you find me
my supper? Be damned I've traipsed my feet off half over Wapping with questions; and got never an answer for my pains.'

'There's a game pie; and a cut off the sirloin.' He bent over to
take a light for his pipe from the candle. 'It's common talk Kemble
was alive when you got to him. Couldn't he speak a word or two?'

'Nothing of any sense,' I said. 'The poor devil was near gone and
never saw who struck him. I doubt we shall ever discover the
villain. And for now I'm more concerned with a bed for the night.'

'They say Dr McGrath was with him too. If he could do nothing
nobody might.' He seemed to reflect on that and then added, 'As
to a bed you must suit yourself. We ain't a post house and don't
have much in that way. There's Mr Colville in the first chamber,
and a young lady in Number Two, with her gentleman next along.'
He gazed over to where Rosie was wagging her rump and grinned
at me sideways. 'Rosie might accommodate you if you're in the
mood. She's a lively piece, and I daresay she'll make you snug
enough.'

'Then Rosie it is,' I declared. 'If the accommodation's what it
looks like nothing'll suit me better. But who's the young lady and
her gentleman? Would that be the couple who came in a post
chaise just when I left today?'

'That's right. They're waiting for a ship as I understand.' Offering
no more on that he said, 'I'll take a sounding with Rosie and send
her over to you,' and added with a laugh, 'We do our best to oblige.'
Then, starting to move away, he stopped once more to ask, 'How's
the old captain with this wench he picked up?'

'There's nothing in it,' I told him. 'Some sailor's doxy that got
herself mishandled. But you know what Isaac Bolton is as well as
I do. As tender hearted as a baby and makes a romantic tale out
of pissing against the wall. I've advised him to have the wench
away to Bart's Hospital and be done with her.'

He turned away on that, and then in some few minutes more

Rosie came bearing a tray and platters which promised a very fair supper; and a manner with it which offered a lively enterprise later, for I never saw a bawdier little bitch. Giving her tits a swing and a bounce as she set it out before me, and herself with it, she enquired, 'Be you the gentleman who's asking for bed room?'

'If you can spare it, my dear,' I answered. 'And if it's as plump and downy as it looks I couldn't wish for better. I'll not ask you to sleep upon the boards.'

'La, you're saucy,' she retorted. 'You'd have small hope if you did.'

There were several more such pert exchanges, which I shall not report here as being common to such occasions, but at last she left me to my game pie, another pint of claret, and my own reflections. I had plenty of these by now, and for the first time today leisure to consider them; and for what these were, as is always my habit I have set down everything most precisely for your consideration so you may judge them for yourself. I was in no great hurry, but sat at ease smoking a pipe, contemplating the company and Rosie bouncing about her business, turning over certain stratagems in my mind and several naughty but not unpleasing anticipations. In the Art and Science of Detection a man must be all things to all women.

It was another hour or so before Master Maggsy appeared; and you never viewed such a picture. Limping, the knees of his fine new pantaloons black with mud and his beaver dinted, blood and snot half wiped from his chaps, one eye closed in as nice a shiner as I've ever seen, and stinking very near as bad as he did when I first found him; yet not without a kind of triumph. Gazing at him horror struck I demanded, 'What of hell have you been up to?' and then added, 'Be off this instant and clean yourself in the horse trough.'

He glowered at me like a wild cat from a gorse bush but went off obediently enough, only beseeching that for God's sake I bespeak him a pot of ale, and I called to Rosie for a dock of Madeira for myself together with small beer and a plenitude of pie for my clerk; not without some further forward exchanges from the trollop. He was already back, damp but sweeter though cursing and muttering, when she returned bringing it, and she cried, 'Save us, is that your clerk then, the saucy toad. You'll have some rum entries in your ledger if it is.'

'You'll have some rum entries in yours before I've done,' I threatened her, but not ill humoured.

She flounced off in a fit of giggles, and Maggsy fell on his supper like a ravening wolf only pausing to observe with a further glower, 'You're at it again, are you? Making up for a rollick with Rosie whiles I do the work and damn near get killed for it. Well, if you ask me, you've bit off more'n you can chew this time.'

Whether the rascal was speaking of Rosie or this singular mystery I did not enquire, but left him to eat and drink his full. Then giving him the remainder of my Madeira to finish for a kindness— and also as I had a busy night before me—I said, 'Now we'll hear how you came in that state.'

'It warn't playing kiss-in-the-ring, nor yet Ride a Cock Hoss like you're up to with that Rosie. Nor you won't never get nothing out of that boy as put Copperknob ashore neither. He's corpussed; found first light today, and the back of his nut stove in, and that's corpussed enough for anybody. I dunno as I like the look of this lot.'

'Be damned,' I said. 'That's another setback. But let's have your tale in due order.'

I shall spare the most part of it, and his elegant observations. Save that in one store yard he had found a watchman of whom the girl had enquired the way to London and asked was it far. Then in the Grapes Tavern he had seen that mulatto who was in the crowd at the Prospect this same afternoon, but had not stopped for discussion on perceiving the said mulatto and several sailors regarding him with close interest. Thereafter he had hurried on his way with one eye over his shoulder, the cowardly little wretch. 'Reckoned out one thing anyway,' he finished. 'Copperknob's heading for London; Copperknob says she's agoing to Mr Moxon. So Mr Moxon's in London.'

'Now who'd have thought of that,' I asked. 'Maggsy, you're a living miracle. We shall have to have you at Lady Dorothea's soirée for a philosopher. But if you can spare a minute from your profound reflections, what about the boy; and the jacket?'

'I'm acoming to it, ain't I? Found the wherryman in a beer house close by Limekiln Dock, and that cost me a pint of beer only to find as some boy had come ashore deaded t'other side the Isle of Dogs, and it was the same one and found by a mudlark name of Billy Snape. So I don't fancy that neither but trudged all across there and wore my heels down to my arse about it; and this mudlark Snape was three times as big as I am, and lives under an old boat turned keel uppards. Well the corpus'd already been took by the dead cart, but I says it's a golden sovereign for information, and that set him talking quick enough, and he reckoned the boy'd got himself bounced on the back of the nob and chucked in the river the night before at some place called Bow Creek.'

'It's another vexation,' I said. 'We're baulked at every turn. Was there any more to it?'

'Oh no; nothing much. Not a lot, save Snape very near killed me. He says what about the sovereign, and I says what sovereign and what about the jacket, and he got a bit low and vulgar then so I hit him in the eye.' The dreadful creature drew a deep breath. 'God's Tripes, I thought I was a goner; he was atossing me like a bull with a terrier till I recollected Mr William Makepeace's advice that it's all very fine to fight fair if you fancy it, but safer to kick 'em in the cobblers; and this I done. Then while he was awhooping and yellocking I got astride of him, and by the time I'd rubbed his nose in the mud about six times he changed his mind about matters, and seems he'd sold the jacket to a slop shop, so I give him two or three more for a blessing and he screeched to cry quits and I should have a button. Seems he'd took a fancy to the buttons and cut 'em off to keep for himself.'

'Maggsy,' I told him, 'you're a sweet child. A singular sweet, pretty child. For God's sake what good's a button?'

'It's better'n nothing, ain't it?' he demanded.

I drew the candles closer to examine this treasure. It was nothing very uncommon, made of brass and stamped pretty clear with a device or coat of arms such as you sometimes see on servants' livery, though a shade bigger than most. It looked little enough; yet on reflecting over it I fancied I saw some way in which it might be made of use, and was then pleased to commend Maggsy. 'You've done pretty well,' I told him. 'You might even learn your trade yet if you don't get yourself hanged first.' He was now engaged scratting up the last crumbs of pie from his platter, and I finished, 'So when you've done stuffing yourself we'll set to work again,' gave him certain further instructions, and turned to the stairs myself to go up and join Mr Colville and his friends.

They were seated in the bay window, sovereigns and cards on the table; but it seemed to be an idle game and far from the style of any you'd see in the clubs of St James's, for they had just finished a hand and were talking at their ease before taking up again. For a minute I stood in the shadows watching them. Mr Colville as described before and then a squarish teak and ironwood fellow they addressed as Captain Furlong, of middle years, hard face and rat trap mouth; another I acquitted on the instant of any part in this business, being too fat, easy, and lazy looking—though I have known some uncommon wicked fat rogues in my time—and the last who might well have fitted the bill. Somewhat younger than the others, dark, lean and wiry, of a foreign cut and with black hair caught in a club at the back of his head; a man I'd reckon an uncertain friend and an ugly enemy. His name, as I learned later, was Mr Lopez. But villainy is not to be read in the face; or if it were no small part of our Members of the Commons would cease from troubling us the sooner, to say nothing of the Lords.

They were discussing matters of shipping—from which I discovered that Mr Colville, Captain Furlong, and Lopez all had ships in the river—the peace and trade and the strange dull weather.

While I was still standing unseen Captain Furlong asked, 'Where d'you sail for then, Mr Colville?'

'The Ivory Coast,' he answered. 'When I've settled my business and the confounded calm breaks. Your weather wise fellows give it another day or two yet.'

'Did you find the war harmed trade much, sir?' the fat fellow enquired. He seemed somewhat tight of breath and wheezed as he spoke.

Mr Lopez barked a short laugh. 'It depends on the trade.'

'Aye,' Captain Furlong agreed. 'So it might with yours. But how long d'you give the peace?'

At this one of the serving men came clumping up the stairs in his oafish way and Mr Colville turned to see me standing by. 'Hello there, Mr Sturrock,' he said. 'Come and join us, sir. And tell us what they say in London. How long do they give it?'

'Why, sir,' I answered, 'twelve months or less. Bonaparte's stretching out his claws all over Europe, and there'll be no rest till they're clipped. He's a rascal as signs a treaty with one hand and throttles you with the other.'

'Stake me,' Mr Lopez observed, 'a politician as well as a thief-taker.'

'No, sir,' I returned, keeping civil. 'But repeating the common talk. I'm more concerned with Lieutenant Kemble. And as to that, if anybody can tell me anything, little though it be, I shall be obliged; as I'm at a right loss.'

Mr Colville looked around at all of them. 'Well now, gentlemen, what can we tell Mr Sturrock? Has any of us seen or heard anything? No matter what?'

Seemingly none of them had, for nothing was offered, and at last affecting as somewhat shy of it I ventured, 'Yourself, sir; you said you'd thought to find Kemble a berth, as Second Mate. Wasn't that a bit sudden? On such short acquaintance.'

'Short acquaintance?' he repeated. 'How d'you get that notion? I knew Kemble since years back; many years, and I've heard much of him since. I was shocked to find him fallen so low.' Reflecting

on this I nodded as humble as a bumpkin with the squire, and
Mr Colville went on, 'I'll go further. I said I'd a proposition, Mr
Sturrock, and so I have. Gentlemen,' he announced, 'I've a mind
to put up a purse. A hundred guineas to find out who killed
Kemble; a reward to Mr Sturrock. Do any of you care to join me?'

You never saw such mixed dismay. For my part I announced I
was most gratified, but you'd have thought he'd asked the others
to give him their ships with wives, daughters and doxies thrown in
for good measure. Only the hard faced captain was plain about it,
saying, 'No, I'll be damned if I do. It's all very fine for a ship
owner, Colville, but I'm a poor sailor, and I never knew the man
from Adam. There's a seaman gets himself killed in some port or
the other every hour of the day, and the most part of 'em ask for
it.'

'No, now, that's unchristian,' the fat one cried, as near to agitation as his weight and wheeziness would let him be. 'Though with
me the spice trade's never been worse; prices too high to buy the
stuff and money too tight to sell it. Yet I'll not be outdone. I'll offer
five, Mr Colville.'

I was watching the dark Mr Lopez from the corners of my eyes,
and he gave another of his short laughs. 'Is that how high you
rate the fellow's guts, Simpkin? Well enough, Colville,' he said, 'I
don't have your money but I'll throw twenty in,' and then added,
'Wait though, Master Sturrock. I like to know what I'm putting my
odds on. D'you have any tricks to turn up at all?'

'Only the one,' I confessed, now taking out Maggsy's button and
laying it under the candles, where it lay shining among the cards
and sovereigns. 'But it might hang some rogue yet. It was found in
Kemble's lodging; as he might have snatched it from a seaman's
jacket.'

No man can watch three others at once. So far as I could observe
Mr Colville studied it with only slight interest, but I could swear
a quick sharp look and some puzzlement passed between Mr Lopez
and Captain Furlong. Then Mr Colville said, 'I wish you well, but
I don't see what you'll have of that.'

'As Dr Samuel Johnson has observed, sir,' I told him, 'knowledge is of two kinds: we know a subject ourselves, or we know where we can find information upon it. There's a certain office in London where I might discover the name this crest belongs to.'

'God bless us, so there is,' wheezed Mr Simpkin. 'Begod that's smartish. Herald's Office; the College of Arms by Doctors' Commons.' He gave a fat chuckle. 'I'm acquainted of it as Mrs Simpkin, the vain creature, is forever at me to apply for patents. Think little of such flim-flams meself, but she will have a coat of arms. Considers a clove and two nutmegs proper would be most appropriate.'

Forbearing to tell him what a clove and two netmegs would look like, or that Mrs Simpkin must have some damnation comical notions, I could have nutmegged him to hell for giving the others time to think. The moment, if there had ever been one, was passed now; but continuing genteel I said, 'That's right, sir. And I shall be there first or second thing tomorrow's morning.'

Neither did that produce any fresh response save that Mr Colville turned the button over idly in his fingers, while Captain Furlong knocked out his pipe to take a fresh fill of tobacco and Mr Lopez demanded, 'What're we at? Cards or a sea lawyers' meeting? Don't you fellows want your money back?'

So being dismissed I thanked them again for their kind offer of reward and assured them of my best attention, took the button and my leave, and descended once more to the common-room. Here Master Maggsy was already seated at the settle; moreover with a fresh pot of small beer on the board at my charge. 'Don't stint yourself,' I advised him. 'Call for a quart of finest brandy while you're about it. Now then, what did you get?'

'Nothing partic'lar,' he confessed. 'Fust door was locked fast, next was voices beyond though couldn't catch much for all I got my ear hard up against it, but the last come better; that being open a bit so I crept in. Candles lit, gent's coat'n travelling capes tossed down, and a brace of pistols, also another door open to next chamber and they was still on the go in there, a wench and a cove, and I thinks "What ho, here's a bit more rolling and rollicking, I'd admire to have a look at this." But not so. Wench is atalking kind of oddsy, she says "I do not like it, I do not care for this countree, why does it take so long?" and the cove answers "Be hanged, Consooela, these damned bankers always keep their fingers on your money till the last minute." I dunno as I never heard a name like that before, it sounds Frenchy to me.'

'Consuela,' I said. 'More like Spanish. Continue.'

'Ain't a lot more. He says "There's things we never reckoned on and no good falling into the vapours," and on that it sounds like he's acoming back into this chamber where I am and I get myself out quick.'

'It might mean much or little,' I mused. 'Very well then, Master Maggsy; I shall ask the landlord to find some corner where you may sleep. But for choice with the potboys, as I now wish you to discover all you can of three more gentlemen.'

'What?' he screeched in a rage. 'You'll have me with the potboys while you're ariding and rollicking Rosie? I'll be damned if I will.'

'You'll be damned if you don't,' I warned him. 'I've told you, the mystery of this wench is all for you. Why it's a signal privilege, and I expect you to do your duty as I shall do mine.' The little whelp snickered at that, but I finished, 'Remember these names. Captain Furlong, Mr Simpkin, and Mr Lopez. And likewise keep a watch on the time, for I want you ready to come away with me again by three o'clock.'

It was now growing late, the company down here falling off to a scant half dozen, and cutting short the contumacious wretch's further protests I moved on to settle his accommodation with Mr Comber. I next considered whether to take a peep at the woman Consuela and her gentleman by the simple ruse of tumbling into their chambers as a drunken roisterer but decided against it, especially as he had a pair of pistols lying handy. Neither was there much chance of it, for pretty well on the minute as I moved Rosie was at my side saying brisk and businesslike, 'Well then, come on; and bring a pot of something up with you.'

There must be a genteel veil across the best part of that encounter or I shall have my publisher demanding 'What, sirrah'—for this is how these brass faced and flint hearted taskmasters commonly address their poor scribblers—'What the devil has this lewd romp with a strumpet to do with the Art and Science of Detection?' As to that, Rosie was no mystery being very plain and simple in her desires, manners, and performance; but in the course of our charges and counter-charges, retirements and parleys she gave me several intelligences; of which one, be damned to it, at a single stroke demolished the only conclusion I had so far reached.

I never saw a lustier nor more impatient bitch. I was barely ready for the jump myself before she was out of her clouts, stripped, and back on the pallet bed, arms and legs grappling and saying again, 'Well come on, then; d'you want to take all night?' So we were at it in a cavalry charge on a rolling mount, sabre forward and head down, no quarter asked and none given, spike the guns and home. 'Begod,' she cried with a half nelson lock on me and damned near taking a bite out of my neck, 'you're a thrusting rider.'

'You're no tender footed yearling yourself,' I retorted, disengaging for air, taking a draught of the claret and giving her a mouthful to quieten her. 'D'you rear like that with Mr Colville? Or ain't he had a ride yet, as I fancy he came here only today?'

'Only today?' she repeated, giving a heave with her rump that lifted me like taking a five barred gate. 'Why he's been in and out of the Prospect the last week or more.'

'He's what?' I demanded, getting a grip on her buttocks, a handful on each side to stop further plunging. 'Are you sure of that?'

'Course I'm sure. He's a gentleman any lady'd notice. Though keeps himself to himself. Not but what I've surprised a kindling look about him once or twice. Here, what're you at?' she enquired on a fit of giggles, 'you're a tickling. Are you another that takes but one dip at a bob apple and then spends the rest of the night in tickles and chat like a hedge parson? 'Cause if you are I'm agoing to sleep.'

'Not yet you ain't,' I promised her. But seeing how quick she was with her teeth I rolled her over tits and belly, and plenty of all of 'em, to mount for a fast downhill canter, roll, bounce and lift for the fence at the bottom; this merry exercise to the accompaniment of squeaks, giggles, curses and squeals and a last 'God's sake, go easy you naughty rogue, you'll shake the house down.'

Never did a man work harder for his information, but we broke out of the grapple at last and I gave her another pull of the claret and finished the rest of it myself, while she lay panting and licking her lips with a look in her eyes that boded worse to come. What that wench needed was a troop ship all to herself, but I said gallantly, 'Mr Colville don't know what he's missing. To have been in the house all the week and not try the snuggest chamber of them all.' I affected to be teasing. 'But maybe he fancies the Spanish lady better.'

'Ain't been in the house all the week. I said in and out; like you,' she added with a fresh giggle. 'He's only lodged here tonight. And one day he rode out to the country, as I heard him telling Mr Comber so. As to that other, he's welcome to her; she's a hoity-toity bitch. Nothing would suit but that she must have her supper to her chamber and I brought it up myself and scratched on the door and carried it in, and God help us you never saw such a look as I got for reward. She was writing at the desk, copying from one bit of paper to another as I thought, but I never had much chance to see as she got her arm across it on the instant, and her eyes flashing at me like she might've been a tiger. "You should wait till you are bidden before you enter," she cries. "In my contree you would be whipped for this."'

'It's a heathen Spanish custom,' I told her. 'Did you get a sight of the other gentleman?'

But now the smoulderous ember in her eyes was fanned to a flame. 'Rot the other gentleman,' she announced and launched upon me incontinent with another half nelson; doing her best to mount me herself, the indelicate creature, and what was worse very near taking off my left ear in her teeth. I cannot put up with for-

ward women, and responding in the spirit of the jest I gave a
mighty heave and roll which fetched us clean off the pallet and on
to the floor; where I set to work with a will to quieten her ardour
and have done with it, while she kicked and scratched and cursed
that the splinters in the boards was making a pincushion of her
arse. A pretty scene; and not improved by then hearing a scuffle
and sniggers from beyond the door.

Disarrayed and deep engaged as I was my rage still got the
better of me. Heaving free of the bitch and leaving her to kick and
curse, in one step I flung the door back; to reveal, as you might
expect, Master Maggsy and a pot boy cackling and scuffling for
possession of a knot hole to peep through. One I despatched down
the passage with my foot in his breech—and stubbed my toe as
I'd forgot I had no boots on—and the other I dragged into the
chamber, where our naked Venus in the candle light was legs
and arms akimbo, hair down over her shoulders and tits, and belly
heaving. 'Why, here's our little clerk,' she cries. 'Come in, little clerk.
I likes it younger and tender.'

'No you don't,' I said. 'I'll not see innocence affronted.'

Yet disregarding me she fell upon the child. In a trice she very
near had the shirt off his back and his britches half down; while
the little monster himself by no means unwilling made the most of
whatever he could reach, and I strove to part them with one hand
at the scruff of his neck and my other arm round the wench's
passionate middle. I was fast losing patience when a voice from
below bawled, 'Lay off your bumping up there or I'll come and
quieten you with the chamber pot.'

That was the end of it, for seeing a lull I presented her a brace
of sharp smacks on her naked backside as must have sent the blood
to her head, and she fell back on the pallet panting and giggling
and saying, 'That's Mr Comber. And he would too; he's done it
afore. Well then, I'm going to sleep; and it'll be a crown piece.'

Suiting the words she turned over, drew the cover up to her chin,
gave a snort and another giggle, and in another minute or two was
snoring like a little farmyard. Close on that too a church clock

somewhere struck three and it was time to leave; and not without some thanksgiving. But I left the five shillings.

The streets were silent and empty now, neither candles nor lanterns to be seen, though lit with that mysterious coppery moon riding behind the mastheads and throwing deep pits of shadow and here and there patches of strange light. Master Maggsy was somewhat sulky and he said, 'You was puffing a bit that last go. That pot boy says they sometimes put a green'n on to Rosie for the fun of it as she's a regular tiger, and he's knowed strong sailors be carried out of there in the morning, but I says not old Sturrock, he's more'n a match...'

'Maggsy,' I ordered him, 'be quiet. I was about better business than doxying.' He gave a grunt at that which made my fingers itch on my cane but I went on, 'And, be damned, it was a business which destroyed all of my conclusions at one stroke. It seems Mr Colville's been in and out of the Prospect all this last week.'

'You don't reckon it's him that's after Copperknob, do you?' he asked. 'He's a gentleman. Least he looks like one.'

'They're always the worst when they turn wicked; and I fancy he wouldn't let much stand in his way if the fit took him. But it don't add up to sense, be hanged to it. Consider that canting chanty Kemble was singing. "I says to him Captain and how do ye do?" and then, "Says he none the better for seeing of you." A man telling the truth in a drunken jest. He'd recognised somebody, Master Maggsy. And that somebody was most certainly none the better for seeing Kemble; so little the better that the fellow had to be put out of the way.'

'Well, ain't that what I told you?' Maggsy demanded. 'I said he'd got the words wrong.'

'You're uncommon sharp, and so you did. But you didn't reckon out what it meant. It takes my intellect for that. Yet Kemble couldn't have seen Mr Colville in and out for a week and then recognised him to call it a prodigy only on the last day. So we must turn elsewhere. What did you glean of the other three.'

'Mr Simpkin, spice merchant, right old softy, forever in the

Prospect, and got a warehuss in Cinnamon Street,' he recited. 'Captain Lopez, master of the *Santa Theresa*, trades to Italy and North Africa and such places, into London every three months about, but reckoned a rum un and best left alone. Captain Furlong, tight fisted old bastard and ugly tempered with it, the *Louisiana Belle*, mostly Bristol and New Orleens but turns up every so often, been here better'n a fortnight now.'

'Be hanged again,' I said, 'that accounts for them too, and for the same reason; Kemble must have seen 'em all time and time again. No more I don't fancy the woman Consuela and her gentleman,' I mused, 'for when they came to the Prospect he'd already gone. Be damned, if we're left with some stranger nobody knows we might hunt for a lifetime. So we've but a single thing left. To take or capture one of these villains, and then by God I'll have the truth out of him in half an hour.'

Maggsy stopped, his big mouth agape. 'God's Tripes, you ain't out for trouble again, are you? Ain't you loosed off enough wind and piss for one night? You ain't in no shape for mischief, not after that lot with Rosie.'

His outcries were enough to awaken even a watchman, and I silenced him short and sharp. We were now close by the Widow Rooke's house, and I drew him down the passage by its side to the shadows of the old warehouse, where we concealed ourselves to watch and listen on a rotting wharf; a strange spectacle, for the ships hung black and motionless in a kind of infernal glow, a wraith of mist drifting here and there, scarce a ripple on the water, and never a sound but the rats scuffling behind us and Master Maggsy muttering like a dissenting parson.

But I had concluded the villains would come by the river with the tide; and so they did. It was not long before we observed a boat drawing in silently to the water steps at the Widow Rooke's little garden, and then no less than six of the rascals ascending; and one of them, as I saw clearly even in that sultry light, the mulatto who has already been noted. 'So ho,' I breathed; and Maggsy whispered, 'God's Whiskers; we ain't agoing to take that lot on, are we?'

'Needs must,' I returned. 'And I fancy we shall find the physician awake and waiting.'

Their ruse was clear and impudent. Five of them stood close against the wall of the house while the last set to knocking on the door and crying, 'Dr McGrath, sir; you're wanted. It's Mr Sturrock.'

The doctor was awake and waiting sure enough, for in another minute a window above opened and he put his head out saying, 'Wheesht there, be quiet. What's that you say?'

'Mr Sturrock,' the rogue repeated. 'He's found the villain as done for Lieutenant Kemble, but stabbed near enough to death himself and calling for you.'

Master Maggsy must needs guffaw, but I roared, 'Stabbed to death, is he? By God, we'll see. Hold there, McGrath,' I added, 'they're all about you;' and on that the battle was joined.

A rough encounter it was. With Maggsy screeching behind we plunged into the garden, and at once no less than four of the rogues fell upon me. There was no time for niceties and the first I kicked firm and sound where he would remember it the longest, awarded the second a cut with my cane, flung it aside, and flattened a third's snout for him. But by now the fourth had his clutch around my gullet to throttle me from behind, while the mulatto came in from the front. Him, however, Master Maggsy disconcerted with a two handed St Mary le Bone cricket stroke from a stave he had found somewhere, and then set to roaring round the garden with the mulatto after him, a useful diversion but cowardly; while though somewhat puffed from my night's exertions I contrived to fling my own rascal over and then tread a thought carelessly on his face as he fell.

Wasting no time the physician dropped from his window, flailing his fists like a windmill and engaging two of the rascals from me as I laid one more back with another snouter. But straight on that came a dismal yellocking from the edge by the river, where I observed Maggsy hard pressed by the mulatto and a little dwarfish fellow, one with a glint of steel in his hand, and there was nothing for it but to break off my own engagement and go to his rescue. It was a short and sweet business. The mulatto I met with a right footed salutation between wind and water which sent him flying backwards into the river, while Maggsy fetched such an uncommon dirty stroke on the other that he let out the wail of a stuck pig and reeled away in despair until I plucked him back, quietened him with a merciful blow, and left him to lie in peace.

Old Isaac had now joined us, roaring and stumping round from the front of the house and brandishing a blunderbuss in such fashion as to strike me in more terror than all the cut-throats in Wapping, while from the upper window the Widow Rooke was busy tossing down pitchers of water; a strange female perversity, but we were lucky it was not something worse. Advising Isaac to be careful with that cursed armament or he'd pepper all of us I joined in with the doctor and shoulder to shoulder we set into the dogs while, uttering his own impolite observations, Maggsy struck in a wicked blow or two as he could. 'Don't kill 'em,' I cried. 'Save me one for questioning.'

So it might have turned out and all ended well but for a most provoking accident. Beside himself with battle and excitement, no doubt in fancy fighting off pirates in the China Seas, Isaac seemed somehow to catch his wooden leg, uttered a fearful curse, went arse over tip, and exploded his devilish hand cannon. Ladies, I beg of you, never put your trust in a blunderbuss. It went with the roar of a broadside and such a shower of nails, bits of lead, shot, etc., that it was a wonder we were not all discommoded. But Isaac, the old fool, lay there black in the face with rage and gunpowder, waving his stump and cursing like a bosun, and there was nothing more for me and the physician but to run to his aid lest he had done himself a mortal mischief. And on that diversion the rogues broke clear and fled.

Dripping wet the mulatto appeared at the steps bawling at them to beat about, and stopping only to catch up the dwarfish wretch that I'd laid cold off they went. Flinging Master Maggsy aside with scant courtesy, the whole gang was tumbling down to their boat before we'd done hauling our impetuous captain to his feet. By the time we reached the brink they was well away, pulling for dear life downstream on a racing tide; and myself left with never a prize to show for my trouble.

CHAPTER FOUR

I have since reflected that for a time Providence must have turned
His Eyes away from me; most likely in reproof as instead of presenting myself at Divine Service in St Giles last Sunday I took leave
to attend a pugilistic contest at Edgware. Providence may not be
mocked; yet a rare good match for all that, as I had my money on
Sir Tobias Westleigh's man and the other fellow lasted for twenty-
two rounds before they carried him off the field. But for this occasion never was I closer to a seizure. Maggsy has often said since
that many of my observations were both poetic and instructive; it
was canticle and chorus with me and Captain Isaac, and even the
physician had the grace to look as sheepish as one of his own Scots
muttons. 'Wheesht, man,' he said, 'ye'll excite yourself,' and added,
'Aye; hrumph; I'd best be away to look to the lassie. That com-
motion might well have disturbed her.'

'Be damned to the lassie,' I said.

But on that he was already halfway to the house and there was
nothing more to do than sit to get our breath back and cool our
tempers—sending Maggsy in to find some liquor to assist in the
matter. It was plain now that a fresh stratagem must be devised,
and while Isaac still simmered and rumbled I remained pondering
on it until Dr McGrath returned; now looking more lovelorn than
ever. 'Pretty well,' he announced, as if his soul's salvation hung on
the words. 'Aye; verra well conseedering. I persuaded her it was a
wee rabble of drunken sailors brawling.'

I was pretty near to forgetting my gentility. 'And did you per-
suade her that the captain's blunderbuss was one of 'em dropping
a fart? Come now, doctor, this is no business of a rabble of bully
boys after a wench. There's a damned quick and wicked villain
somewhere giving the orders and your lady can tell us who he is.
In short, if she's very well considering, can I question her?'

'No sir, you may not,' he retorted. 'Not yet. I'll have her sleep for as long as she can.'

'You'll have her sleep till some rogue cuts her throat,' I observed. 'And she's just as much a danger to Isaac and Mrs Rooke.'

'Haul your braces,' Isaac roared. 'We'll fight 'em then; we'll not have these sons of Pondicherry whores put us down.'

Nevertheless that took our good doctor across his bows; doting as the man might be he knew the pretty tricks of villains as well as I do. 'Be damned,' he groaned. 'Ye've got me pulled both ways.' He considered it and then demanded, 'You wouldna say they'll try again tonight?' With this at least I was pleased to agree and he continued. 'Well then tomorrow I'll have the house watched and guarded by a dozen fine stout fellows.'

'And the morrow's night?' I enquired. 'What then?' But already I had taken a most excellent notion, for Jeremy Sturrock is seldom at a loss. Lady Dorothea might well be our Hand of Providence. 'There's only one thing for it,' I announced. 'She must be removed away from here.'

'To a hospital?' He shook his head. 'I'll grant we must conseeder it. But I'm not easy. I don't like the places and I'm damned certain they don't understand this ailment.'

I could have answered that neither did he, but said, 'To an elegant establishment in Hanover Square. Where she'll have all care and attention.'

Isaac set up a fresh roar. 'Be damned and blasted and keel hauled, we'll stand by to repel boarders. By God, we'll have their cods off if they try it.'

The old gentleman was growing over excited again, and I recounted short and simple what had happened to the boy Henry. 'They ain't playing lift the lady's smock to see what's underneath,' I finished. 'But have it your own way. I'll tell you again, I'm more concerned with Lieutenant Kemble.'

I left the physician to reflect on that and at last he muttered, 'Aye. I canna deny you've got the rights of it.' It was clear what was troubling the poor fool; that once taken away from him he might never see the wench again. You could see Cupid and commonsense fighting for mastery, and like a man giving up his last hope he enquired, 'It's a respectable house?'

'God's Teeth,' I demanded, 'd'you think I'd take her to a doxy shop? It's so damned respectable it's a wonder they admit me. Lady Dorothea Dashwood; Lady Dorothea Hookham that was. A female Whig to be sure, but an excellent woman for all that. She runs wild to do good, whether wanted or not, and I'll engage she'll fall over herself on this.'

'Jer'my,' the captain said, 'what poops me is why you don't set out and take this mulatto. He's plain enough to get a bearing on.'

'Never find him,' Maggsy answered for me. 'Not in this place. Pickle me, it's near enough as bad as Seven Dials. That's what we say, Sturrock and me. Once let your rogue go to ground in a warren and you'll never flush him out.'

Our physician did a masterpiece of harrumphing. 'Lady Dorothea Hookham. Is that to do with a Lieutenant Lord Hookham, killed in an engagement against the French off Antigua in '98?'

'The same,' I told him. 'And if you knew his Lordship you're set up for life. We'll have you attending the half of the nobility with your own carriage and coachman before you've done.'

So it was concluded. We passed the remainder of the night with what comfort we could, while I gave the physician and Isaac further advices and instructions. First to put it about for her own safety that the wench would never speak again; second to enquire after any strangers seen yesterday, though I had little hope of this; next to find the *Mary Carson*, if there was such a ship; and last that as soon as my own business permitted I would return with a carriage to bring the girl away.

Next to the Prospect to settle our score. It was too much, but we improved the occasion by a ride in Landlord Comber's gig as far as Smithfield Market, where he was going early to purchase his provisions for the day. He enquired kindly after my entertainment with Rosie, which I assured him had more than passed expectation; I proposed she should be sent to keep Bonaparte quiet. Lastly I went on to tell him that it was now certain Captain Bolton's wench would never utter another sensible word again, and turned to my question about strangers. But I expected little good of it and did not get any; the mystery was not to be solved this way.

Refusing an offer of refreshment at Smithfield, we parted company and I now sent Master Maggsy off on a fresh enquiry; this in brief to comb through every single coach inn and station between Ludgate and Holborn to discover whether a red haired young lady coming perhaps from the west had been noted at any one of them lately. As you shall see I had my notions already, but for now I must hurry to Bow Street and inform my master Mr A, the Chief Magistrate, of these affairs. It is ever our duty to show respect to them set in authority over us.

I was a little late, and as I entered the outer chamber our old clerk, Abel Makepenny, looked up from his scribbling and whispered, 'God's sake, Jeremy, where have you been? He's roaring like a baited bear, and you'd best tread light, for he's in a pestilential tetchy mood. I wish to God he'd keep away from the port a bit and take to Madeira.'

'Easy now, Abel,' I advised him. 'I'll soothe the gander down. First tell me quick; is there any complaint yet of a young lady kidnapped or abducted at some place unknown, about last Saturday?'

He scratched the end of his nose with his quill in agitation. 'Not as I knows of; never a word. What're you after now?'

But before I could add more there was a slamming of doors and Mr A's rasping voice within, and I said, 'Be damned, you're right, Abel; he was at the port again last night.'

Admitted to his closet it pleased the good gentleman to be in his third or sarcastic manner. 'Well, good day to you, Mr Sturrock,' he observed. 'So you've condescended to honour us, have you? You was detained at St James' Palace or Kew House very like; doubtless taking tea with His Majesty.'

There were several such exchanges until reflecting that if Mr A had time for 'em I hadn't, also that he'd work himself into a tantrum and upset his gout again if he went on, I said, 'I've been about Bow Street business, sir. In short the murder of a Royal Navy lieutenant, and the abduction of a young lady some days since. An American, I fancy.' Seeing then that I had his ear I continued, 'Or at least a stranger. She's never heard of Bow Street, and there's nobody in this country that don't know who and what we are. Yet she speaks English as clear and plain as you or me. I wouldn't swear to it, not yet; but I'd take a wager she's American.'

Mr A grunted. 'If you'd take a wager, Sturrock, it's damn near a racing certainty.'

Whereupon I launched into the whole tale, excepting only Lieutenant Kemble's letters which for my own reasons I considered were best left in obscurity, and at last finished, 'A young lady of that quality wouldn't be travelling without a servant and very likely a duenna as well. So why haven't they enquired after her? To say nothing of this Geoffrey, and a certain Mr Moxon.'

'To say nothing of another damned impudent highway robbery at Hounslow last night,' he complained. 'I'm over stretched, Sturrock.' Shifting his gouty foot and cursing he said, 'If this young woman's got fifty thousand in the Consols she'll be well advised to have it out, quick. Is that what you're after, Sturrock?' he demanded. 'You can smell a reward, eh?'

'I'd never so much as thought of it,' I declared. 'To my mind our lieutenant's the more important, whether he's much to do with this young lady or not. The more so as *The Times* and *The True Briton* go sounding off every other day about the way we treat our laid off sailors. With all respect, sir, if they get wind of this and nothing's done they'll make a fine tantivy of the business.'

'You're a cunning rogue, Sturrock,' Mr A observed. 'Ye think you're too grand for mere highwaymen now. Very well then: I'll give you two days.'

So reporting to Abel that the storm clouds and gout was somewhat lifting, I then took myself on to my next port of call, this being the court or college so much advertised by that fat ass Mr Simpkin yesterday; an ancient office in Bennet's Hill off St Paul's Yard, where they keep the records of coats of arms, badges and crests of the nobility, gentry and otherwise. Here there is a certain clerk, one Mr Ashmole Fossdyck, well known to me as being seen often in the pit at Drury Lane Theatre and a most persistent damned scribbler of tragedies himself; but thank God Mr Sheridan has never been rash enough to put one of 'em on. A curiously learned man, though as mad as a March hare and more than over fond of the gin.

A dim and antique closet lined with mouldering tomes, and Mr Fossdyck himself of a general greyish brownish figure and a whitish wig, looking like nothing so much as a phantom compounded of his own dust. It took him a minute's peering to determine whether I was real or a figment from the past and then he cried, 'Why, 'tis Mr Jeremy Sturrock as I recollect perfectly. Well now, Mr Sturrock, you won't be looking for one of your footpads, not lurking among my records?' Even his cackles were as dry as the leaves of one of his own tragedies being rustled over.

'In a manner I am,' I said. 'Though more than a mere footpad. In short I want you to name a coat of arms.'

'No more'n that?' He sniffed. 'Still the damned things're my trade. I breathe 'em, eat 'em, drink 'em, and sometimes fancy I piss 'em. And talking of that I'm just about to take a snicket of gin. Will ye join me?'

I never much fancy the stuff, considering it fit only for scribblers, but said, 'It'll keep the dust down.'

'And needs to in this damnation place. Near on fifty years I've been here, and it gets dustier every day.' So having dragged a flagon out from behind his books, filled two pots and tossed his down at a gulp, thereafter rewarding me with a belch of it in the eye, he continued, 'That's better. So now, Mr Sturrock, what's your coat of arms then?'

'To you a simple matter, Mr Fossdyck,' I replied, laying before him the button.

'What,' he cried, 'a common livery button?' But he trotted over to the light of the one dusty window, pushing up his spectacles on

his forehead the better to see it. 'And not much neither,' he pro-
nounced. 'A chevron; then a lion passant guardant dimidiated
with the hulk of a ship; and two falcons. There's no rank there.
Creation of the second Charles; very likely some wench as let her
shift slip for him. Anything more I can do for you, Mr Sturrock?'

'Why, yes,' I answered with some impatience. 'The name.'

'The name, dammit?' he asked. 'Well that'll want some searching
out.' He took a further snicket of gin which might have steadied
a Dutchman, and then fell to dragging out one volume after
another, slapping them on his desk and raising fresh clouds of
dust, muttering and sniffing to himself. But you must never in-
terrupt these historians in their delvings or they might fly into
a passion and do you an injury. I sat quiet until he crowed in
triumph, 'We've got the rascals. Peregrine, with a connection to
Ryde. That do your business, Mr Sturrock?'

'Near enough,' I said. 'You're a remarkable man, Mr Fossdyck.
But where's their seat; country or town house?'

'God's Wounds, you want the Gospels and the Creed,' he complained, but fell to rustling over his leaves afresh and at last crowed
again, 'There it is then. James Edward Peregrine, second Baron
Falconhurst; born 1710, married Augusta Ryde 1731; issue five
children. Four sons and one daughter. Seat: Wolcot Hall, Hunting-
don.'

'We're doing very well, Mr Fossdyck,' I encouraged him. 'But
that Peregrine's ninety years back.'

'You're a most pertinacious man, Mr Sturrock. Ninety years ain't
nothing in this place; more like yesterday. That's Almon's *Peerage*
so now we'll look to Debrett; only come out this year, and if it ain't
in here it's nowhere,' he muttered, dragging out a new volume and
once more sniffing through its pages. 'Well then,' he demanded in
the end, 'does this suit you better? First and second sons died
without issue, third Lord Falconhurst the Reverend Matthew
Thomas Peregrine, incumbent of St Ethelburga's, Ponder's End.
Your man's a parson.'

'A parson?' I repeated in astonishment. I could think of little

73

less canonical than the goings on at Wapping. and said, 'It don't make sense.'

'Commonplace enough,' he retorted pettishly. 'Specially where there's little money. First son the Navy, second the Army, third the Church and the fourth whistles for what he can get. There's the fourth boy here; Hayward, but no later record of him. And then a daughter Lydia as married another Ryde.' He peered back at the book sniffing with yet more disparagement. 'They're mere nobodies. A demnition irregular title too. I wouldn't have much to do with that lot if I was you, Mr Sturrock.'

'It's in the way of business, Mr Fossdyck,' I told him, 'and I'm particular obliged. But begod you've set me food for thought. Now will you write it all down for me? I shall never carry that in my head.' Then while the good gentleman was scratching, snuffling and scribbling away I added, 'And I must recollect to send my clerk with a pass for Drury Lane. There's a new play going on as they promise shall be better than most of late.' We should all be at pains to encourage the learned and diligent; it's about all most of 'em ever do get.

But it is always the same with them. Promise so much and they want more. 'Sarah Siddons,' he babbled, making a snatch at my coat tails as I was half out of the door. 'That's what I'm after. Sarah's new revival of Lady Macbeth; get me a billet for that, and begod I'll find you all the coats of arms you can ever wish to see.'

I was not best pleased, but Mr Fossdyck's importunities no doubt saved my life, for had I walked straight out to the court this tale had had a sharp and fatal end.

Bennet's Hill is a narrow and quiet lane going down from St Paul's Yard to Upper Thames Street; Doctors' Commons and the doctors' lodgings on one side, the Herald's Office on the other, and little traffic at any time save a few old fustians shuffling with eyes on the ground and pondering on the mysteries of Law. The Herald's Office itself is built about a courtyard, with an arched passage out to the lane, and like that thoroughfare not a soul in it; a place deep in the sleep of ages.

It was the most impudent and outrageous attempt you ever heard of, yet safe enough for a quick and audacious rascal. I was disengaging myself from Mr Fossdyck, explaining that half London was clamouring for tickets to the incomparable Sarah's Macbeth when my sharp eye caught a movement in the passage, not fifteen yards away. I could scarcely make out the man, as he was hugging close to the wall and hidden, but I know the gleam of a pistol barrel coming down with deadly intent when I see it.

The rogue must have paused on seeing Mr Fossdyck clinging to me, and as sharp as only I can move I thrust the old gentleman back into his doorway and myself after him. There was a flash and bang, sparrows rising in a clatter from the yard and a cloud of dust from the stone beside my head. He was shooting close, and when I put but the corner of an eyebrow out to have a view of him a second discharge came with the movement, his ball humming past my beaver and smacking into the closet beyond; while Mr Fossdyck uttered cries like an expiring goose and scrabbled away on his hands and knees to the shelter of his desk and books.

Then came a clatter of hoofs from the street and spurning further concealment I hastened out to the archway, but to no purpose; only the whisk of a tail as the rogue pulled his horse hard round the churchyard corner by the bottom of the hill. He was gone and there was no sense in running bawling and hallooing after him. Neither were the bystanders any better service; three or four musty old bookworms and a small urchin. All agreed on the horse, but beyond that none told the same tale; a youngish fellow running out, declared one; a shambling, squat, darkish rascal, cried another; a villainous rogue with mustachios like a cavalryman, said a third. There was nothing to be had out of any of them and the Herald's Office yard now filling up, heads poking out of windows, and Mr Ashmole Fossdyck declaiming in the midst like a broken down actor making the most of his first and last chance, I left them to their amazement and turned away about my own further occasions. It was very plain I had started a hare with Master Maggsy's button, and a damned ill mannered hare; but which one?

I had instructed the child to wait on me at Mr Hackett's eating house by Stevenson's Brewery, and arriving there I found him already seated on the doorsteps exchanging the pleasantries of his kind with several other street arabs. These I dispersed with my cane, and then seeing that the creature was alight with triumph allowed him to tell his tale while we settled to a moderate dinner of capon, steak and oyster pudding and a nice Double Gloucester cheese. Commonly I find his elegant style unsettling on an empty stomach.

'Found 'em,' he announced. 'Doing it all for you again; but likewise,' he added handsomely, 'you was right; dunno how you reckon it out, damned if I do. Anyways they was at the Belle Savage on Ludgate Hill, and come on the coach from Bath and Bristol. Three of 'em; Copperknob, another wench uncommon airs'n graces, and a black man. Would you believe it? A black man done up particular fanciful, yaller trousers, blue frock coat, and a beaver; what d'you make of that?'

'It don't surprise me,' I told him.

'Nothing never does,' he grumbled. 'Nor I don't suppose nothing never will till you get your liver took out, and then you might cry "God's Tripes, I'm surprised at last." Well then they fetched up at the Belle Savage a week ago last Saturday; that's what a big Irish ostler tells me and he recollects it perfect on account of Copperknob and the blackie and an heap of baggage as must've cost 'em a pretty penny in extra weight on the coach; and likewise that self same day this ostler's wife pupped for three all at once and he reckons at least one of 'em ain't his. I never heard of that before,' he marvelled.

'Maggsy,' I said, 'let us leave the misfortunes of the Irish and keep to your tale. Did this fellow or any others have their names?'

'Says the airs'n graces spoke to Copperknob as Miss Lydia. Says they was all of a fluster, and one of 'em says she hopes never to ride a coach in England again so long as she lives.'

I cut him short. 'Lydia? You're sure of that, boy?' I took out Mr Fossdyck's paper to study it. There was a Lydia, the only daughter of the second Lord Falconhurst, born 1738 and married a Percival Ryde Esqre 1756; but thereafter lost to sight as Debrett don't notice commoners. 'What this means I don't know,' I observed, 'but it gets deeper every minute. Well then,' I demanded, 'where is this other woman and the negro now?'

'I dunno likewise,' he answered. 'But not at the Belle Savage. They left, all of 'em. Didn't get no more from the ostler as a coach come in then and he got took away, so went inside and got my head clouted by the landlord, but found a chambermaid after who recalled 'em on account of the blackie man scaring the daylights out of her; she thought he was a Frenchy. Well, this wench says they was only there the one night, complained of the racket and clatter of the coaches starting from five o'clock in the morning, went off again the next day and there's an end of it.'

'Not by any means,' I said. 'You can go back to the Belle Savage and stay there till you've discovered where they went.'

'What?' he screeched. 'I've told you. Nobody knows.'

'Then find somebody who does. Chairman, hackney man, porter, servant or what you like.'

So I was left in peace to smoke a pipe and reflect, though with little profit. To be sure we had two Lydias now; the Lydia Peregrine on Mr Fossdyck's paper and Captain Isaac's wench. But the dates, which Mr Fossdyck had most carefully set down, would make the first sixty-four while the other could not be a day worse than twenty-one; it was no more than a guess that she might be the older woman's granddaughter. Then again I had the best of reasons to suppose that one or another of those four gentlemen at the Prospect did not much care for my enquiries; but which of them was another question. As also was how far this same fellow had swallowed my subterfuge that Master Maggsy's button had been found in Kemble's lodging. As also once more why Kemble must have seen those four in and about the tavern for a week yet chosen not to recognise his man until the last day. That stuck in my throat like a fishbone; and more like a cod's than a herring.

But there was one thing plain which brings us back to Lieutenant

Kemble, and I took out the poor man's letters to make sure of it. Miss Georgiana Woodforde was going to entrust her first most secret message in 1771 to a certain Tristram Peregrine. Here yet again Mr Fossdyck's paper came handy. It gave Matthew and Hayward Peregrine; Matthew the third Lord who had married another Ryde—Hester this time—and had one son by her named Mark, and Hayward the younger brother of whom nothing more was entered; one being forty-six in 1771 and the other forty-five. Then where the devil did Tristram Peregrine appear? It set my head in a whirl, as it well might yours.

I am never a man to wear out my thinking cap in fruitless speculation, and time was pressing. My next port was Lady Dorothea Dashwood's; first to engage her interest in the wench as I had promised, next to make certain further enquiries, and most important to procure for myself a free chaise, horses and driver, as I could foresee a vast deal of travelling before this business was done. It was a brisk walk down Oxford Street surveying the bustling spectacle, and very different from Wapping; young bloods in their curricles, carriages, tradesmen's gigs and sedan chairs, gentlemen going to their clubs and ladies to their milliners, the street vendors crying their wares and whores promenading to pick up a soldier or two, with shifting crowds along the pavements by such multifarious shops as make this street the wonder of the kingdom. A wonder for many other things too, and I kept a sharp eye about me for unwelcome attentions, but at length arrived at the sedate and porticoed quietness of Hanover Square without incident.

From the carriages and chairs outside, together with a knot of rude drivers and chairmen lounging by the railings, it seemed my lady was engaged about one of her philosophical conversaziones. Such assemblies are the very pink of learned fashion these days, and where at the coffee houses you will find your play actors and modish wits here you may observe any condition of starve gutted Grub Street hacks to a belted earl or two; all are welcome so long as each has some fresh whimsicality to air. As Mr Masters admitted me to the drawing-room this gathering was much to the rule; Lady Dorothea herself and Miss Harriet, gentlemen of several sorts from foppish to the scribbler's livery of ink, snuff and stink, and ladies after the style of the famous blue stocking Miss Hannah More.

Lady Dorothea's particular fantastical was always Noble Savages after that prating prattling Frenchy, Jean-Jacques Rousseau—a nonsensical rascal who has already done enough harm and will do more yet wherever his notions can find a cracked wit to drip through—and she was well at it now, while Miss Harriet pecked at her needlework and cast eloquent little black parrot looks down the sides of her nose. For my part I sat quiet and took my tea, though reflecting that any time the good soul fancied I could show her a mixed handful of Wapping savages whose nobility would startle her into the vapours before one of her philosophers had time to take a pinch of snuff. However, as Doctor Samuel Johnson has observed, a woman's preaching is like a dog walking on its hinder parts; it is not done well, but you are surprised to see it done at all.

I was in some impatience, but at length the company broke up in twos and threes and I was left at last to present my compliments, to enquire most kindly after Mr Dashwood—who was not present—and to finish, 'I'm here to beg a kindness, ma'am; or indeed several kindnesses. Likewise to ask a question or two; and to tell a most singular and curious tale.'

'Then of God's love let's hear it,' Miss Harriet demanded. 'I'm near asleep of tedium from all this stuff. If a savage is noble he ain't a savage and so contrariwise and there's an end of it. What mischief're you up to now, Mr Sturrock?'

'An uncommon ugly piece,' I said, and so encouraged told the story; and made an opera and chorus about this beautiful and mysterious young American lady of quality and poor Lieutenant Kemble; but again with no mention of his letters, as Lady Dorothea might have been over nice about those. To be short about it, and about the ladies' exclamations, long before I'd done there was no matter of begging favours but only saying what I wanted.

For once in her life Lady Dorothea seemed speechless. Can such things be?' she enquired. 'Cannot you apprehend these men?'

'What with?' I asked. 'A Parish Constable and a handful of watchmen who're afraid of the sound of their own rattles?'

But before I could continue my own views on our need for a strong and widespread force of police, whether the unruly public likes it or not, my lady cut me short. 'This cannot be permitted. Be so good as to pull the bell, Mr Sturrock.'

In another minute the butler appeared, to receive such a broadside as you never heard. 'Masters, please require Gedge to put the horses in the town carriage,' Lady Dorothea commanded. 'He is to wait on Mr Sturrock and drive at his instructions. And have Mrs Tibbets prepare the Chinese bedchamber for a guest. We must have her physician too, Mr Sturrock,' she continued, 'you must beg him to accompany the lady.'

'I fancy he might be so persuaded, ma'am,' I ventured.

'Then we shall also require the old tutor's room prepared, Masters; everything a gentleman may need. And have Jagger and Hobbs saddle horses to ride with Mr Sturrock.' Then she was off on a fresh tack. 'Harriet, you recollect tomorrow Mr Dashwood and myself must leave to the country for a few days. You will look after her, will you not?'

'I daresay I might,' Miss Harriet answered equably. 'I've looked after many another naughty young miss in my time.' Her sharp glance caught my eye, and she added, 'A young woman that gets herself into this kind of scrape and with looks as Mr Sturrock describes 'em ain't exactly milk and water.'

'Fiddlesticks,' Lady Dorothea retorted. 'You think the sharpest of everything. Is there anything more, Mr Sturrock?'

So invited but with proper modesty I came to the matter of travelling, and in this again all my requests were granted with a perfect passion of good works; a light chaise, cattle and driver to be freely at my command as ever I might need them. The good Mr Masters was something more than commonly wall faced as he looked at me, but made his bow before he left to give this array of orders, and then I came myself to the real heart of the business.

I said, 'You're kindness itself, ma'am. But might I ask yet more? Do you know of a certain Lady Motley; wife of Captain Sir Charles Motley?'

'Eh?' Miss Harriet exclaimed. 'What're you about now?'

Lady Dorothea was no less curious. 'I know of Captain Sir Charles. He's at sea as I understand, but has a house at Highgate. Why do you ask, Mr Sturrock?'

There are none so quick to close together as the gentry when they catch some impertinent fellow coming at them with questions. 'In the matter of the lieutenant,' I explained. 'I must needs know if the poor fellow left a family behind; and I've a notion also that the reason for his death may lie somewhere in his past. To uncover that I must talk with Lady Motley.'

Being all for equality she was plainly shocked by my forwardness. 'Do I understand you, Mr Sturrock? Are you saying this unhappy lieutenant, of Wapping, was in some liaison with the wife of Captain Sir Charles Motley?'

'Dear Heaven, no,' I assured her. 'I wouldn't think of it. They were childhood friends; and it seems they had some common acquaintance with a certain Tristram Peregrine. I'm bound to ask what Lady Motley can tell me of the Lieutenant and that gentleman. In short, ma'am, I'm asking yet another favour; a letter or note from you commending me to her.'

Miss Harriet let out an ill timed cackle while Lady Dorothea gazed at me astonished, and by no means over willing. But in the end, and by persuasion of a nice diplomacy, she consented to write an introduction in such general terms as I desired; this to be brought to me by the driver of my chaise in the morning. It was a necessary stratagem as a mere Bow Street man is not always welcomed in the most genteel establishments; unless they need his assistance.

That concluded I could now turn to my last question. 'Ma'am,' I asked, 'do you or Miss Harriet know of a Lord Falconhurst? The family name Peregrine.'

'Falconhurst?' she replied. 'There is a title I fancy.' But then she was off on her distractions again, saying, 'Tut now, I should have told Masters to ask Mrs Tibbets to request Mrs Asher to prepare a light supper. I must speak to Mrs Tibbets myself. You should ask Miss Harriet, Mr Sturrock,' she added, bustling away. 'She is a veritable compendium of families.'

Miss Harriet cocked another of her wicked looks at me. 'There's nothing puts her in a tiz quicker'n some tale about a poor wench mistreated. But it's no harm, for the house is full of people biting their fingernails for want of employment. What're you after now? I recollect a Falconhurst of Wolcot, but God's sake that scandal's forty years dead. I was a gal meself at the time.'

'Forty years dead,' I mused, 'but I wonder if it left a ghost? What scandal was it, ma'am?'

'Bad blood and gambling,' she answered. 'Jimmy Peregrine. His father got through one fortune by the time the lad was twenty and James married another to get through himself. A rake hell; and some tale as he murdered his wife but nothing ever proved. End of it he tossed in Wolcot Hall and lands, such as there was left, on a last hand of cards at Hoxton's Club. Flung his last few guineas down for a dozen of port, presented each of his cronies with a brace apiece, drank the final two himself and blowed his brains out. Recollect my old father saying as any man'd shoot himself after one bottle of Hoxton's port, much less two.' She fetched a snuff box from her reticule, took a hearty pinch and finished, 'That was '57 or '58; a long time back. Men was just as big damn fools in them days as they are now.'

'D'you know of the present Lord Falconhurst, ma'am?' I enquired. 'He's a parson as I understand; at some place called Ponder's End. Wherever that might be.'

'Never heard of him,' she answered. 'But if he's a Peregrine he'll be a damned odd parson. Ponder's End's out by Edmonton, on the York road?' She took another pinch of snuff and regarded me with her head to one side. 'Is this wench a Peregrine?'

'We don't know, ma'am. It seems she might be on a grandmother's side. And seeing that Americans don't commonly invest in British Consols I fancy she's here about a legacy; which legacy some certain other person or persons are out to get their fingers on, and none too particular how they do it. Well then, our good physician won't permit me to question her, but he can scarcely stop you as one lady to another. Likewise,' I added with a cough, 'she may not be acquainted with our London custom of granting a reward for any considerable sum of money saved or recovered.'

Miss Harriet gave me another sideways parrot look not without admiration, but further discussion was cut short by Masters returning with an eye as cold as a publisher's. 'My lady requires me to advise you that the carriage is ready, sir,' he announced. 'Together with wraps and cordials should they be required. My lady further requires me to request you to make all haste.'

My lady, in short, had the bit well between her teeth and was off at a bolt, but it suited me well enough. In a few minutes' more we were rattling at a spanking pace along Oxford Street with our two mounted grooms riding abreast behind; and a damned fine turn-out with cattle to the admiration of every beholder, my men in livery and cockaded hats, and an elegant carriage with a crest upon its door panels. It was a style of life for which Providence and my own talents had always intended me.

CHAPTER FIVE

I directed Mr Gedge first to Soho Square, where I have my own
chambers above Mrs Spilsbury's genteel dispensary for domestic
disorders, debility in bed, failing powers and general disappointment, etc. Considering the rude customs of Wapping my own brace
of pistols might not come unhandy, and I desired moreover to see
whether Master Maggsy had yet returned from his latest embassy.
As he had indeed, the thieving wretch, for I found him at ease like
a lord in my particular chair, smoking a pipe of my tobacco and
sampling my Madeira.

That was a matter firmly corrected, bundling him down the
stairs and into the carriage with a flea in his ear, and we set off
again while I made a number of moral and philosophical observations on his manners and habits and his certain future and end.
But there is little you can do to instruct the young; it must be left
to the Awful Hand of God, and at last I asked, 'Now then, what
good did you have of your work; if any?'

'Kicks, cuffs, clouts and cussings,' he answered bitterly, 'that's
the good I had of it.'

We were rattling into the press of High Holborn then with a
coach crowding us as the villains sometimes will for devilment
when they see an aristocratic carriage; the rogue of a guard winding his horn, the outside passengers cheering, and our eloquent
Mr Gedge exchanging politenesses with the driver. But we were
forced to fall back; and observing that there was a damned unruly
spirit growing up among the lower orders, and if something wasn't
done about our London traffic before long the place would tangle
itself up altogether, I said, 'Cuffs and curses are the common lot
of all such little monsters as you. Did you discover where Miss
Lydia and her friends went?'

'Some Mrs Bedales,' he replied in a sulk again. 'Keeps a genteel lodging house for ladies in Bloomsbury.'

'We're getting on,' I observed. 'By degrees; as lawyers get to Heaven. Whereabouts in Bloomsbury?'

'Dunno,' he answered indifferently. 'And got my arse kicked for asking; that's a plain enough answer for anybody. Anyways,' he continued in a sudden hurry, 'I've got one thing you don't know, not yet, and I've a bleeding good mind not to tell you neither.' But then warned afresh by the look in my eye added, 'T'other wench, the airs and graces; I'll wager you can't guess what her name is. Copperknob called her Consooela; and lest you've forgot that's the same as the one at the Prospect.'

'So ho,' I mused. 'Nor that don't surprise me very much, but you've done pretty well. Let's have it all in order.'

'I was keeping an eye out for that landlord,' he started, 'who's an uncommon nasty tempered man if you ask me, pretty near as bad as you are. Well then I come on two or three chambermaids in a kind of pantry, it's a big place this Belle Savage, and I let on as the red haired lady'd been particular pleased with one of 'em and she'd given me a sovereign to bring to her but, be damned, I couldn't misremember which it was. You never see anything like it, there was seven or eight of 'em all at me like flies round a muck heap, and all yacketting at once till I says "Not so; the one to get the sovereign's got to prove it in telling me the ladies' names and where they've gone." On that one of 'em screeched that it's her as she was in the chamber that Saturday night taking hot water and looking to the bed, and the blackie man's sitting outside in the passage and Copperknob says to Airs and Graces, "We'll go to Mrs Bedales first thing, Consooela; the landlord says it's in a place called Bloomsbury, and promises we'll be well satisfied as it's a most quiet and genteel lodging for ladies."'

He scowled at me. 'You ever tried offering a dozen or so chambermaids a sovereign only to discover you don't have it about you? God's Whiskers, it'd steady even you. Got me upside down in a trice to try and shake it out and one of 'em near enough had my cobblers off; they'd got no manners at all and I think there's never going to be no Rosies for me, not in this world; and there wouldn't never have been neither but the landlord come up then roaring like a bull. He struck 'em away fast enough and quick as thought I says like you do, "Bow Street and the King's Law, and where's this Mrs Bedales' genteel lodgings in Bloomsbury?" But seems he didn't reckon much on Bow Street nor the King's Law, as he took a running canter with me and a toe in my breech and I come to earth no more till I land in the yard. After that anybody can have Mrs Bedales for me; and after the mudlark Snape and fifteen or sixteen chambermaids I ain't never going to speak of golden sovereigns no more neither. It ain't safe.'

'A pathetic tale,' I said. 'But it's no great matter.'

'What?' he screeched in a fury. 'All that and you say it's no great matter?'

'Mrs Bedales, you captious little rogue. If we must and if we have time we can find her fast enough. It's Miss Consuela that matters now. Why,' I added kindly, 'you might have brought us a quick end to the mystery.'

We were coming to the Prospect by this time and I had Mr Gedge halt here to let his noble animals slake their thirst at the trough, while I got down and thrust through the inevitable knot of vulgar idlers which gathered to gaze at our equippage. It was plain Mr Gedge did not like the look of it; and no more did I, for by their lowering manner some of 'em were in an ugly mood, but stationing Maggsy by the door with orders to come and fetch me if I was needed I turned inside. Once more the place was well attended, the candles lit and a haze of smoke, though for my first set-back no appearance of the landlord. Nevertheless Rosie was at my side in a minute lifting her lecherous tits. 'What there, Master Hard-Rider,' she enquired, 'are you back for another bout tonight? By God, you'm a fine randy game-cock.'

'I've no time,' I told her, sharpish. 'Where's Mr Comber?'

She tossed her curls at me. 'Away to a Free Vintners' supper in the City. You'll not see him till morning.'

'It's no matter,' I said. 'Quick, Rosie. The lady and gentleman then. Are they upstairs; in their chambers?'

'La,' she cried, 'so it's that bitch you fancy, is it? Well, you'll have no good of her, for they've gone. Both of 'em.'

'Be damned.' I was impatient, and at the door Maggsy was looking back at me over his shoulder. 'When was this? And where did they go?'

'How should I know?' she demanded. 'They went off the forenoon, bag and baggage in a wherry from the steps here, as I should know for I helped to carry...'

I cut her short. 'Tell me then, did you ever catch their names? And who was the wherryman? Let's have it now, you lustful slut; I'm about the King's business.'

This seemed to displease her. You'd never have thought the hot little strumpet had such tender sensibilities. She advised me what I could do to the king, added further what I could do with myself, and then flounced off with several more observations about farting old shove-bellies who'd ride a poor wench near enough to death and then leave a miserly crown piece for her pains; there is seldom much good to be had out of whores. I was of two minds to go after the bitch and administer some sharp correction, but thought better of it as having no wish to start an unseemly encounter in a respectable house; and also as having further short affairs if I could be spared another minute or so. Regardless of Maggsy who was now calling and beckoning me back I turned to the stairs.

Here I was more fortunate, or so it appeared. Mr Colville, Captain Lopez, and that sharp nosed little ships' chandler Mr Dombey Wells were all seated together, this last with the candles pulled close and scribbling away for dear life in his ledger. As once before I held for an instant in the shadows to watch them while he recited, 'A dozen of salt pork, very good; the same of beef, excellent. And all prime I promise, Mr Colville; none of your stuff that's rotten already as you break the casks. I love a properly found ship.'

'A well fed crew's a loyal crew,' Mr Colville observed.

'And that's true; there's no mutinies with good vittles,' the fellow agreed in another rush of scratching. 'The finest biscuit; there's no weevils in my bread, Mr Colville. Now the powder I must bring up in a barge from the Arsenal Yard. Lord, it's a lot of powder; it's a big load altogether.' He rubbed his hands together and did a merchant's cackle. 'Not as I mind. But I dunno where you'll find stowage for it all.'

'Let me see to that,' Mr Colville answered shortly. 'I'll have her towed up with the tide and warped in by forenoon tomorrow.'

I was to recollect that powder in its due occasion, but for now my time was short and I stepped out into the light, causing Captain Lopez to give a start and jerk as he perceived me. 'God's Blood, man,' he rapped out. 'You move like a cat.'

Mr Colville was more composed. 'Why, Mr Sturrock,' he said but then continued to the chandler, 'I want it all snugged down by nightfall tomorrow. I aim to sail with the tide on Saturday; if we get an air of wind by then. Well then, Mr Sturrock,' he asked, turning back to me, 'have you any news for us?'

'Not a lot,' I confessed. 'Save I've got three or maybe four who might fit our bill. But I don't know the name of one of 'em. Can you tell me, Captain Lopez? The lady and gentleman who lodged here last night?'

'What're you at, my man?' he demanded, half rising from his chair, and damned ugly with it. 'Why the devil should I?'

'No reason at all, sir,' I told him in a hurry. 'It was no more than a notion I had.'

Mr Colville regarded him somewhat curiously. 'You seem to take it hot, Lopez. But what is this, Mr Sturrock? You've got a cock that won't fight there. I fancy the young couple were no more than a pair of runaway lovers. The lady kept close in her chamber, but for what little it's worth I heard Comber speak of the gentleman as Mr Thwaites.'

'And Mr Comber's away at some supper of his trade and can't tell me himself,' I mused. 'But it's no matter. I can send my clerk to ask him first thing tomorrow. Where are Captain Furlong and Mr Simpkin, sir?'

'Come, Mr Sturrock,' Mr Colville answered, sharpish again, 'your

questions get a thought impertinent. God's sake you can't rig Furlong and Simpkin with Lieutenant Kemble? You'll be a fool if you
try. Did you have any good of that button you were so pleased with
yesterday? Does it lead you anywhere?'

'Why yes,' I said. 'In a manner of speaking it will lead me on a
longish journey tomorrow.'

But before I could say more—and my next question was to be
about Captain Blackbird—there was a clatter on the stairs and
Maggsy's ugly face peering up, crying, 'Here, you'd best come
quick.'

Behind him was one of the two grooms, Jagger, who announced
in a rush, 'Mr Gedge's compliments sir, and says he'll be thankful of your attention in haste to get out of this lot. One of 'em's
raised the cry that we're carrying off a wench to Bedlam and
they're looking right ugly.'

And ugly it was. I doubt if all of Lady Dorothea's philosophers
will ever explain the workings of the mob. Bedlam, as you must
know, is the Bethlehem Hospital for the insane, and a truly dreadful place, worse by far than Newgate gaol; you may have some
escape from this, even if it is only by way of the rope, but there
is none from the other. It is a common pleasure of the lower sort—
and of those who should know better—to go there on Sundays for
mere entertainment, to peer and mock at the poor distracted
creatures confined here in their fetters as if they were beasts in a
wild animal show. Yet such is the fickle spirit of the commons
that let but a rumour be put around that some poor soul is about
to be taken away to Bethlehem and it will often start a riot; no
doubt as it is a common belief that more than enough have gone
there for no better reason than to be rid of them for good. But this
was no time for moralising. If our unknown rogues had considered
it for a month they could not have hit upon a better plan to stay
us from getting the wench out of Wapping.

Upwards of a score of them I judged. The other groom still
mounted, holding the reins of Jagger's animal, causing both to
kick and plunge and laying about him with his crop, was keeping

some at bay, though with no great stomach for it. The carriage horses were straining and pawing and might have been off at a bolt but for Mr Gedge holding them in hard, while cursing valiantly and flicking out with the whip in his other hand. Here too the rogues were keeping their distance, but others were about the carriage, rocking it on its springs and heaving to tip it over; which is a common pretty practice with these unruly rascals. Moreover if they got inside and discovered my two pistols only God could guess what might happen. It was near enough dark and some of 'em had torches, which I misliked, others again bawling 'No Bedlam', and from a fine safe distance away the sound of a watchman's rattle; and much good that was to us.

In the event it was all over short and sharp; for this part. They did not see me come out in a rush. One I awarded a backhanded stroke with my cane, dragged another away by his scruff as Jagger put down a third and flung one more aside unkindly. What Maggsy did I do not know but several screams and curses seemed to be his handiwork. By this time I had the door open and my pistols already in my hands, Jagger flooring yet one more to swing up on his horse, my fine brave clerk himself bolting past me into the carriage like a rabbit. Not raising my voice overmuch I said, 'Well then, lads, you've had your frolic; if you want something heavier, here it is.' Even in uncertain torchlight a pair of Wogdons is a sure quietener, and that stopped 'em just long enough for me to get in and cry 'Let go there.'

Let go Gedge did. We was off with a jolt which damned near broke my neck, Maggsy rolling atop of me and adding his curses to mine, swaying and rattling over the cobbles like a carriage demented with the clatter of our two grooms close each side; but the yells and howls were left behind. Indeed I was afraid Mr Gedge had lost his hold of the horses altogether—as I never entirely trust the creatures—and I was constrained to put my head out and bawl, 'Hold 'em in, man, easy now; we're near enough there.' God only knows how we stopped in time, but so we came to Widow Rooke's and the pursuit outdistanced; but not for long.

I was out in an instant, pulling Maggsy after me and catching up the wraps and cloaks Lady Dorothea had provided, the two grooms close in with their horses snorting, and Mr Gedge looking down from the box none too good humoured. 'Hopes there ain't too much of that,' he observed. 'My lady won't take it kind if the horses are foundered; nor yet if our coachwork's scratched.'

'I'll go bail,' I promised. 'But more you can be certain of; maybe worse.' There was no time for debate. Giving him one pistol and Jagger the other I warned them that the mob would come sure enough, but if I knew the manners of such rabble would hold back for a bit till one bolder than the others led the attack. The armament would keep 'em off, I said for encouragement. 'But don't discharge unless you must; we might need our fire later on. And all of you,' I added, 'look out for a mulatto. He'll be here and he's the ringleader.'

Physician, Isaac and the Widow Rooke were all awaiting, the door pulled open to admit us, the physician yet again as dour as his own dark mountains. 'Losh, man,' he demanded, 'what's the matter noo? Ye came up like a Fire Office machine.'

'The matter,' I informed him, 'is a riot worked up against us. As riots go it's not much yet, but it's more than enough. Isaac,' I asked, 'did you go blabbing about at the Prospect that we was going to take the wench away tonight?'

'Why, I might've done,' he confessed. 'I thought no harm of it.'

'You didn't say she was to be carried off to Bedlam?'

'That I did not,' he roared, touched to anger. 'I'd never say such a fearful thing.'

'Bedlam?' the physician repeated. 'God's sake, is that what they say?'

'It's what this rabble's howling. And you know what they'll do. There's only one thing; we must have the wench away up the river. I want Isaac to go out by the back and the wharfs to find us a boat and boatman. And quick about it.'

The fellow was repeating like an echo. 'By the river? At this time o' night? You're out of your wits, man. The lassie'll never do it.'

'Then the lassie will have to,' I retorted, 'like it or not. The lassie's more damned trouble than enough with her vapours.'

To be plain I spoke out of turn. The wench herself had appeared at the stairs, though not until Widow Rooke commanded me to hush did I look up and see her; standing with a bed-robe held close, a damnation wicked glitter in the blue eyes, chin like the prow of a frigate sailing to engage, and hair glowing in the light. Well in her right wits, and none of 'em much taken by me. 'Am I so then, sir?' she enquired.

A man should stand boldly by his word, even in the face of such an apparition as this. 'Presently you are, ma'am. Though I'll own you can't help it.'

'You're pesty generous with your kindnesses,' she rejoined.

'And better when there's time for 'em,' I promised, turning back to McGrath who was struck speechless; though whether by Miss Lydia or me I could not tell. Widow Rooke likewise started some protest, but I cut the good lady short to tell them quick and simple of my stratagem; in brief to have Miss Lydia carried secretly with Captain Isaac to some place up river close by the Tower—where we might all be safer—while Dr McGrath should lead us and the carriage by a roundabout way to shake the rogues off and meet her again; with a part in it also for Master Maggsy. It was not of my best but better than nothing.

The physician set to grumping and rumbling, turning sheep's eyes on the wench once more, but Widow Rooke gave it a brisk approval and Isaac thumped his leg and roared out like a true old sea dog. 'Haul away then,' he cried. 'And I knows a bosun's mate who'll take us. Parson's Stairs, by Goodwyn & Thornton's brewhouse we'll come ashore Jer'my. And you, Doctor Ian, bring 'em there. By God this beats cribbage,' he announced stumping off, but adding back over his shoulder to Widow Rooke, 'asking pardon, Mrs Captain.'

'Get along now, Captain Bolton,' the good sensible creature told him. 'And be quick.'

'Do I have no say in this?' the wench demanded. 'I will not be carried off so. Let me have a pistol and I'll give my own account of myself.'

'Ma'am,' I advised her politely, 'if there's one thing I fear more than God it's a woman with a pistol in her hand. You'll do as you're told.'

Could blue fire burn I'd have been cooked to a turn on the instant, but the physician rasped his hand over his lantern jaw and rumbled, 'Aye; he's an unceevil callant, mem, but he's got the sense of it. Ye'll be safer on the water with Captain Isaac.'

She turned a melting look on him, and no wonder the poor fool was down by the bows. 'And what of your safety, Doctor Ian? I shall come with you, I say.'

'Ma'am,' I said, 'you might not have heard me before and you've never met a London mob. There's upwards of a score of 'em out there and could be more yet. Most part are idle rogues primed with a few quarts of beer and the promise of a shilling or two. If you're very fortunate you might escape from them with little worse than a frolic. But there are three or four in it who're out to cut your throat.'

Widow Rooke squawked out at such plain speaking, but it sobered the wench well enough; though I was bound to admire her spirit. She took her time considering it but at last answered, 'Very well,' like a February frost. 'Then if you will sit with me, dear Mrs Rooke, we will wait for Captain Isaac. But I'll warn you, sir,' she added to me, 'I do not thank you for your manner.'

'That's my loss, ma'am,' I replied, all gentility again, 'and I'm grieved of it. But you'll not sit with Mrs Rooke yet neither. While we've time you'll answer me a question or two.'

'Sir,' she said, 'I will not answer questions for you were the end of the world to come.'

A pretty speech, and what I might have answered I cannot say as on that came a chorus of shouts from outside, running footsteps on the gravel, and the groom Hobbs was at the door frightened out of his life and too breathless to speak. Stopping only to thrust Lady Dorothea's wraps at Master Maggsy and saying in a voice which brooked no argument 'Get these about you and be quick,' I went out with the physician close behind me.

There was more of 'em now, clustered across the street, and blocking it in the way they fancied we must go back past the Prospect; ugly and muttering yet keeping their distance, not much in the way of stones and dung being thrown so far, though the worst of them at the back were still bawling about Bedlam. They were safe enough for a bit, but the horses were nervous once more —as being accustomed to more refined company they might well be—and Mr Gedge and Jagger were barely having the best of holding them. Seemingly not in any great hurry I passed out to the carriage, stopped for a word or two of encouragement to my two good fellows, took my pistols and then with the physician beside me walked across the fifteen or twenty paces to confront the rabble.

Some of the rogues set up a fresh yell as we approached, howling, 'The thieftaker,' and I answered in good humour, 'That's right, lads. And if any here fancies a ride to Newgate he's welcome. It's transportation you get for rioting, and there's none of you would much care for Botany Bay. They say the beer there's sour and not much of it.'

So long as you can keep their reason before they run mad you can sometimes hold them, and I shall confess handsomely again that our physician played his part. Once more I noted his authority with the rascals, cursing them for damned fools as we had no thought of carrying the wench off to Bedlam, calling some by name, and telling a tale about another which raised a roar, while I scanned their faces. But it was too dark and the torchlight too uncertain to make out much, and at length I said aside, 'We've quietened 'em for a bit. Back to the carriage now, but in no haste.'

Once there, and conversing like two gentlemen with never a care in the world but with an eye to the rogues across the street, I said, 'That wench is as clear in her wits as you and me. So has she told you anything?'

He was for him uncommon chastened and perplexed. 'You'll

mind we don't understand the workings of this ailment; or if it is
one. Aye. Nonetheless I ventured one question myself; to do with
Kemble. I asked her did she know or had she heard of a Captain
Blackbird.'

'Well,' I demanded sharpish. 'And had she?'

'Oh aye,' he answered. 'Aye, she'd heard of him. It was plain in
her face. I didna press and at last she begged please to give her leave
to think. But I'll still thank you not to fret her further, Sturrock,'
he added with a sudden fresh fierceness. 'She's doing verra well,
but I'll not see her put back.'

I considered our rabble before I spoke; they was remaining quiet
enough and one or two even starting to edge away. 'There'll be no
need. That's told me all I want to know. I'll engage never to trouble
the chit more; and thankful. But I'll yet tell you her whole tale
before she tells it herself. And I'll give you one bounty to start
with. You may call her Miss Lydia.' With some pleasure at the good
simple fellow's astonishment I went on, 'Now one more matter.
Have you or Isaac discovered a ship called the *Mary Carson*?'

He shook his head. 'The captain's been stumping up and down
with his cronies all day. There's no ship of that name.'

'I fancy there is,' I mused. 'But I fancy also that she's many,
many miles away from London.'

On that the house door opened a crack and old Isaac summoned
us in the windy bellow he considers is a whisper. Keeping a careful
eye on the street we drew back to him and, rosy with excitement, a
cutlass under his arm for all the world like going off against his
China Seas pirates, he announced, 'Crew mustered and waiting
to give way.'

It was another Drury Lane spectacle. The wench muffled in a
boat cloak and hood, still flashing blue fire but softening when the
physician went to say something in her ear and take her hands, a
most pathetic farewell; Mrs Rooke the other side of her to support
the poor shrinking creature; and Maggsy like nothing you have
ever seen before. The little monster gave even me a turn; a monkey
dressed up in purple velvet and a woollen shawl over its head,

face wickedly compounded of cowardice, mischief and sniggers, and clutching a cudgel under his queenly robes. If that mulatto ever got sight of him in the dark he'd cut his own throat first for fear of the grues.

But there was no time for admiration, and I said to the captain, 'We'll meet at Parson's Stairs then. Only one more thing first Isaac. Tomorrow forenoon there's a ship warping in to Wells' victualling yard to take on stores. I want to know her name and if you can discover it where she's sailing for.'

Then they were gone out to the back, Isaac stumping and chuckling and fancying himself forty years younger, the wench with one backward look at the doctor but never a glance for me. We were well shot of her, and as a good general freed from encumbrances I could now make my dispositions. The groom Hobbs being little use to us I would have up on the box; the physician I desired first to instruct Mr Gedge which way to start—away from the mob, in the direction they least expected us to go—and then to take Hobbs' mount and join our bolder fellow, Jagger. If the rascals rushed us at all, as I thought they would egged on by the worse villains behind, it would be as I took Maggsy out; the physician and Jagger would then block the street with their horses while we got away; finally when we were off at a fair gallop they would break off and catch up, Jagger then to fall in at the rear of the carriage and Dr McGrath to take up in front to lead the way.

Seeing us about to move the crowd set up another growl and swayed forward. Yet once more McGrath seemed to quieten them. As cool as a melon he spoke a few words to Mr Gedge and then swung up on to Hobbs' animal; that fellow now being in a muck-sweat of fear. There was a fresh surge, a deeper growl and more yells, but the physician and Jagger turned their horses flank on against our rascals; a shifting mess of dark figures and faces half seen under the wavering torches and brassy moonlight again flooding us. It was plain that the rogues in front were ripe for mischief but bashful of starting it, and while the doctor's authority seemed still to be holding them I hustled Maggsy out with Widow

Rooke slamming and bolting her door after us.

It brought a yet uglier howl as they took him for the wench. One fellow I saw grappling with Jagger to pull him down, another from behind whirling and flinging a torch, the physician swinging his horse's rump against the press; and Master Maggsy wailing, 'God Christ, they'll rape me first and then gut me when they find how they've been tricked.'

I thrust the wretch incontinent into the carriage, bundled after him myself, and as a bolt released our cattle went away. It was a rattling business, with Maggsy making the din more hideous with his complaints, me offering up a prayer that my pistols might not explode in the shaking and swaying or that we might not run full tilt into some belated carter. But Providence put out His Hand to us and the way was clear. The hell's chorus of shouts, howls, and curses was dying behind, and at length in the darkness I contrived to find a grip of the door and get my head out to view the battle.

It was still a scene of running confusion, but my men had broken clear. Jagger was coming on and striking one last obstinate fellow away with his crop, the physician riding hard beside him. In another minute they had caught up in a clatter of hoofs, and then with a lurch which very near tipped us over we wheeled to our left to come into a broader thoroughfare. Here there were a few lights in the beer houses and chandlers' shops and people abroad about their mysterious errands, but none with further interest in us.

We could settle to a more sober pace and dispose ourselves in better comfort; though broken by Master Maggsy's curses and Mr Gedge expressing his opinions on Wapping and its inhabitants from the box above. Having the physician riding ahead and Jagger behind we pulled again to the left into a still wider mercantile street, with manufactories, rope walks, and a tavern or two on either side; but before long we discovered ourselves once more passing into an uncharted wilderness of meaner and darker lanes returning to the river. It was here Dr McGrath came back, calling on Mr Gedge to stop and dismounting at the carriage door. In his plain

Scots manner he demanded, 'D'ye ken where we are?'

'If my nose don't lie, close on Goodwyn's brewhouse,' I answered.

'Aye,' he said. 'A hundred yards or so and the next cut to the right. There's a long dock, ye'll understand, with but one bridge across it; and damnation narrow. Aye. And that's where the devils are waiting for us. I kenned they would,' he added with a kind of dark satisfaction. 'When we broke away yonder I obsairved a number of 'em setting out to run back. Ye've no' been so smart, my man.'

'I can't foresee all things,' I told him. 'Is there no other way round?'

'Not if we're to come out by Parson's Stairs. And I'll not have the lassie left there.'

I forebore from advising him what he could do with the lassie and asked instead, 'How many? Can we drive straight through 'em?'

'Not as many as the last tussle. A dozen or more mebbe. But they'd have the coach over in the dock in a trice.'

I made up my mind on the instant. 'Then we must clear the bridge. We'll go forward to see their force.'

'Here,' Maggsy screeched on that, 'you let me get out of this clobber afore you start fresh trouble. If them villains come at me looking for a pair of tits and finds what I've got instead I shall never be the same again.'

Silencing the creature's outcries I took my pistols—though in general I am opposed to shooting in the streets—and we went on afoot leaving Jagger, the horses, and the carriage itself to come after us as quiet as they could. It was a close lane of ancient tenements slanting together above our heads, in stinking darkness but crossed here and there by rays of that unearthly moon, and a chink or two of light from behind tight closed shutters; a place for people to lie behind locked doors and mind their own business. With the carriage creaking behind us, but now on earth instead of cobbles so muffling the sound, we came to the corner by a leaning clapboarded hovel with a sign board hanging over us like a gallows.

A bit below us down a little slope lay the bridge, scarce more than wide enough for a dray and with nothing but a low parapet on either side. At the far side was the street down to the river and the famous brewhouse, with a lantern burning in the archway to its yard and a few lights half obscured by vagrant wisps of steam in the buildings and sheds; for these fellows work night and day about their alchemy. In the dock several barges, and a cresset flickering on the wharf; on this side an open space of twenty paces or so for wagons to turn about in; and our fine gang of villains blocking the nearer end of the bridge. As McGrath had said, not so many but enough; two or three still carrying torches, some with sticks and cudgels, and one with the glint of a knife in his hand. Behind me the physician muttered and grumphed, Master Maggsy broke into one of his genteel curses, and Mr Gedge gave vent to fresh opinions on the manners and customs of Wapping.

I counted up to fourteen, reflecting on my tactics, and then said, 'I'll not have the horses or carriage put at risk. One of us must get across to the brewhouse and beg help. We may cause a diversion from the other side.'

'My man,' the physician announced, 'we've had enough of your divairsions for one night. They're too damned divairting by half.'

With that he seemed to go mad. Swinging the spare horse about he mounted and charged past me down the slope roaring like a cavalryman; and on the instant Jagger followed him, uttering his own wild cries. I caught a glimpse of our villains' eyes glinting, heard their astonished cries at the sight of these fearful apparitions, and then physician and groom were upon them with awful carnage, the excited beasts squealing and rearing, plunging clean through the rogues and thundering on the timbers of the bridge. It was a stirring spectacle, but vexatious; in that mêlée I dared not use my own armament for fear of hitting one of the horses, a circumstance which might well cause Lady Dorothea some annoyance. There was nothing for it but for me to join the fray myself, and I advanced with Master Maggsy trotting behind, even trying to hold me back by my coat tails and crying, 'God's Tripes, he's at it again.'

By now McGrath and Jagger were wheeling on the bridge pre-
paratory for a second charge, coming back like a squadron of
Hussars turned raving; and, be damned, that impatient physician
was laughing. But I had no time to wonder at miracles, for several
of the villains rounded on me. One I disposed of neat and simple
with a shot which caused him to clutch at his shoulder before
plunging over from the bridge to the dock below, while Maggsy
quietened another with a blow from his cudgel and a dreadful
curse. The third, however, was the mulatto and him I marked down
as my own for all that he advanced on me crouching, his teeth
agleam and knife held low but point upwards for the dastardly
lower belly stroke. I would have winged him at ease had not our
hasty physician chosen to come roaring back to ride the rogue
down. I was forced to hold my fire and in some impatience cried,
'Be damned, sir, have a care with that animal; you'll do a mischief.'

Those were my final words. A fresh rascal engaged me, and while
I was awarding him a snouter with my pistol barrel one more
struck me a cruel blow from behind. The last sound I heard above
the din of battle and the roaring in my ears was Master Maggsy
screeching, 'God's Whiskers, they've done for Sturrock; there goes
my bread and butter.'

CHAPTER SIX

What followed I do not know. After some interval I was next by degrees aware of riding in a carriage with a light or two passing by; another coach now and again with lamps flaring, a sedan chair and link boys with torches or lanterns, the better kind of shops, coffee houses and taverns. By the same degrees I became also aware of a head on me like the finest surfeit of Madeira you have ever had in your life; then of Master Maggsy muttering and complaining about his bread and butter, and lastly of the physician on the opposite seat and of the wench reclining asleep with her head upon his shoulder. No doubt an affecting spectacle had I been of a mind for it. But I was not, and demanded, 'What the devil happened then?'

'So ye've come to?' the physician enquired. 'Aye. Well your beaver saved you a fine bonnie dunt on the head, that's what happened, my man. But ye'll be none the worse by the morn.'

'He's come to,' Maggsy screeched. 'I thought you was corpussed; God's Whiskers I did. I says "He's got it at last, as I always knowed he would, and what's to become of me now?"'

'Be quiet, you little imp of Satan,' Dr McGrath admonished him, 'ye'll disturb the leddy.'

I do not advise a rush of blood to the head when you have lately taken a murderous blow. It sets all the hammers of Hell pounding. But I answered, 'Be damned to the lady.'

Even in the dim light of a passing lamp I perceived the blue glitter as her eyes opened. 'That is a pesty uncivil observation, sir,' she announced. 'But I'll acquit you of it. I hear you fought most bravely for me.'

I very quickly corrected her on that. 'For Lady Dorothea's horses and carriage.'

'You'll permit me to say that you do not go out to make people

101

care for you,' she replied sweetly.

'He never does,' Maggsy complained. 'Never did and never will. Anyway,' he continued to me, 'I saved your pistols, you should be thankful of that; I says "If he's corpussed they'll be worth a guinea of two, or likewise I might turn highwayman myself, as with old Sturrock gone it'll be an easy trade.'

On that most improper observation the Devil himself gave a stroke with his own particular hammer, and fearing lest my head should fly apart like a case shot I felt it wise to say no more. Moreover by then we were rolling into Soho Square and in another minute stopping with a jingle of harness at my own door. Here the physician saw fit to offer me medical advice. 'Away to your bed, my man; and mind now, no sperits or wine. I'd as soon you came on to present us to Lady Dorothea Dashwood but ye're in no state for it. Aye. Ye'd best lie quiet a bit the morn and I'll come about to see how you do.'

But I had the last word. Clambering out, with Master Maggsy so much assisting that he damned near tripped me over, I said, 'I've no doubt you'll manage well enough with her ladyship, but pray present my compliments. As for tomorrow, you may save yourself the trouble.' I addressed myself to the wench. 'I'm off to Ponder's End tomorrow, Miss Lydia. First to find a certain negro servant named Geoffrey if I may; and then perhaps to discover who Captain Blackbird might be.'

I was rewarded by a sharp catch of breath, but by now quite out of patience stopped only to desire Mr Gedge to remind my lady of the letter she had promised and the chaise, and then ordered him to give way.

Damning the lot of them roundly, with Master Maggsy pushing from behind and more hindrance than help, I ascended to my own snug chambers. Here also damning the physician's whimsical advice I ordered the monster to set out my pipes and tobacco and a bottle of Madeira with two glasses—for I am a forgiving man—to take off my boots and then tell his tale of how the battle ended. It served to wear away a few minutes while I was recovering my humour, though there was little enough of it and of no great importance.

'I've knowed you do better for a start,' he said, 'I reckon you shouldn't ought to go arolling and rollicking with wenches like that Rosie at your age, it throws you off your form; you only put two down as I see. I done for three myself and I don't reckon to fancy fighting, not all that much, and never would if you didn't keep getting me into it. Well then the doctor and that groom was laying about 'em with hoofs, teeth and arses, and a crowd come out of the brewhouse to see the fun and then stopped to join in; seems one of 'em knowed McGrath on account of his youngest getting seized with the chokings awhile back, and her'd been a goner but for the physician. So that was the end of it and the villains took to their heels.'

'Thought you was a goner too,' he continued, 'lying there with your trap open but not saying nothing. I says "Sturrock's corpussed", but the physician says "Not so, they snores when they're bad", so we heaves you into the carriage and comes on to Parson's Stairs for Copperknob. She's there on the steps with Captain Isaac and a wherryman, and seems he's telling her one of his tales for she's alaughing to split herself, and then she flings her arms about his neck and kisses him and says he's the grandest old gentleman and when she's settled her own business, as she means to do, she's sure to come back to visit him and Mrs Rooke.'

'When she's settled her own business, as she means to do,' I mused. 'Well then, we shall see who settles it for her first. And to that end, Master Maggsy, we'll be off to bed. We both have work to do tomorrow.'

It takes more than a light tap from a villain to discompose Jeremy Sturrock, and I arose betimes with little worse than a claret headache; which is a mere nothing. Stirring Master Maggsy up I arrayed myself in my newest coat—a curious cut but nothing foppish—and a particular fine neckcloth, took down my best beaver and had our little wretch shine my boots until a cat could see to break its neck in 'em. Then after an early but substantial breakfast I instructed

Maggsy in his duties for the day. These being to return to Wapping and first make certain enquiries as to what Lieutenant Kemble was doing in the week before he was killed; next to seek out the wherryman who had transported Miss Consuela and the gentleman and discover what ship he had put them aboard; and last to glean any more he could of Captains Lopez and Furlong and what business they had with Mr Colville. That accomplished, I added kindly, he might return by way of Lincoln's Inn Fields and pry about there in the hope of hearing of Mr Moxon; this as I now considered that same might well be a lawyer.

'I dunno that I ain't had my bellyful of Wapping by now,' the impudent rascal observed. 'And supposing I don't get myself triped while I'm about it, what do I do with the rest of my time?'

'If I'm not returned from Ponder's End,' I told him, 'you'll try to keep away from my tobacco and Madeira. Then on the day following, Saturday as will be, at the earliest in the morning you'll report to the servants' entrance at Hanover Square; where I shall contrive to send you fresh orders.'

How often do we make such plans for Providence to dispose of? But for now scarcely had Maggsy's complaints died away on the stairs before the rattle of wheels and hoofs heralded my own conveyance, and taking a light valise which contained my pistols, powder flask, shot, and other small necessities I descended at once. Here Jagger greeted me with the sealed letter addressed 'To Lady Charles Motley, at Highgate', and an anticipatory grin of fresh excitements to come, while I directed him to head first for Bloomsbury. We were looking, I explained, for a lodging house kept by Mrs Bedales; and since it was reputed to be uncommon genteel we should most likely find it somewhere hard by the British Museum.

So we set off in another spanking turn-out—murrey and dark blue with a crest on the panels—and I sat at ease composing a moral observation or two on the spectacle of London rolling by; the which I have described several times elsewhere and no need to repeat it here. It was still a strange calm day with the same brassy sky; and the ships, I reflected, would still be hanging idle in the river. But we had a pleasant air from the passage of the chaise, as there was not a lot of traffic yet and Jagger kept up a smart pace; nor was it a long journey, for after but three enquiries my good fellow discovered the establishment in Upper King Street, close by Bedford House. Not quite the modish elegance of Hanover Square, but very proper. Nor could anything be more genteel than Mrs Bedales when she received me in her private parlour, conducted there by a little blackamoor page dressed up in a green robe and pink turban. A woman at one time a housekeeper or butler's wife, I judged, all bombazine and jet beads and a face not unlike a chamber pot half filled with cold tea; but all prunes and prims once she had taken in the cut of my coat and neckcloth and got a quick look through the window at my equippage waiting in the street.

There is a nicety in these matters, and I let it be seen that I knew my place and knew hers; affecting to be a man of business concerned with great affairs and great families, but now in some vexation. 'Moxon, ma'am,' I told her. 'Attorney at Law, the civil practice you'll understand; I want no scandals in my legalities. Though be hanged it looks as if our wilful chit Miss Lydia's doing her best to raise one.'

'Miss Palmer?' she enquired.

'The same, ma'am,' I cried. 'That's what I said; Miss Lydia Palmer. To speak nothing of the duenna; a wench who'll lead her into mischief if we're not careful. Confound it, what's she called now? I've got better things to think about than servant's names, but I've got it writ down somewhere in my Lord's latest letter. Consuela something.'

'Consuela Smith,' Mrs Bedales volunteered. 'And if I may say so an impudent baggage. Several times I observed to myself that young woman's got notions above her station.'

'That's what I'm told,' I hurried on. 'Lord Falconhurst's beside himself. And now I've a fresh message hot from Boston.'

'Boston?' the woman asked. 'But as I was informed they came from Philadelphia.'

'Why so they do,' I answered all impatience. 'Boston was the first port the family could find a fast packet sailing.'

No man of sensibility would wish to linger on Mrs Bedales a minute longer than he must, and I shall use as few words as I can on her tale. It was simple enough. As we know from Master Maggsy, Miss Lydia, Consuela, and the negro servant had arrived here from the Belle Savage on Sunday September 7th. On Monday morning Miss Lydia had sent out early to bespeak a post chaise, but Consuela Smith had pleaded that she herself must remain at the lodging to look to their clothes after the long journey, and Miss Lydia had set off attended only by the negro whom she addressed as Geoffrey. She had then returned at a little after six of the evening somewhat fatigued, and her travelling cloak dusty from the roads.

Tuesday she had required a town hackney, and Consuela had now declared that she must remain to clean and sponge Miss Lydia's cloak from yesterday; accordingly Miss Lydia had again gone alone save for Geoffrey and on this occasion returned before dinner and in better spirits saying—as Mrs Bedales chanced to hear—that all was arranged though it seemed like to take longer than she had thought it might. Wednesday both ladies had ventured out to view the sights and shops, but had returned discreetly before dark with Consuela complaining of a migraine brought on by the heat, noise and crowds. Then on Thursday another chaise was fetched after an early dinner, but Consuela's migraine continuing Miss Lydia had once more departed accompanied only by Geoffrey; after advising Mrs Bedales that she would not return until Saturday.

By Friday Miss Consuela Smith's migraine seemed miraculously to have passed away, as she went out herself to take the air in Bedford House gardens; and on Mrs Bedales' remarking this she retorted that Miss Lydia sometimes had affairs of her own which rendered a migraine a polite necessity. On Saturday a note was brought by a post boy, and this Miss Consuela was good enough to show Mrs Bedales, somewhat with an air that it did not surprise her. It announced simply that Miss Lydia had settled to remain at Lord Falconhurst's house, and she now desired that on the Wednesday following Consuela should settle their accounts in full, procure a conveyance and bring herself and their remaining baggage there to join her.

I put a few further questions to the woman, but she had never seen any of Miss Lydia Palmer's handwriting herself, neither had she observed any sign of a gentleman concerned in the matter, and at last I finished, 'That's what it is, ma'am, depend upon it. A runaway elopement, for the chit never went near Lord Falconhurst. And what the young are coming to in these wicked days I can't reckon.'

So taking leave of her, and thankful for it, I directed my good Jagger to our next call and reclined at ease reflecting on this intelligence while we trotted briskly out of town to more verdant fields. We now knew where this confounded troublesome wench had come from, though be damned her name being Palmer and not Peregrine, as I had thought, seemed a fresh confusion; yet I could now perceive most part of the plot and what lay behind it, though how much it had to do with Lieutenant Kemble was yet uncertain. But no doubt my own wits, Providence, and perhaps Lady Motley would unfold that also in good time, and I was not ill satisfied with my conclusions as we came to climb the long hill to Highgate; a pretty village of the better sort.

Captain Sir Charles Motley's residence proved to be a commodious house in the latest style, red brick decorated with white windows and portico, some good stands of the new trees now much affected by the landed gentry, to the left a very fair range of stabling, and on the other hand the arbours and walls of a garden. In short Captain Sir Charles was a baronet of substance; and a good thing too, as such men guarding our shores have the best of reasons for taking care that the Frenchies never get vile thieving fingers on their property. Just as plain his household staff was of the same ilk, for the fellow who came in answer to my summons had a manner of gazing over your left shoulder as if he fancied you might have come about the dog's meat, but this softened somewhat as he took in my turnout and Jagger in his livery and cockade standing by the horses; and I put the rest of it to flight by presenting my letter and announcing, 'From Lady Dorothea Dashwood.'

Within a minute or two he came back, this time essaying a bow, and led me round the front of the house and through a brick archway to a spacious garden and a stretch of well clipped grass, where there was a little temple or pavilion done with pillars and balustrades in the Italian fancy. It was a very picture by the late Sir Thomas Gainsborough, the lady on a marble seat, a lap dog at her feet, a fan in one hand and a wide hat to protect her from the sun; and lounging at the back a young fellow having a fowling piece under his arm and an ugly looking gun dog at his knee. The lady herself was much as I expected her; somewhat overblown but the same girl as had writ those letters much taken with a baronetcy thirty odd years ago; and still much taken with it.

The boy was a very different basket of fish; a lowering look and an air of 'Who the hell might you be?' about him. Considering which was the most dangerous, the gun or the dog, I reflected that but one word out of place and unless I defended myself— which I should dislike, having a proper respect for the gentry— I might soon find myself beating a retreat with one at my heels, a charge of shot from the other in my arse, and a vulgar loss of dignity. This was to be a matter of nice diplomacy and I did my best bow while my lady cried, 'La, sir, I vow here's a mystery. For though I know of the family, as who don't, I've never met Lady Dorothea Dashwood.'

'No doubt a lack she'd wish corrected,' I replied, 'for she speaks in most approving terms of Captain Sir Charles. Soon to be Rear Admiral Sir Charles when we set about Bonaparte again.'

'La, sir,' she simpered at me, 'that's a secret.'

'Not to my Lords of the Admiralty, ma'am,' I assured her.

'You come from their Lordships?'

She puzzled over Lady Dorothea's letter again which must have said little, but enough, and I hastened in, 'It's a matter which most deeply concerns them.' As you shall see in the end I was speaking nothing but the most precise truth. In the Art and Science of Detection you must always cling to truth as ladies cling to modesty; so long as you know how to wrap both up. 'But that's true, ma'am,' I continued, 'it is in a manner secret. I'd be obliged of a word for your ear alone.'

'Egod, sir,' she answered, 'you grow more mysterious by the minute, and I'm all agog. Rodney, dear boy, pray have the goodness to retire.'

He cast me a devilish unfavourable look and moved off with an ill grace and only as far as another bench, out of earshot but well within sight. An unfortunate circumstance for if I could gauge my lady her face would change from sweet lemon pie to cold mutton fat before I'd done, and I did not want that young sprig at my back when I least expected it. But I set about the business briskly. 'It concerns a certain Lieutenant Robert Kemble, ma'am.'

That shot went home true enough for one hand flew to her amplitude of tits, and the other to her mouth. Nonetheless she tried to face it out. 'Lieutenant Robert Kemble? Who is that? Some officer of Captain Sir Charles?'

'No, ma'am,' I said. 'He was not. He was an old friend of yours. Let me not remind a lady of the years, but a fair time back. To be plain Lieutenant Kemble's met with a sad and vexatious accident and there's bound to be a coroner's inquiry. Moreover there was several letters discovered in his sea chest. They was signed by a Miss Georgiana Woodforde.'

She gave a little squeal at this, pressing her hands yet tighter to her tits. In another instant she'd have screeched for Master Rodney with God knows what result, and I begged her, 'Pray compose yourself, ma'am. There's no harm in 'em; or very little so long as they're not read out in court. That's what I'm here to stop if I can. It'd be no pleasure to Captain Sir Charles if some of the newsprints and rascally lampoonists got wind of 'em and set out to make the worst of an innocent love affair.'

'You're an odious wretch,' she whispered. 'What is it you want? Money?'

'Why, no,' I told her, much offended. 'I wouldn't think of it; not with an introduction from Lady Dorothea. Just plain answers to a simple question or two.' To set the woman more at ease I added, 'I'd as soon not offend your delicacy, ma'am, but Lieutenant Kemble was done to death for no rhyme nor reason that yet appears. I mean to find out why and I mean to have the man who killed him or gave orders for it. Now then, who was Tristram Peregrine?'

Her eyes widened at me, yet also seemed to gaze back over the years. 'Tristram? What're you at now? It was all so long ago,' she cried pettishly.

'To behold you now it might have been but yesterday, my lady,' I told her. 'Whether Tristram Peregrine had much, little or nothing to do with Lieutenant Kemble I don't know; but I'm bound to ask. So who was he? "Tristram is my *devoted slave*, tho *very young* and I think *wicked* and Mama will not bear me to speak of him."' I said, 'That's from your own letter, ma'am. Why was he wicked?'

She cast a glance at that ugly looking young fellow and for an instant I thought she was about to scream for him, but she changed her mind on it and answered, 'He was hard, even as a boy. He had a way of command and would let nothing stand in his way.' Contriving a blush beneath the powder and raddle on her cheeks she added, 'I did not learn of it for years after; my dear papa and mama would never permit it discussed. He was a ... His mother was his father's sister-in-law; Hester Ryde.'

'It sounds indecent,' I observed, and then begged, 'Ma'am, I become confused with these family matters. Let's go back to the Lord Falconhurst who shot himself over his last two bottles of port. As I understand it he had four sons and one daughter: Lydia Peregrine. The first two died without issue.'

'One was killed at sea and the other in India.'

'So we're left with Matthew Peregrine, the heir to the title, and Hayward the younger son. Where does this Hester Ryde come in between the two of 'em?'

My lady gave vent to a sniff which would not have disgraced Miss Harriet. 'From one to the other turn and turn about. Hester fancied Hayward more than he did her, so my dear mama told me at last. But Matthew had the expectations, so she married him; and not six months after gave birth to a son by Hayward. Being a doting fool Matthew admitted the child as his own, while Hayward took himself off to Barbados to make his fortune. Whereupon Hester Ryde gave Matthew a son of his own a year or so later. But by then the old Lord had shot himself; the expectations was no more than an empty title and she went off to Barbados likewise, after Hayward. Where he would not have any more to do with her; or so it was said.'

'So there was two boys,' I mused. 'What became of 'em?'

'They went as midshipmen to the Navy; both the same time. And I'll warn you, sir,' she added, 'I'm growing tired of this. In a minute I desire my son to summon our men or put you out himself. Moreover I shall complain to Lady Dorothea Dashwood.'

'I should dislike to see your letters get into the hands of the scandalous printers, ma'am,' I said. 'Or even to have them read out in the Coroner's Court.' But I could see my welcome was wearing thin, and though I much wanted to ask more about the two young midshipmen it is never genteel to over stretch a lady's patience. I allowed myself one last question. 'There's another name appeared today. Palmer. Was there a Palmer family concerned with the Rydes and Peregrines also?'

She sniffed once more. 'The Palmers of High Beech. Always marrying in and out with the Rydes. I can promise you my dear papa and mama had little truck with people of that kind.'

'I can see they wouldn't, ma'am,' I agreed. 'I can see you yourself are a lady of particular good sense, and I'm obliged to you. And as one favour requests another I'll engage to send your letters back to you in private when this business is all over and done with. Likewise I'll present your compliments to Lady Dorothea Dashwood.'

With this politic speech I took myself off, not in any unseemly haste but still keeping a sharp eye on that young fellow with his gun and dog, and on reaching the chaise instructed Jagger 'Now, my lad, make for Edmonton, where we'll take our dinner; and then on to Ponder's End. Don't flog the horses but don't let 'em loiter neither.'

So we took a smart pace into scenes of deeper rural solitude while I pondered on the ways of English country families; and then turned with some relief to philosophise on the Profundities of Nature and the remarkableness of trees and vegetables. I also reflected on the difficulties of the Art and Science of Detection when so much travelling is called for, and speculated on what fresh intelligence Master Maggsy might be discovering in Wapping; or more likely what fresh devilment he was getting himself into. But to be plain and short I was more concerned with considerations of a cut or two off the sirloin and a pint of claret when we reached the Bell at Edmonton; which is a well spoken of coaching house.

We were soon there and I kindly advised Jagger that he might refresh himself at my charge with a quart of ale and bread and cheese and pickles or even pie if he fancied it, while I repaired to the travellers' dining-room. It was pretty fair, and I made a tolerable country repast of goose, beef, pie, cheese, etc., though the claret was little better than indifferent and overpriced. But I did well enough, all considered, and at length we set out again men and beasts alike refreshed for the last short pull to Ponder's End.

This was now on the London to York run, and a confounded dangerous stretch of road it is, what with ruts, dust and coaches. To any gentleman with his own equippage these pestilential four-in-hands are a curse and a rudeness, for all their proud names such as the York Highflyer, the Stamford Regent, the Rockingham, or the Truth and Daylight. Get through at any cost, their rascally agents tell the coachmen, and get through they will, thundering by at ten miles an hour or more, expecting you to clear the way at the first sound of their horns, and giving you the lash if they fancy you're crowding 'em; these vain and impudent rogues with their capes, coats, whips and white top hats consider themselves the kings of the highway.

But by the Mercy of Providence we continued without incident, now passing through a landscape of still greater rural solitude; of flat and marshy nature, with here and there a sluggish water course, clumps of willow trees, and ever and again a melancholy pool or mere enmeshed with reeds and sedges. In short a damned good place for fevers and the ague. I have already done my philosophising on the countryside—as is properly expected in any genteel composition—so no more of it here save only to observe that this prospect looked like the last place God made, and He forgot to finish it or lost interest.

Nor did Ponder's End appear a lot better as we rolled up to the inn there, being assured by a yokel that this was the place we sought. It was called The Two Brewers, promising good livery and bait by a board hung over the stables, and a pretty enough tiled and brick built house with several gables and bay windows, but small and somewhat over rusticated for my taste. For the rest there was a cottage here and there, a farmhouse by the roadside, and some little way on the tower of a church beyond further groves of melancholious willow trees hanging over what seemed to be a dark and slow river. None of it much enlivened by a disconsolate cow or two, a dog of two minds whether to bark or return to sleep, fowls scratting in the dust, and the whole lying under a still breathless air and lowering sky. But there was no hint of the fearful happenings soon to come.

An ostler also seemingly half asleep came to the stable door to survey us, and I charged Jagger with his latest instructions. There was no need of his remaining, I said, and he might return to London either with his own cattle or by taking fresh horses from here if he thought fit. He was to pass the word through Mr Gedge to Mr Masters and on to Dr McGrath that it would be well to keep a sharp eye on the young lady as she might be expected to have designs of her own. Then he was to return to Ponder's End at the soonest tomorrow bringing any new information with him and my clerk, if this little rascal had by then reported at Hanover Square; but not to wait for him if he was late as I might have more urgent need of Jagger himself. It was a simple arrangement which served both to keep my intelligences open and save me the cost of his lodging the night.

So leaving Jagger to arrange his own mysteries with the ostler I took myself with my valise into the tap. It seemed respectable enough, plaster walls and oak beams, a red tiled floor and well sanded pewter, one ancient rustic with a face like a wicked old goat mumbling over his beer, and the landlord leaning on the counter; neither better nor worse than most of 'em but maybe honest enough when it suited him. Being in doubt about the claret I called for a pint of strong ale and was of half a mind to invite the pair of them to the same but thought better of it. These suspicious country savages incline to think you're after something if you're too open handed.

The landlord was a man of few words but we reflected on the weather which he considered was fair to lowering, on the state of the roads which he opined was moderate to wicked, on the coach services which he announced was poor and getting worse, and on the government which he said was bad and going rotten. 'Well,' I offered for comfort, 'you've got a lot of water here. Though no doubt a lot of bone ache with it.'

'Crippled,' he assented. 'All of us.'

'Some sort of river maybe,' I proposed, whereupon after deep consideration he confessed that was very likely, and I asked, 'Would it come out by London?'

'River Lea,' the old gaffer piped up. 'Everybody knows that; even a babby knows that. Why we gets wherries up it. We gets wherries all the way from Bow Creek to near Crooked Mile.'

'So ho,' I said. 'It comes out at Bow Creek, does it?'

The landlord gave me a sharper look than I'd have thought he had in him. 'Been a lot of mud of late years.'

'Be damned there ain't,' the gaffer screamed, flying into a rage.

'You'm a most contrary man, Thomas Coote. You know as well as I do as we gets wherries reg'lar.'

'You chatters too much, Gaffer Gudgeon,' Master Coote interposed, on that staying to listen as a voice within called out a summons to him, and then adding, 'Like a magpie and no more sense in it. A gentleman don't want to listen to your babble.'

He went out, leaving me alone with the old rascal, who made a naughty gesture after him and whispered, 'I could fancy a pot of strong ale while's he's gone. Thomas Coote don't never serve me better'n small beer and it rots my bowels.'

'You shall have a treat then.' I tossed a few pence down and while he scuttled round to the barrels with an agility distasteful in one of his years enquired, 'With such a lot of water you'll very likely have a mill or two hereabouts?'

He came up from the pot with a suck and a gurgle, shook the drops from his goat's beard, and agreed, 'That's right. Mills in plenty. Was a windmill too, but it got blowed up.'

'One way and another,' I observed, 'you lead a wild life in Ponder's End. How did that happen?'

Gaffer Gudgeon cackled heartily. 'On account of it being uncommon hot and windy that Sunday. And the flour dust.'

'What's that got to do with it?' I asked.

'Why, don't you know that neither?' he asked. 'Flour dust is rare bangable. Partic'lar of a damnation hot Sunday and Ezekial Coffin singing in the church with a mighty voice and got himself a wicked thirst. Ezekial's thirsts was monstrous and come nightfall he'm as drunk as a sow in a cider press. Well then us gave'n a candle lantern to light his way back to the mill. So by what us reckons he must've got the door open and then fell over and broke the lantern for the whole lot banged up with one walloping whump. And that was the end of Ezekial Coffin. Found him atop of Farmer Pottle's cow byre and took the better part of an hour to pick the broken tiles out of his arse. Not but he was past caring by then but Parson says it wasn't proper to lay him in his grave arse uppards.'

Reflecting that Master Maggsy would find a boon companion in this old gentleman, I demanded, 'Ezekial Coffin, did you say? Coffin? When did this happen? Would it be last week or so?'

The old scamp gazed at me dumbfounded. 'Last week? Why, master, you're simple for sure.' He fell to reckoning on his fingers, nodding and mumbling to himself and at last finished, 'Eight and twenty year ago. The year Parson Peregrine's lads went for sailors.'

I was breathing a prayer to the Almighty for preservation when Master Landlord returned. He cast another sharp look on us and asked, 'What tale's he been telling now? You should be warned, sir; he'm a wicked old fancifuller.'

'No I ain't,' the gaffer screamed again. 'I be a very smart old man for my age. I be telling him of Ezekial Coffin's flour mill that got blowed up eight and twenty year ago.'

'Ezekial Coffin was it?' The rogue turned a strange gaze on the old crackpot, but then said, 'I see you've posted your man back to London, sir. And nice cattle you've got there; they're no common post hosses. But I'll see they're well looked after. Will you want a lodging yourself for the night?'

'God help me, yes,' I said.

'Well, there's a nice chamber above,' he announced. 'Save a leg comes off the bed if you get too bouncy on it, and Moll's a bouncible wench when she takes a fit. She's had the itch on her for a week or more now. On t'other hand Mrs Coote's suffering a gripe of the colic and goes farting claps of thunder day and night. Still there's a prime bit of treacle cured ham if it ain't gone off by now. Or if you'd sooner there's what's left of a laying pullet I had for my dinner. I broke a tooth on her, but you might do better.'

'No,' I said. 'Not by any means. A clean farm'll suit me. Or some good woman who knows how to cook a supper.'

'Ain't it to your taste here then?' he enquired. 'So you'd best try Mrs Matcham. Her husband's a sailor away to sea and she'll sometimes oblige us with a gentleman when we've got a coach stuck in the snow.'

'Well,' I observed, 'I don't see any snow yet but nothing'd surprise me now. Mrs Matcham'll do.'

Gaffer Gudgeon let out a cackle like a mainsail splitting, and I turned a cold eye on the old goat while Landlord Coote explained, 'It's a step or two up the road but nothing to hurt. By the river and up the green and close against the rectory and church. It's called Glebe Farm; only it ain't a farm.'

'No,' I agreed, 'in Ponder's End it wouldn't be. I couldn't expect that. But you said the rectory and church. Is that where I find the Reverend Matthew Peregrine, Lord Falconhurst?'

The fellow scratched his head. 'Well, you do and you don't, as you might say; likewise you could or you could not. On the other hand he commonly writes his sermon for Sunday of a Friday night.'

Words choked in my throat, but before I could utter even one Gaffer Gudgeon piped, 'He'm as mad as a snake, poor soul. But for all that Nicodemus Scrope declares he've come into a bucket of money. Be that what you're about, master?'

'That's right,' Mr Coote advised. 'You'd best consult Nicodemus Scrope.'

'Quite so,' I got out through my strangulation, 'so I will,' and seizing my valise, thankful to be out of it while I still had the half of my wits left, turned out to the passage. But I still had wits enough not to latch the door, clatter out to the entrance and then move back as silent as only I can, to get my ear to the crack. I was in time to hear Landlord Coote awarding the old gaffer a fine dressing down. Speaking low and hard he was saying, 'You crack pated old zany, you damned bag of pig's chitterlings, keep your trap shut about Coffin's Mill, can't you? I don't like the cut of that'n.'

But then by the sound of it he was coming to the door himself, and just as quick I was out with my valise to the road; and little to be seen save the ostler sitting on a bucket by the stables and an aged crone hobbling across the meadow like a badger caught in daylight. I set out to find Mrs Matcham's reflecting on what further oddities I might yet discover in this Bedlamite place; reflecting also on the Reverend Peregrine coming into a bucket of money, and on the strangeness of Ezekial Coffin's exploded flour mill.

CHAPTER SEVEN

Glebe Farm was one of a cluster of dwellings about a little green, with the coach road and river at one end, church and rectory at the other. A cottage done in whitewash with dimity curtains at a window on each side of the porch and two more up under the eaves, not bigger than a hatbox, and by the look of it scarcely room enough for me and this Mrs Matcham unless we got close together; but if the inside matched the out it would do well enough. God knows what I might have expected after that addle wit inn and the fellow most patently determined to be shot of me, but no sooner was the door opened than I perceived that I had come safely to a snug berth.

Providence which casts us down with one Hand will raise us up with the Other and so He had now, for it was a warm and welcoming woman and never a sign of a crackpot about her; not all that big, but of a conformable shape and fullness, a merry face and most inviting eye. I had scarcely more than asked the comfort of a night's lodging before she burst out with a perfect flood, crying that she was ever ready to oblige a gentleman from the coaches, and there was a good goose feather bed; moreover she'd got a nice stewed eel already simmering and she could very likely find a duck, with her own pickled walnuts to a bit of cheese for afters. All the while leading me up the stairs to a little chamber under the roof and then descending again to urge me into the parlour where, she declared, I could take a dish of tea or a bottle of her elder flower wine whichever I fancied best. The dear good soul was a jewel among women, but at this I begged her leave to stretch my legs and take the air to whet my appetite for her supper; there was still two hours or so of daylight left and much to do. Mrs Matcham would be a treasure afresh by candle light.

Safe outside I turned first to view the river, flowing slow and dark under its willows twenty yards or so beyond the coach road. As I stood here this highway ran to left and right; right past The Two Brewers to Edmonton and London—that great city ten miles or more distant—and left to the wilder solitudes of the north. Before going by the inn the river turned away through meadows but to the left it kept pretty straight by the road, though some little distance off it and concealed by thicker groves of trees. Save for a few philosophical cows, however, there was little more to observe, and I turned my footsteps back up the green towards the lych gate entrance to the churchyard; now pondering several more matters. The chief of these being the boy who must have released Miss Lydia from her leg irons, who was said to have been done to death and cast into the Thames by Bow Creek, and who was setting out to find Geoffrey in some place which he might expect to reach before daylight. There was no lack of fodder for thought here.

I paused again to survey the church, graveyard, and vicarage; this last approached by an overgrown and grassy path between the tombs and save that it was bigger looking pretty much like one of them itself; all lying oppressed under the heavy sky, deep in funereal yews and just as deep in neglect and solitude. The proper and improving moralities for such occasions are well known and I can turn one with the best, but Mr Thomas Gray has already made the most of all of them in his pathetic Elegy and I shall not set out to rival him. In short here the ruder forefathers of the hamlet slept; and if they were anything like old Gaffer Gudgeon at The Two Brewers, it was the best place for 'em.

For the rest I discovered no evidence of any newly dug grave such as might have sheltered the lost Geoffrey, and little else of profit save for this following inscription on one rudely sculptured stone. 'Here lie the Mortal Remains of Ezekial Coffin, 1735–1774. A Man of Mighty Voice ever Raised in Praise of the Lord. And the Lord stretched out His Hand and Carried Ezekial on Wings of Flame to the Eternal Choir'; where no doubt the Lord is still requesting him not to sing so loud in the bass. Beneath was added, 'Also of Mary Coffin, beloved wife of the above, 1737–1797.' So, I mused, Master Ezekial was thirty-nine and married when he exploded himself; and if I know anything about country pastimes in the long winter nights and the price of candles there must have been a brood of little Coffins about by then; of which one was very likely still about and now working a water mill. A handy water mill where you could get a wherry all the way from Bow Creek; a water mill which Master Coote of The Two Brewers was over bashful about, and which the wench in her confusion had thought was Coffin Mill when it should have been 'Coffin's'.

Reflecting on this I turned next to the church and the door being open passed inside to what was once a noble edifice, but now reduced to flaking whitewash and dull and dusty pews, with the windows of a greenish cast and the light growing dim. Here memorials of the better sort were all around the walls; Palmers and Rydes in plenty—though no Peregrines yet that I could see—many a crest and heraldic device, many a pious text, and inscriptions praising the virtues of the dead; for the most part of us are granted more kind words when we leave this world than we ever get while in it. But from all of them only the last was of much consequence. A plain white tablet which announced, 'In Memoriam, William John Palmer. Died October 15, 1785, aged 29 years. And I looked, and beheld a pale horse: and his name that sat on him was Death.' And then carved below that, 'To the Memory of his wife Lydia Palmer (Born Lydia Ryde 1757) who departed this life in Philadelphia Anno 1794.'

'So ho,' I said, taking out Mr Ashmole Fossdyck's paper on the Peregrine family to study it afresh. For what little more it was here we seemed to have our red haired chit's mother; a Lydia Ryde who must herself have been daughter to Percival Ryde and Lydia Peregrine, so making our present reverend lordship in that gloomy vicarage great uncle to the wench. My own sure wits, Mr Ashmole Fossdyck and Master Maggsy's button had brought me to the seat of the mystery; but what part a fancy captain's crest had in it was yet to be disclosed.

I was still musing on this—and might have heartily damned such a confusion of families had I not been in the House of God—when I heard a light sound behind and turned to discover myself closely regarded by a darkish little rascal standing at the door in the last rays of light from the porch. A weasel faced fellow with britches and gaiters of earthy colour, a fustian coat in some sort of livery, an old-fashioned bag wig and Newgate chin fringe of beard, and an uncommon cunning look about him. 'Who be you then?' he enquired with scant courtesy.

'You'd best mind your manners, my man,' I advised him. 'If it comes to that who are you?'

'Nicodemus Scrope,' he announced, 'manservant to the reverend. And likewise verger and sexton of this church.'

'A fine handful of holy offices,' I answered. 'Well then it's Mr Moxon, attorney at law. And here to wait upon your master.'

'Mr Moxon is it?' He gave a sharp scratch under his wig. 'Then be buried and rotted here's a comical go. Reverend's a'ready been to you; along with Miss Lydia.' Counting on his fingers like addle witted Gaffer Gudgeon he added, 'Last Friday, a week gone this very day, as I recollect on account we had eel pie to supper. So what d'you want of'n now then?' he asked.

'That's your master's business,' I told him sharpish. 'And you may take me to him. Is he at home?'

The rogue routed at the fleas under his wig again and regarded me more cunningly than ever. 'Her is and her ain't, as you might say. Her's home sure enough, but contrariwise not to any sense.'

'God help us,' I cried, 'do you all talk conundrums in this pestilential place? Let's have it plain, sirrah.'

'Bottle heavy,' Master Scrope said. 'Couldn't have it plainer nor that. Drunk as a fiddler's drab. Leastways her was; her's sleeping it away now.' He took another rout at the fleas, pushed his wig askew over one eye, and continued, 'Not but what her might rouse up to write his sermon later whiles. Reverend writes a powerful sermon when her's got the sins on him, but won't talk to none when her's about that. Best leave'n bide till the morn; her'll be bright as a button by then. But for now I'm to shut the church up and I'll thank you to be off, master. There's witches hereabouts and I don't reckon on 'em roaring and roosting in here the night.'

I regarded the impudent rogue with some disfavour. 'You've a congregation of Bedlamites hereabouts. But still we'll have some sharp answers to simple questions. Miss Lydia Palmer was here last Friday. And was she also here any other day?'

He set to counting on his fingers again. 'Monday, sure enough. I recollect as we had a sheep's head to dinner. Mrs Hodge's partic'lar tasty with a sheep's head.'

'Be damned to your sheep's head. Miss Lydia Palmer came and went on the Monday. But on Thursday and Friday she must have found a lodging. Was it at the vicarage?'

'God save us, no,' he exclaimed. 'Us couldn't do with a lady like that and her blackamoor man. Give Mrs Hodge the screaming hoots first go off he did, as she feared he was a Frenchman. They lodged at The Bell in Edmonton.'

'So they did,' I told him. 'You're doing very well. But now then, has the negro man been seen about here since?'

'Never a sight nor sniff,' he avowed. 'I dunno what you're about, master, but the last I see of'n was as they brought the reverend back from London Town about this time of day the Friday. Then they druv off to Edmonton and Miss Lydia saying they was to return to London theirselves the Saturday's morn.'

I mused on that while the wretch shuffled and scratched in his impatience and at last said, 'Very well; you may advise his reverend lordship that I shall wait on him in the early forenoon of tomorrow. But one last word for now. Where's Coffin's Mill?'

The fellow started as if a dog had taken a nip at his arse. 'Coffin's Mill?' he repeated. 'What's about Coffin's Mill?'

'Why, nothing,' I replied. 'Save I thought to walk that way. What of damnation is it? Wind or water mill?'

'Coffin's was a wind mill once,' he said in a sudden surly fit, 'but now it's water. You leave Coffin's Mill be.'

I regarded him with yet more care, sorely tempted to lift the dust out of his coat with my cane. But there is little profit to be had of these country savages when they turn sullen and in my kindness I spared the rogue, leaving him to his own devices and taking myself off through the graveyard.

Without doubt there was madness stalking this village; or something worse, for as I returned to the green what should I see but Master Coote of The Two Brewers coming out from Mrs Matcham's cottage, a devilish furtive manner about him and glancing up and down as if in fear of being observed. Daylight was now fading fast, the sky hanging heavier in a dun canopy of cloud, and he did not perceive me concealed there under the lych gate but hastened off down the green to the road, where he turned away to the right under the willows. 'What,' I asked, 'is our good Mrs Matcham in league with these naughty rascals?' and then set out to follow him; though in no great hurry, for I could hazard a guess where he was off to.

Sure enough the poor fool led me straight to the mill, keeping close by the trees for a space and then gone from sight like a rabbit down its burrow. It was a scant two hundred paces further. A rough and rutted wagon track leading across the narrow meadow and the building itself squatting low by the water; two sightless windows and a dark entrance, a barn at one end surrounded by yet more of these gloomy willows, with the river beyond, a shallow weir, and the leat or water course coming to an undershot wheel. In the strange light from a dying ray of sunlight striking level from beneath the clouds it was a forbidding picture, at once inky and lurid, and standing in the concealment of a riven tree trunk I considered the scene. There was fifty yards and more of open grass with no more concealment in it than a whore's chemise, and I concluded that the best time for this damned mischancy and insalubrious place would be at first light of morning; but search here I must.

Nevertheless I was not to waste my small trouble. With that care which has raised me to my present eminence I turned some attention to the road and track. The ground was of a clayish nature now dried hard and not much to be observed on it, save what might have been a rut made by the narrow iron tyre of a post chaise which seemed to have stopped here, backed, and turned again towards Edmonton. It was little enough. I would not hang a mongrel dog on such evidence. But I chanced also to perceive a screwed up scrap of paper lying caught on a thorny twig in the ditch or drainage cut between the roughage at the roadside and the trees, and in the countryside you rarely see paper cast aside; these frugal people have many other uses for such a valuable commodity, even small pieces. It might have been no more than some way-bill flung from a passing coach, but I turned it over with the tip of my cane and bent closer to examine it, making out a few lines of handwriting on either side, and then taking it up to smooth it out. Though much besmeared and stained and the ink run in the dews and dampness of a week, the superscription was plain enough. It said, 'Mifs Lid.... ..lmer ˙ At the. ..ll Inn'.

Well satisfied, with nothing more to do here and the sky now darkening quicker, I returned at leisure to the green and Mrs Matcham's hospitable cot, where there was a fine and promising aroma of supper. Yet it did not escape me that the good soul herself was flustered and eyed me somewhat askance, though the candles were lit and the table set out in her parlour; together with a black bottle already opened. It seemed that the womanly arts were just at their nice point and nothing would satisfy her but that I should take a taste or two of her elder flower wine while she was bringing them to their consummation. 'Don't stint yourself,' she cried, bustling off to her mysteries and blushing like a maiden with one lover in the closet and another under the bed.

With a lively recollection of the Widow Rooke's parsnip drench I took a little glass to try it; and, be damned, if that was a country liquor made from innocent flowers I was Napoleon Bonaparte, which God forbid. It was laced up to the bung with proof spirit, and a touch of laudanum for good measure if I was any judge; not a lot of harm in it to a sound head, but a bottle or so would lay you speechless for a long night. I've known it done in whore shops with intent to robbery—they'll sometimes strip a fool of his fine clothes and leave him naked in the gutter—but had never thought to see the trick played in a rustic hamlet, nor from such a warm soul as Mrs Matcham. I was disappointed of the creature, and could but pray that she was as innocent as I hoped she might be. As to that I should find out in time; and for the rest their stratagem was plain enough and just as easy to foil.

Dismissing the mischief for what little it was worth I carried my discovered paper to the candles. The inside was just as run and stained as the out, but there was enough of it plain. It said, 'Mifs ... pardon to trubble at this hour ... Parson Peregrine being here ... the goodness of your hart ... The old woman Alice Spurge being nurse and maid to your dere mother lying here in last ecstremity ... entreats you ... come and say to her how your dere mother does in Amerika...' There was a line or two lost here, and then it continued: '...if it pleases you best to come the morning tho Parson declares she will not last so long ... we has given home and shelter to Alice these many years ... me likewise honored by your respected father as we was young lads together...' And then the signature was lost.

'It wouldn't take a baby in,' I said; and then added, 'but it would a warm hearted wench with a wilful mind of her own.'

There was no time for more as Mrs Matcham came bustling back to lay the supper, plainly trepidacious but yet with a simple pride in her cooking; and a country feast which would have melted the heart even of a publisher. First the stewed eel, then a duckling which must have quacked its last on a benediction, a quince pie that melted in sharp and sweetness, and a crumbling home pressed cheese the like of which I'd never tasted before; and the whole washed down with a careful mouthful or two of that kick guts liquor, for it could have little effect on a well filled belly. 'Ma'am,' I announced in conclusion, 'you're a jewel among women. And you'll permit me to observe you grow some damned fine elder flowers in Ponder's End. It's a rare love potion.'

'Lord, sir,' she cried, blushing red, 'there's a naughty specch.'

'And a naughty liquor,' I replied warmly. 'Why, don't you know?

Have an elder flower wine laced with fine French brandy and a touch of laudanum and it'll rouse a hedge parson.' I presented her a frightful leer. 'And I'm very far from that, ma'am. I'm a proper warm man. In short I'll have you to bed.'

She let out a little squawk, though I fancy not displeased. 'Indeed you'll not. I've your supper things to clear away and wash.'

'Let 'em wait,' I said. 'Ain't that what Mr Thomas Coote was after? To keep me quiet for the night?' As pretty as a bride about to drop her shift she turned a dozen colours, blushing down to her bodice and I continued, 'I'll not do such a thing with you, ma'am, for I'm tender with the ladies; but I could carry Mr Coote off to Newgate to find out what he's up to. Shall I do that, I wonder? Or will you tell me?' She did not answer and I asked, 'Or shall I tell you? Come, me dear, you've but to nod or shake your head and no harm done. It's contraband, ain't it? Brandy and claret most likely brought up the river from London and stowed at Coffin's Mill.'

For a space she stood at the table, gazing at the dishes and platters and rattling them together, biting her nether lip; but at last she nodded.

There was a tear glinting in her eye for her own unfaithfulness and as a gentleman should I sprang up on the instant to comfort her; and the good soul herself by no means unwilling of it neither, though she whispered, 'Do mind where your hands are straying, Mr Moxon.' She fetched out a sigh that would have blown a ship of the line off course. 'I'm a lonesome woman and defenceless.'

'Not with me,' I promised her. 'Neither one nor t'other. And I'll tell you a secret. In short I don't give a rap for contraband; I'm no excise man, and wouldn't sink to it. But tell me now. Are you certain sure that Thomas Coote's in nothing worse than a few ankers of smuggled spirit?'

'Lord, sir,' she cried, pulling away from me with her tits heaving afresh, 'what're you after now, and who are you? Coote's a good man for all his dumpty ways; and looks after me as well as he might with my own husband away to sea and not heard of these five years.'

Reflecting on these village customs I answered, 'Only give me leave, my love, and I'll look after you myself. But I see your mind's on domestic matters, so do you clear the table off and then bring a bottle of your own wine and we'll sit to a gossip. I dearly love country tales.'

Seeing that she was forgiven her naughty prank, and might expect fresh favours to come, the good soul lost no time about it. She was back very near before I had done reflecting on that mischievous letter which had lured Miss Lydia to Coffin's Mill last Friday at some hour after our chit had left the parson. So with fresh candles alight, a bottle of more innocent brew, and a manner between demureness and rosy invitation the dear creature set out to entertain me, while outside drum rolls of thunder started to grumble in the distance.

Thomas Coote was shortly dismissed. Observing my concern with Coffin's Mill the rascal had taken me for Customs and Excise, or some such low creature, and had at once concluded to warn one Jabez Coffin at the mill, to disperse their present stock of contraband in the dark of the night. While this Jabez of the brood of Coffins was eldest son to Ezekial of the windmill explosion; who after that calamity had removed to the ancient water mill, and was now carrying on the family trade there—and several more besides —by water instead of wind. A dour, silent rascal Mrs Matcham made him, with fingers in many another pie besides smuggled liquor, but well enough so long as he was left alone. I had a hearty laugh at the tally of their customers for miles about and said, 'It's no affair of mine. But tell me, my dove, have you ever heard the name Lieutenant Kemble in the business? Or maybe even seen him? A thin, darkish, sourish looking fellow?'

'Darkish for sure,' she mused, 'as he's about at The Brewers now and again, where I sometimes do a turn to oblige Thomas. But not Kemble. A kind of foreignish name.'

'Would it be Lopez?' I asked.

'Why so it is,' she cried, and then added, 'I declare I don't know what you're at, Mr Moxon.'

'Nothing, me dear,' I assured her. 'Good luck to the captain I say. If a gentleman can't get his honest liquor without these damnation taxes invented by the rascally politicoes to pay for their own follies it's a bad lookout for all of us. Moreover,' I promised, 'when I've done my business I'll relate you such a tale as you've never heard before. But for now, my sweetbread, tell me of these families hereabouts. The Rydes and Palmers.'

She conjured up another blush at that, announcing warmly that I was the comicalest lawyer she'd ever set eyes on, but went off in another spate. 'The Rydes and Palmers? They've been here since time out of mind. Marrying one to the other, fighting and falling out and kissing and making it up again. There was Rydes many years back who went off to find their fortunes in America.'

'And a Lydia Ryde?' I prompted her. 'Who must have been niece to your parson, the Reverend Matthew Peregrine; and who married a Mr William Palmer.'

'A wild young·devil,' she sighed. 'Oh they was all wild young devils. Jabez Coffin and William Palmer and the parson's two boys; save one of 'em wasn't his but only half and half as you might say. Born of his wicked wife.' The good creature fetched up a fresh sigh for her lost years. 'I was no more than a slip of a girl then.'

'You're no more than a slip of a girl now,' I told her, 'and a country rosebud with it. But didn't Mrs Lydia Palmer, Lydia Ryde as was, go off to America herself after Mr Palmer died?'

'After he killed himself,' she said shortly, 'the vain, silly creature. There was a party of his mohock friends here from London, and nothing would suit but he must needs wager he'd jump his horse cross Coffin's Mill leat bareback for five hundred guineas. Miss Lydia begged and implored him not to do it. But do it he would. And took a toss off the creature, struck his head on the stonework, was swept down beneath the wheel and killed' on the instant. Whereupon Miss Lydia declared she wanted no more of this place and but a month or two later went off to Philadelphia taking their baby daughter with her. And that's it,' she cried. 'For the younger Miss Lydia's come back, and that's what you're here about. Tell me the truth now, Mr Moxon, you naughty tease. You're here about the parson's money.'

'In a manner of speaking,' I said. 'But I'd thought it was Miss Lydia's inheritance.'

'They was to share it,' she answered in impatience. 'Or so Nicodemus Scrope says, and he should know. Nicodemus Scrope and Fanny Hodge, who's cook to the parsonage, both listen at doors.'

'It's a useful occupation now and again,' I observed. Then to forestall further questions cried, 'But come, my treasure, you're as tender as a bit of crackling, and the night's made for sweeter things than burning candles,' at the same time approaching her and getting one hand to her generous tits and the other at the back of her bodice. She let out a little squeal, but not unwilling, while afire with gentlemanly intent I set about the buttons.

But it was not to be. Before we could come to there was two frightful noises. One a roar of thunder and the second a loud sharp bang. 'God help us,' Mrs Matcham cried, giving a wild start in my arms, 'what's that?'

'That,' I announced, 'was a pistol shot,' and was out of the parlour, up the stairs to the bed chamber, seizing my own weapons, and descending again all in a gallop. This was no time for ceremony, but I said, 'Ma'am, I fear our pleasures must be delayed.'

Leaving her in full voice behind, I hastened out to be greeted by a wicked flash of lightning as if the Devil himself were at work. It lit the church and rectory, the yew trees and tombstones like a Sadler's Wells perspective, and in the brief silence which followed came a screech 'Murder!', which was in turn drowned by another monstrous roll of thunder and the rain. Cursing Ponder's End and all its madness, and fearing for the priming of my pistols, I hastened across the green as another cry rang from the rectory and lights appeared here and there in the cottage windows.

It was near enough my end. As I approached the lych gate some villain concealed there fired on me, and I'll swear the ball near enough parted my hair. I felt the wind of its passing but discharged my right hand armament at the flash; and the damned thing mis-

fired. Cursing, I followed with the left, to be rewarded this time
with a scream. Then others was upon me; four of 'em at the least.
It was a troublesome business for even as I struck one down with
my pistol barrel another had his forearm round my gullet from
behind, while from before I caught the glint of a knife. True I
gave a good account of myself, but Mrs Matcham's overflowing
entertainment was not the best prelude for an affair as rude as
this, and the sheeting rain, lightning, and thunder was no help. I
flung one aside, awarded the next a blow which must have spoiled
his guts, rattled a third's teeth for him, and commended my soul to
my Maker; though the rogues themselves were disconcerted, for
one whispered, 'God blast it, finish him.'

I was hard pressed, yet Providence looked down upon me; even
in the form of Master Maggsy. Never was a man so astounded; and
no time for questions. There he was howling, 'God's Tripes you
lot; gouge 'em,' lit by another flash of lightning, brandishing a boat
hook like a demon in a deluge, and making the night more hideous
with his coarse yells; and behind him old Gaffer Gudgeon hobbling
up with a candle lantern.

With the little rogue laying about him and Gaffer Gudgeon capering with his lantern I returned to the charge, and hard on that
came a sharp whistle from the streaming darkness. Only then one
of the villains cried, 'That's the captain; haul off,' and they took to
their heels and were gone. I was left half winded, demanding in one
breath, 'How the devil did you get here?' and saying in the next,
'After 'em,' while Master Maggsy howled, 'You won't catch 'em,
they've got a boat. I knowed if there was mischief anywhere you'd
be in it.'

But Master Maggsy's tale must wait, for there were still shrieks
of 'Murder' from the vicarage, and with one sharp glance at the
villain sprawled dead under the lych, noting in a fresh lightning
flicker that it was the mulatto, I turned into the churchyard to
stumble through wet grass between the tombstones in a witch's
night of black and dancing shadows and silvered rain. We passed
into a rank and sodden garden where from the dark building before

us one light was glowing in a downstairs window, another from an open doorway and the man Scrope peeping and snivelling, while from a casement under the roof two female heads was screaming themselves silly. Out of all patience by now I roared, 'Be damned to you, be quiet,' and that together with another roll of thunder silenced them. So we reached the window and the pitiful spectacle which lay within.

The candles guttering, but lighting a big table with papers, quills, inkstand and open books on it, leather chairs and other such old-fashioned furniture; the dusty closet of a country parson where the harmless soul would sit to write his improving observations. There was one high backed chair thrust as if he had turned it aside to look round; the unfortunate gentleman himself lying in a sprawl on his back amid a litter of papers scattered on the floor. A most cruel, unnatural and wicked crime for he was an old man; well on in his sixties; the face careworn but once handsome though now stilled in the shock of death, his hair white and lying loose, a mess of blood, and one clenched hand still grasping a broken quill.

It needed little of the finer Art and Science of Detection to make out what had happened. The villains had crept up to the window and there perceived him sitting at his table writing. Then some one of them had smashed the leading with his fist or a stone, and on that the parson had turned to see what the noise was, so presenting himself a plain and simple target at a distance of not more than four paces. 'God's Tripes,' Maggsy observed, 'he won't sing no more hymns.'

We hastened on to the open door, where there was a stone flagged hall beyond, and Scrope still shaking and weeping with a face like tallow melted untidy. Him I viewed with some displeasure, but said kindly enough, 'Now, my man, let's have your account of it.'

I might have saved my words for the shaking rascal told me no more than I could see for myself. The hour being nine o'clock he was going to his bed and the parson alone in his closet, and by now roused up enough to set to writing his Sunday sermon; the com-

mon Friday custom. But Scrope had then heard the noise of breaking glass, had opened this chamber door to see what it was, and had
been rewarded by a monstrous flash and bang and the sight of his
master falling. Whereupon he had slammed the door again and
clung to the outside of it very near in a faint until he came to his
senses enough to yell for murder. A pitiful tale, and not improved
by Gaffer Gudgeon's goatish interjections.

Losing patience with the pair of them I paused only to command the fellow to stop those damned women caterwauling and
passed into the fatal chamber myself, where Master Maggsy was
already feasting his eyes on the horrid spectacle. 'Dunno as I never
see a corpusser corpus than that,' he announced. 'Must've turned
his toes up without a squawk.'

The sweet little monster was right enough. Tossed aside by the
force of the ball, a frightful wound in his chest, the reverend lordship had died on the instant, and plainly had no need of further
examination. There was nothing to be done, nor any sign of the
deadly weapon—which I did not expect to find and was not surprised—and I said, 'Now then, Master Maggsy, I want any papers he
was writing, all the letters you may find, and most particular anything of Miss Lydia Palmer or Mr Moxon.' I regarded the ugly
wretch still in some surprise. 'And how in damnation did you come
here?'

'Lucky for you I did,' he retorted, 'else you'd ha' been gutted and
all by now. They was after you as well. And what I been through
today's to turn your bowels over.'

'Then we'll let it wait,' I told him and returned to the hall to
catch up Gaffer Gudgeon's lantern and pass out to the graveyard
once more. By God's mercy the rain was abating, the thunder
rolling away into the distance, and by now a huddle of villagers
about their cottage doors; Mrs Matcham still in good voice, others
of the women wailing, and half a dozen or so men. These I soon
put to work; ordering one to run and fetch the Parish Constable for
what little good he might be, others to get a hurdle and carry away
the mortality under the lych gate, and the strongest stomached

of them to return to the rectory to take up their vicar and lay him decently on his bed. I like everything to be done orderly.

Then I went myself to examine our mysterious mulatto sprawled there on the wet stones. Throwing the feeble light on him I reflected that here was one villain done with, though a pity to cheat the hangman and rob myself of forty guineas for his neck. Never a maiden's dream in life he was now still less pretty, for my shot had taken him at the base of the throat and a ball from a pistol by Wogdon is no love tap; what with the blood, lips drawn back in a grin from the teeth, and staring eyes, lying there with his own single pistol still clutched in the right hand, he was by no means a picture to hang on the family staircase. But very fair shooting in the dark nonetheless.

The single pistol perplexed me, and I bent closer to detach it from the cold fingers and then study his hands as best I could. Even in that dim and flickering light there was little doubt that the right was more work hardened than the left. Yet whoever heard of a right handed man discharging his left hand armament first? As it seemed he must have done if his was the ball which struck the reverend gentleman down. And as pistols commonly come in pairs, where was the other? 'So ho,' I said, turning to his pockets. But they brought little of note; only a few coins, a plug of tobacco, and a sheath knife about the bigness of that which had killed Lieutenant Kemble. There was no more the rogue could tell me.

By now the men had returned with their hurdle, and instructing them to carry him to some place where he could be kept safe from the rats until the coroner's officers came for him I retraced my steps to the rectory. Here Gaffer Gudgeon and Master Scrope were taking alternate pulls at a black bottle like ancient demons sucking at a witch's tit, while Master Maggsy was fanning his mouth with a handful of papers and gasping and choking plainly from a draught of the same wicked brew; rude experimentations will be the death of that child before he's done. This I soon put to rights with a sharp back hander which sobered him and said to Scrope, 'Now, my man, is there some place where there's a handful of fire?' For the night was turning cold after the storm.

Grumbling and muttering he led me to a fairish sized kitchen, dusty and shabby, but with a few embers still glowing in the hearth, and I ordered, 'Make that up with fresh logs and bring more candles. And fetch another bottle of that stuff with 'em; I need a warmer myself.' His gaze shifted sideways to Gaffer Gudgeon, and I added, 'I know where it comes from and I'm not particular. Nor your master won't miss it now, poor soul.'

This ordered, with Gaffer Gudgeon peering at the several pistols and Maggsy in a pet of his sulks, I took the papers he had discovered and laid them out on the table; two or three letters, what seemed the start of a sermon, and an information from Coutt's Bank. But these could wait presently, as I was more curious about the mulatto's weapon. It was an uncommon pretty piece of work, somewhat shorter than a Wogdon but most nicely made, and the name was in English yet unfamiliar to me; 'S. North Midln Con'. I mused on this for a minute and by then Scrope having finished his labours, also producing another bottle and glasses, I told the rascal he might take himself off, adding to Gaffer Gudgeon, 'And so may you. I've seen enough of you for one day.'

'You leave him be,' Maggsy cried. 'If it warn't for him I'd be in the river now, and my belly full of mud.'

'That's right,' the horrible old rogue agreed. 'And promised me a sovereign to set her free. He'm a rare wonder, that'n. God's Truth, I never hear such cussing since the day Thomas Coote got his cobblers catched in the privy door.'

'Be damned to your lewdness,' I said. 'And your sovereign. And you, sirrah,' I told Maggsy. 'We'll have it at last. How d'you come to be here?'

But before he could start we had another interruption; there was no end of 'em tonight. Quick footsteps in the hall and a voice demanding, 'Helloa there. What the devil's amiss here?'

I opened the door myself on a tall young fellow of some twenty-eight to thirty years; a coaching coat and capes, a beaver set to one side of his head, damn your eyes, handsome, and high nosed; very clearly a gentleman. 'What's amiss?' he demanded again. 'I came upon some clods out there carrying another away on a hurdle, and devilishly mishandled by the look of him.'

'A small mishap, sir,' I told him. 'And who are you?'

'What's it to you?' he asked. 'But if you must know, Hamilton Ryde; of Charleston, Carolina.'

'So ho,' I said. 'Another of the family. And what's your business here, sir?'

'Now confound your questions,' he protested. 'I might ask who the devil you are too.'

I told him in short order, and concluded, 'So there you have it, sir. I've the power to ask.'

'Why then, if you have I'll tell you,' he offered. 'I'm here to wait on the Reverend Matthew Peregrine; and to discover from him where to find Miss Lydia Palmer. Dammit, don't I have the best right? She's my cousin and my promised wife to be.'

CHAPTER EIGHT

I advised him that Parson Peregrine was somewhat more than dis-
composed and explained the unfortunate mishap—as much of it as
I thought fit to explain—but even in that dramatic moment I could
spare a thought of pity for our poor distracted Dr McGrath and his
hopeless case. With such shabby habiliments and cracked boots,
gaunt manner and not two pence to rub together he'd have never
a chance against this gallant young sprig. Making his own proper
exclamations, and looking curiously at the pistols and papers on
the table, Mr Ryde tossed his beaver down and flung his capes aside
to disclose a dark blue coat fitting to perfection, tan breeches without a wrinkle in them, fine lawn neckcloth, and well boned boots
though now spattered with mud. He was all in the very pink of
fashion, and as befits politeness in the presence of wealth I
moderated my own manner. 'Might I offer refreshment, sir?' I
enquired. 'It's an inclement night.'

'I'll be thankful of it,' he confessed. 'You'll permit me to observe,
Mr Sturrock, that you keep some damned strange customs in a
peaceful English village.'

'It's a damned strange village,' I answered, pouring out the liquor.

What that might have meant was lost on him, as he took a
mouthful of the potion and at once fell to coughing, choking, and
gasping until at last he caught his breath to ask with awe and
admiration, 'God's sake, what is it?'

'Brandy, sir,' I told him. 'The pure spirit as it comes from France.
Our rascals commonly water it down for the bottle but that's the
rare liquor. Brought up the river from a certain Captain Lopez, no
duty paid, and half the rascals hereabouts up to their hocks in
the business.' Mr Ryde seemed vastly diverted by this and I continued to Gaffer Gudgeon, 'I've told you once to be off. You cling
like a whore to a banker. Be off and tell Master Coote that if he

137

wants a trip to Botany Bay on a convict ship I'll see to it for him. '

With one last look at Maggsy and a bleat about his sovereign the old goat scuttled off, but now we were invaded by a fresh gaggle of villagers; some reporting that they had laid the reverence properly on his bed, and others bringing the Parish Constable. A gangling fellow more than half simple himself by his looks, yet still striving to wear some air of rustic authority. He was even inclined to impudence at first, but I quickly set him to rights on that and gave him his orders short and simple; viz that he was to wait on me here at a convenient hour tomorrow when I should provide him with messages to be taken to one fuzz-buzz, the County Coroner, and to another, the nearest Justice of the Peace. It was my intention to compose for these gentlemen precise accounts of the unfortunate occurrences here tonight but not of necessity my conclusions; and then to so despatch them that by the time they were received I should be well on my way back to London. There is a nice form and legality in these affairs but no need to waste time upon country officials.

This arranged I turned them all out, closed the door, and announced, 'Thank God for that. Now we can settle to a civil conversation.' Casting a glance at Maggsy which warned him plainly to sit quiet and keep his ugly mouth shut I enquired, 'Will you take a mouthful more of this generous liquor, sir?'

'I'll not say no,' he answered. 'By God it grows on you.' He took his second draught without a blench, kept an astonished meditation for a minute, and then asked, 'Why the devil shoot Parson Peregrine?'

'I don't know, sir,' I said. 'I fancy the gentleman knew too much of something. It's an unfortunate occurrence.'

'Confounded unfortunate,' he echoed. 'I'd hoped to have news of Cousin Lydia through him. Moreover I don't hold with shooting parsons. Mark you, the pesky sermons some of ours preach you could scarcely blame a man, but I still don't hold with it.'

'It ain't an act of a gentleman, sir,' I agreed.

'By God it's not.' He gazed at me appraisingly. 'But there, I never met the poor fellow. And if Cousin Lydia's around anything may happen. What's she been at this time?'

'Not a lot, sir,' I told him. 'Not unless you count getting herself kidnapped and held on a slave ship, thereafter escaping by the help of some poor cabin boy, and then capping it all by losing her recollections.'

'What?' he demanded. 'You're raving, man.' And when I repeated it the second time he cried, 'No, by God, I'll not have it. Even for Miss Lydia that's too much. Be damned, she's a little Tartar. Myself I'd as soon think of trying to kidnap a mountain cat. Come now, Mr Sturrock, what is this? Where is she; and is she safe and well?'

'She's in good hands,' I assured him. 'And safe so long as she stays there.'

'Confound it,' he said, 'I wish you'd stop talking in riddles.'

'So I will in a minute,' I promised, reaching out to fill his glass yet again. 'But give me leave to reflect to have the story straight and simple.'

Among those papers Maggsy had brought from the chamber there was the banker's document which I must needs consider before continuing with Mr Ryde. I was still perplexed by Miss Lydia's talk of fifty thousand in the Consols against the rumour of the parson's legacy and fancied that he might tell me much about it; but gentlemen are often nice about revealing family affairs, in especial where money is concerned, and it would be well to seem to know the most of it before I said much more. I affected to be in a brown study, turning the papers over one by one and laying them face down on the table—a trick which never fails to have the other fellow uneasy however clear his conscience—but while so engaged I asked, 'Tell me, sir, have you ever heard mention of a certain Lieutenant Robert Kemble?'

'I have not then,' he announced. 'Who the devil's he?'

'To be plain,' I told him, 'of more import than Miss Lydia Palmer now she's out of harm's way. But it's of no account if you've never heard of him.'

Like any other high spirited young gentleman Mr Ryde was growing impatient but after the sermon and several letters, which could wait for consideration later, I came to the paper I was seeking. A form of receipt on Coutt's Bank dated Friday September 12, acknowledging a transfer in the sum of one hundred thousand pounds from the Bank of England to the Reverend Matthew Peregrine, Lord Falconhurst, and Miss Lydia Palmer to their separate accounts; and in smaller print advising the aforesaid that the said funds would be encashable on demand as from Saturday September 20. In short and as we were then, tomorrow; the day Mr Colville's ship was to sail. Reflecting on the conversation Master Maggsy had heard in The Prospect of Whitby, when some gentleman unknown had observed that these damned bankers always keep their fingers on your money till the last minute, I said, 'It's plain enough, sir. It's a matter of a legacy. To the Reverend Matthew Peregrine and Miss Lydia Palmer. Where did it come from, Mr Ryde?'

'Be hanged,' he protested with a little hiccup, 'that's family business. You're prying now, Mr Sturrock.'

'The law never pries, Mr Ryde,' I informed him. 'It asks questions; and expects gentlemen of goodwill to answer 'em. Pray let me fill your glass again.'

'Begod it's tangle gut stuff,' he announced, 'but it goes down warm. Dunno much about your law over here; but maybe there's no harm in telling. It came from old Hayward Peregrine of Barbados. Hundred thousand split between the two of 'em, equal and equal.'

'So it'd be on one scrip and need both their signatures to claim and release it. That explains much, Mr Ryde, and I'm obliged to you. A hundred thousand's a fair bait for villainy. This would be the Hayward Peregrine who had a natural son by Hester Ryde? Which son was taken in and adopted by his brother, our presently deceased gentleman, and brought up with his own child.'

'So you've routed out that old tale, have you?' He gave a prodigious yawn. 'It's said Great Aunt Hester was a heller after what she wanted; and Hayward Peregrine never had much fancy for her by daylight, but all cats are grey in the dark. He got her in the family case and then took off to Barbados to escape; there married the daughter of a plantation master and so came into a monstrous packet. Well then it seems he always had some notion of returning to England and set by this hundred thousand in the Consols against the day; then never lived to see it and willed the money as you know. Though damned if I can reckon how.'

'It's a matter of the Art and Science of Detection,' I told him, and continued, 'So Hayward Peregrine left fifty thousand to his brother, our reverend deceased, which was very right and proper. But why the other fifty to a young woman who at best was no more than a far off relation? Why not to his own son; illegitimate or otherwise?'

'Oh be hanged,' he protested. 'You're as bad as a lawyer, rattling the family bones. How should I know? Save Great Aunt Hester chased the poor devil out to Barbados and there made his life a hell to him, or so it's said, before she took up with some Spaniard herself. And his son Tristram was lost and vanished.' He opened his eyes wide at me of a sudden. 'I've no doubt you've scratted up that tale as well.'

'Some part of it,' I agreed. 'Tristram, illegitimate, and Mark Peregrine, his reverend lordship's legal son; who both went off for midshipmen some five and twenty years ago. That Lieutenant Kemble I spoke of was killed and murdered a few days since and one or t'other of 'em can tell me why. I mean to come back to those two boys, Mr Ryde.'

'You'll have the devil of a pother to find either, for God only knows where they are. And we'll not come back to anything before you tell me what Miss Lydia's been up to.'

'That's a simple matter,' I said, replenishing his glass yet again. 'Confounded into a devil's conundrum by all of these families, but plain enough when you perceive they're of no account and sweep them aside. Miss Lydia is left the half share of an uncommon large fortune; but on paper only. To claim and encash it she must needs come to London and present herself together with her lawyer, one Mr Moxon, and the other legatee at the Bank of England.'

Mr Ryde announced with some impatience that this was nothing new to him, and I went on to describe Miss Lydia's travels. Here to Ponder's End the Monday to acquaint herself with our reverend gentleman, to Mr Moxon himself the day following, and out here once more on Thursday when she lodged at The Bell in Edmonton. Then to London again with the parson on Friday, where they ordered their business and instructed that the funds should be transferred to Coutt's Bank in the sums of fifty thousand apiece; and so back to Ponder's End to bring the parson home, when Miss Lydia herself purposed to lodge one more night at Edmonton before returning to London next day.

Here Mr Ryde observed that I'd been about some cursed fine scratting and Maggsy, who appeared to be asleep, emitted a singular snore; but I continued with Miss Lydia's adventures. The summons to Coffin's Mill, being overpowered there and carried down the river to London, then confined on some ship the name at present unknown. 'We shall discover there truly was an Alice Spurge,' I went on, 'and truly one time maid or attendant to Miss Lydia's mother before she went to Philadelphia. You shall observe, Mr Ryde, that the entire wicked plot shows a sure knowledge of all the family affairs. And you shall note that Jabez Coffin of the mill was a boyhood companion of the two Peregrine sons; so they come into the tale again. As also does Lieutenant Robert Kemble.'

He brushed that aside. 'Your Lieutenant Kemble's no concern of mine. What the devil was Consuela Smith and Geoffrey doing? Consuela's an impudent baggage, but older than Lydia and has her head screwed on aright. Geoffrey's Lydia's personal slave and been with her since she was a child; he'd kill anybody who so much as laid a finger on her.'

'I fear he was killed himself; also at Coffin's Mill. Consuela Smith is party to the plot, and advised our villains of all Miss Lydia's actions.'

'What's that?' he demanded. 'Geoffrey's killed? Does Lydia know this?'

'She did not at first. There's little doubt that for a day or two she was confused in her mind, and I fancy she imagined he was held prisoner himself at the mill. But she must know by now.'

'God's Blood,' he exclaimed, 'she'll be beside herself. She was as fond of that saucy rascal as she might have been of a dog.'

'A particular faithful dog, sir,' I observed.

'So they was after the money?' he asked. 'But how?'

'Very simple. Once withdrawn from the Consols and placed to an open account they could force Miss Lydia to sign an order; either by threats or other means. If she proved obdurate they could have Consuela Smith impersonate her; in no manner difficult since they also have all of Miss Lydia's possessions and means of identity. I doubt if she has yet been seen at Coutt's Bank. They could then draw on the account as they pleased or have letters of credit made out to some other foreign bank. But in either case Miss Lydia would then have to be made away with finally and for ever.'

Mr Ryde gave a laugh at that. 'They should have known better. They was meddling with gunpowder to pick on Cousin Lydia.'

'Not so long as they could hold her. There's another ship in this business. The *Mary Carson*. From the chance recollection of a drunken old sailor I fancy she was built in Boston, as I now fancy likewise that she sails the Mediterranean. You'll not know this, Mr Ryde, but there are ports in that region where a well shaped and pretty young white woman will fetch a good price and no questions asked. Have you ever heard of a Captain Blackbird, Mr Ryde?' I asked.

He pondered this somewhat heavily for the brandy was now taking its toll. 'Can't say I have. Sounds like a slaver.'

'Or a Barbary pirate. Very likely one or the other as the occasion goes.'

'Damned if I care,' he said, pushing himself to his feet. 'If Miss Lydia's safe and well that's an end of it for me. I'll thank you to take me to her tomorrow; and I'll have her off back to America before she gets into fresh mischief.'

Once more I reflected on the poor physician, but asked, 'You've travelled far and hard, Mr Ryde?'

'Landed at Bristol four days since, posted to London and so on here to old Peregrine. And a damned fine reception it is. But the hell with it, I'm away to my bed. You'll find me at The Two Brewers, God help me.'

'Do me one last favour first,' I begged, taking up the pistol I had recovered from the mulatto. 'Tell me where does this hail from? The name's unfamiliar to me.'

If the weapon meant much to him he gave no sign of it. He turned it over in his hands, sniffing at the muzzle and examining the butt. 'Simeon North of Middleton, Connecticut. American sure enough, but what's about it?'

'I've a notion it was the fellow to that pistol which killed the Reverend Peregrine. And I fancy he was shot because he might have told me something about the two Peregrine boys all those years back. So we return to Lieutenant Robert Kemble once more.'

'Mr Sturrock,' he announced, shrugging into his capes and clapping on his beaver, 'I'll ask the poor fellow's pardon for it, but be damned to Lieutenant Kemble. I've had my fill for one day.'

'I'll light you through the graveyard,' I offered, taking up the lantern.

The rain had stopped and there was a weeping moon riding through slow clouds to light the now dark and silent cottages; a doleful owl crying to the night, strange shadows among the gravestones, and Mr Ryde cursing it softly for a confounded wanchancy place. He seemed thankful to come to the lych gate and green, but here I stopped him again. I said, 'Here's a strange thing, Mr Ryde. You landed at Bristol four days since, yet Miss Lydia came to England better than a fortnight ago. How was that, I wonder?'

'God in Heaven,' he enquired, 'is there no end to it? It's plain enough. The chit set off without a word. She must have had it planned to the day, for she travelled coach to New York and sailed from there. Seems the Philadelphia family tried to talk her out of it, but the first I heard was when they sent a man riding down to Charleston to tell me she'd gone. I was left cooling my heels for better than a week before I could get a ship; and then a hellish slow one and contrary winds.'

'And very likely in a fever of impatience,' I observed. 'There are several other Rydes in America then?'

'There've been Rydes for seventy years and more,' he answered shortly. 'Some in Philadelphia and another lot in Boston; and ourselves in the South. And there's an end of it, Mr Sturrock; I'll give ye good night, and look to see you in the morning.'

It is always wise to know when a gentleman has answered all the questions he means to answer and I let him go. I watched him going down the green, somewhat unsteady but tacking safely to the right towards the inn, and then returned myself to the kitchen. Here Maggsy was now sound asleep, looking more evil even than he did when awake if that were possible, and I considered whether to rouse him to hear his tale or have myself some peace and quiet for a change. But I doubted there was much he might tell me which could not wait and turned instead to a fresh consideration of the papers from the reverend gentleman's chamber.

First came the sermon or part of a sermon which he seemed to have been engaged upon shortly before the fatal incident. He had taken his text from Mark, Chapter Eight, Verse Thirty-Six, 'What shall it profit a man, if he shall gain the whole world, and lose his own soul,' and I studied this with care for all there was several pages of it and in poor, shaken writing. To be plain it was melancholious stuff—I like a sermon with some belly and fire in it myself, such as preached by our eloquent Mr Roberts at St Giles's—yet of some interest as it made clear that the poor man was in a certain perturbation of mind which was not accounted for by brandy.

This, however, he never got as far as explaining, for as if making up his mind on a decision he seemed to have turned from the sermon to set about a letter; a letter marked by splashes of blood upon it and a great scrawl of ink where it appeared he had broken his quill in a start on the last word. It was directed to 'Their Lordships of the Admiralty', and it began 'My Lords; it is my duty to advise you of certain new information come to light in the matter of the incidents concerning Midshipmen Mark and Tristram Peregrine aboard H.M.S. *Irresistible* off the Carolinas in the year 1777. I have the certain...' And there it ended.

'Be damned,' I mused. 'Yet more history. Twenty-five years back. What incidents would interest their Lordships after so long?'

Pondering on this I turned to the other papers; several more letters and the banker's document. The first from Miss Lydia herself, with a pretty womanliness about it but nonetheless a plain touch of business; expressing a proper sympathy for the death of Mr Hayward Peregrine in Barbados but all the same continuing that for her part she chose to convert her portion into encashable funds to cover letters of credit, as now the war in Europe was over she proposed to travel for a season in Brussels, Paris and Rome, and to this end would take shipment at the earliest convenient to wait on the Reverend Peregrine. 'So ho,' I said, as I turned to the next.

This was an attestation from a Philadelphia attorney affirming Miss Lydia Palmer's identity and signature, stating that the lady would produce a copy of this document, and that a further copy of the same had been despatched to Mr Moxon of London. Then a letter from Mr Moxon himself, in elegant copper plate, and advising his reverend lordship that Mr Moxon was honoured by his instructions and would be just as honoured to receive his reverend lordship and Miss Lydia Palmer, with which lady he had been honoured to exchange a similar correspondence. He considered it advisable, however, to inform his reverend lordship, as he had already advised Miss Lydia Palmer, that the transaction would require some eight days for completion, and he had the honour to subscribe himself his reverend lordship's obedient servant, etc.

The banker's document needed no further consideration, and now stowing all these papers away with care I turned next to my own business, fetching ink, paper, quills and sealing wax from the parson's chamber and setting to my own account of the night's untoward events for the Coroner and Justice of the Peace. I write a particular genteel report, and uncommon good reading, but I shall not set this down here as I have already rehearsed the said events. I finished by craving their Honours' indulgence presently, being now engaged in posting back to London with an end to the speedy apprehension of the criminals. By the time that was done the night was wearing thin and on a short prayer to Providence I settled to get what little sleep I could.

Whether it was the French brandy or my exertions or both together I slept longer than I liked, and when I stirred there was a grey, sour light washing in at the window, with Master Maggsy still sounding off like a whole farmyard. Him I soon stirred up and then turned to cold water from the kitchen pump to freshen myself as best I could, while the little rogue complained of a belly as empty as a drum, yet supposing even that was better than having it filled with mud. 'God's Tripes,' he demanded, 'don't you want to know how I got here last night?'

'We've no time for it,' I told him. 'We've work to do. I shall go to Coffin's Mill, and you will search every inch from that broken window to the lych gate. You're to look for another pistol as might or might not be the fellow to this one. And if you don't find it that'll tell me something fresh.'

'Doing your job for you again am I?' he enquired. 'God's Whiskers, what with that and trying to keep you out of trouble I reckon I earns my bread and butter; and I don't like this going along to that mill neither, you'd best keep away from it, and you would too if you stopped to ask what happened to me last night.'

'What of damnation were you doing there yourself?' I demanded, viewing my soiled neckcloth with some disfavour.

'Not much,' he answered, 'oh no, not a lot. Only waiting to get drownded like a kitten; and I would too if that old funnyguts hadn't come along and set me free on promise of a sovereign; that's all. And what's more they was allaying to do for you along with the parson.'

'I had perceived some such intention myself,' I told him. 'If that's all the tale will keep. And I'll have no more of this extravagant talk of sovereigns. Be off about your duties.'

But still the wretch was not content. 'Here,' he asked, on a fresh thought, 'you was agammoning that cove along wasn't you, getting him pissed up to the eyes and all. D'you reckon he's in it?'

'I'm well satisfied with Mr Ryde,' I said. 'A very obliging young gentleman. He's told me a great deal I only guessed at before. Though he'll be a sore blow for Dr McGrath,' I added. 'Now find me that pistol and no more chatter.'

It was regrettable that my own discharged armament was of little use, as my powder flask and balls were in their case at Mrs Matcham's and it would scarcely be genteel to rouse the good woman at this early hour to get them. There was nothing for it but to go unarmed, and leaving Maggsy poking and dragging and wickedly cursing the wet grass I made my way to the river, where the melancholy willow trees leaned in greyness with their leaves dripping sadly. There was a light mist rising from the meadows, and still not a breath of air; which suited me well if it was the same in London, for a strong wind from the west might bring all my work to nothing. Across the grass there were fresh wagon ruts —doubtless from carrying off their contraband in the night— though the mill itself seemed wrapped in slumber, lying dark and low by the water, and I came to the nearer corner without incident but stopped there close against the wall to survey the scene.

There was no sound nor movement and I passed on to the leat, a deep water-course edged with ancient stone and running to the wheel, this now motionless while the flood poured out through an open sluice. Neither was there any sound here save the rushing water, and I first crossed a plank to the further stretch of meadow and the river. Not scornful of my danger, but daring it, I spent little time here, and soon satisfied myself that the reaches both above and below the weir were too shallow to hide anything with safety. What I sought for would be in the leat itself, where all those years ago the reckless Mr Palmer had tried to jump his horse and so in a manner started the whole trouble.

Close by the wheel I paused again, but all remained still and I next set about finding a needed implement. Here there was a kind of open shed or bothy wherein lay an upturned boat, oars, other such matters, and not least a long pole and hook. Providence could have sent nothing better to my hand, and in an instant I was back at the leat probing with it deep into the water.

For a time it sank only into soft mud. Then it touched something which was at once yielding and more solid. This I essayed to bring to the surface, though not the first nor the second attempt could dislodge it; but at last it stirred and moved, and I then perceived a most awful sight. Floating from the depth a dark face and staring, mildewed eyes; water running out of its mouth, and a shock of white hair now dabbled with slime and filth. My hook seemed to be caught in its shoulder and as I pulled there came up a blue coat and brass buttons with one arm and black hand rising languidly and again falling back with a soft splash. It seemed to be weighted by the feet, and it was none of my business to get the poor mortality out. Releasing the hook I let it sink to rest, but swearing as I did so that I'd see the villains hang for this wickedness, and Jabez Coffin with them. And hard on that a voice behind me said, 'What be you about there?'

I turned to see a squat, dark visaged rogue regarding me. Even among these country savages he was no beauty; a tangle of black hair and beard, barrel chested and one arm dangling to his knees like a monstrous ape; but, what was worse, the other hand was holding an ancient horse pistol which looked damned near as big as a cannon. Still grasping the boat pole, affecting surprise and some indignation, I cried, 'Why, what's this?'

It is a mercy of Heaven that so many of these rogues hesitate before they shoot—a mistake I've never made in my life—and I said, 'There was a big pike basking there and I thought to take a jab at the rascal.' The simpleness of it foxed him and his eyes strayed towards the water, but for all that his finger tightened on the trigger and hoping to God the thing had a hard pull I commanded, 'Drop that now. I've got a dozen men surrounding the mill.'

That paused him again. In the same instant I flung the pole

at him, and even as his shot went off with a frightful explosion
I leapt aside myself and it flew spinning to catch him a pretty
smack in the chaps. But I might as well have teased a bull with a
feather, for he gave no more than a grunt, tossed his armament
away, dashed the blood and snot from his mouth, and came back
at me with arms dangling and hands like legs of mutton. The
fellow wanted a wrestling match, which I had no mind for at all,
and to finish it quick I let him get close enough and then planted
a blow on the side of his skull that should have split a millstone;
but all the good I got of it was damned near breaking my wrist.

I was half behind him and, cursing the fellow for a stubborn
rogue, I got my hand in the filthy tangle of his hair and gave such
a fearful twist that he roared for surprise and pain, though somewhat strangled with my other forearm across his gullet. Yet even
this would not content him, for putting out all his brutal strength
he made to toss me clean over his head and we went down together with me underneath and most of my breath drove out. But
I still had one hand in his hair and as he seemed to have a weak
scalp I gave this another dreadful twist; in any such encounter,
ladies, it is always well to find out your opponent's tenderest parts.
It was rewarded by another frightful screech which seemed to be
echoed by one more, but I had little time to note this for the rogue
was getting too close and I disliked the stink of him. Driving my
free fist in his chaps again I brought my knee up in his belly to take
some of the wind out of him, give me leave to wrench his dainty
maulers away from my throat, and somehow drag myself free.

Gaining speed with his rage he was up as quick as I was, coming
on crouching again but with his arms forward and no very pretty
intentions. The encounter looked like taking an ugly turn, for he
was driving me back against the wheel; but as he came in again
there was one more screech, which I scarce had time to notice, and
another pistol bang. I saw his face change from brutish intent to
pained surprise, and before I could award him even one more blow
myself he swayed and went down like a bull. Somewhat surprised
myself by this remarkable event I gazed past him at the corner of

the mill; and there beheld Master Maggsy capering and cursing, and none other than Mr Hamilton Ryde coolly blowing away the smoke from his pistol muzzle.

For one more instant I observed the hulk, while blood welled out to stain his dirty moleskin weskit still filthier, and then at a loss I exclaimed, 'Be damned, sir, I believe you've killed him. Now sir,' I protested warmly, 'that was untoward. I wanted the rascal. Couldn't you have winged him?'

'I might have done,' he answered. 'But had I winged him I might well have killed you too. As it seems he'd have done himself in another minute.'

'Pooh, sir,' I retorted, 'I was wearing him down. These heavy rogūes tire easy and then you can wade in and finish 'em. I meant to see him hang; and learn much that he could tell me first.' But the mischief was done and assuring myself that he truly was dead and not foxing, reflecting that this would mean another report for the county coroner and that he'd have a butcher's holiday over this affair, I finished, 'Well then, let's put the fellow away tidy. He looks unsightly.'

Mr Ryde stood delicately aside, strolling off as cool as you please, while Maggsy and I dragged the fallen ox into his shed and covered him decently with a sacking. Then I asked softly, 'How did Mr Ryde happen here?'

'Come on me in the boneyard,' Maggsy answered. 'Asks "Where's Mr Sturrock, and when do we start for London?" and I says "He's gone to Coffin's Mill, and I don't like it neither, he's alooking for mischief again, are you game to come along of me and keep an eye to him?" and he gives a laugh and says "Why not?" so we come, and lucky we did; and look at your coat, for all the time I spend brushing it and polishing the buttons. That'n would have filleted, gutted and bowelled you, he'd have picked your eyes out first and then...'

'That's enough,' I said. 'Did you find the pistol?'

'No I never did,' he retorted in another sulk. 'Not though I turned over every bleeding blade of grass in the boneyard.'

'So ho,' I mused, and added, 'well, let it be. We'll go through the mill as we're here. Though there'll be little to see.'

So indeed it proved. With Mr Ryde showing a kindly interest we entered as dirty and stinking manufactory as ever I've seen, and I hope to God I may never eat bread made from grain milled in such a place; London bread is bad enough as it is. The machinery and millstones now standing idle though lately in use, and at one end of the milling chamber marks in the whitish dust where a row of barrels had once stood. Then a dark hole in which bags of corn were stored, with a door to the meadow, and a cut and knotted rope, which Maggsy kicked while looking at me meaningly still itching to tell his tale. But there was little else of any note save a curious tobacco pipe lying on the littered table in Coffin's pig pen living quarters; it had a kind of reed stem and a dried corn cob for a bowl. 'Might that have been Geoffrey's?' I asked Mr Ryde. 'It's a sort rarely seen in this country.'

He examined it somewhat gingerly. 'It might. They're common enough at home. He was here then?'

'He still is,' I said. 'And he'll never sit up and smoke that again. The poor fellow's reposing at the bottom of the leat. Whence as soon as may be I shall have him lifted by the coroner's officers.'

He seemed in no way greatly moved, but he announced, 'By God there'll be a fine tantrum when Lydia hears of this. She'll shoot somebody for it.'

'That, sir,' I observed, 'is what I fear. The sooner we get back to London the better.'

CHAPTER NINE

But there was still much to be done, and this I set about at once, first watching Mr Ryde set off to the inn for his post chaise and then returning myself to Mrs Matcham's to make my peace with that good soul. This was easier than I had feared for plainly she had taken more than a passing fancy to me as the ladies often do, and I promised that when I came to attend the Coroner and Magistrates within a day or two I should return to lodge with her again, and more than make up for past neglects. Thus mollified she bustled to get me and Maggsy hot water and the wherewithal to perform our necessities, and then set before us a most gratifying breakfast of bacon steaks and eggs; which my little wretch gobbled in such style as caused the good creature's eyes very near to pop out of her head. So then leaving Maggsy to watch for my chaise and Jagger, refreshed, with a clean neckcloth and my coat and beaver brushed, I set out again to the rectory.

There was a regular wailing convocation going on there now. One fellow standing by the foot of the stairs, letting other villagers go up two by two to view the body, and in the kitchen a full gaggle of 'em. Nicodemus Scrope applying himself to another bottle of the parson's brandy, a woman I took to be the cook but more resembling a slack boiled suet pudding with the bag still on, and a skivvy maid bawling her chaps off into her groats. With these three or four other women adding their voices to the lamentation, Gaffer Gudgeon making a snatch at the bottle every time Scrope seemed like to loose it, and yet more men examining my pistols; and lucky they was discharged or the blockheads might have done a further mischief with them. This House of Commons I silenced in short order by calling, 'Quiet, all of you, and out. All save Nicodemus Scrope.'

'God Christ,' one of the women wailed, 'here's a man come to take up Scrope and hang him.'

'That's right,' I told them soft and terrible, 'that's very likely true. And I'll do it quicker without your company.'

So I was left alone with the rascal who took another swig, followed by a belch and hiccup, and placed his bottle on the table to lean on it for comfort while he peered up at me out of little ferret's eyes. 'What be after now, master?' he enquired.

'You, Nicodemus Scrope,' I told him. 'When your master was shot and killed he was writing a letter which leads me to think he received another visitor these last days besides Miss Lydia. Why didn't you tell me?'

He gave another belch. 'Didn't ask.'

I felt my blood rising once more, but said, 'We'll put that right now. Who was it and when?'

'God whistle it,' the impudent rogue complained, 'you sets my wits aspin with your who what and when. I recollect we had a pig's head to supper, so it'd be the Tuesday; Tuesday after Friday as the parson go to London. We was a setting to it and the bell go a peal and I says "God's drats, who's to fret us now?" and goes off with a candle. Well then it was Master Mark; save it wasn't Master Mark it was Master Tristram.'

I felt my wits starting to spin out of my ears but reflected that this would be the Tuesday Miss Lydia had escaped from the ship just before dark, while Scrope continued, 'They was always like as two peas, the damned rascals. I cry out "God save us, here's Master Mark come back," and on that parson's door opens and he asking "What's this, Nicodemus?" so takes the candle to look in hers face and says "Father in Heaven, here's Tristram." And he says "So it is, Uncle Peregrine, and home from the dead," 'pon which parson took him in his chamber and there's an end on it.'

'No, my man, it ain't.' For good measure I took him by his shirt front and gave him a rattling shake, adding, 'I'll wager you was listening at that door. What did you hear?'

'Naught but a lot of mumbling and grumbling,' he replied in

a surly fit. 'Seems something as somebody wouldn't sign nor wouldn't tell; and Master Tristram says her could be made to fast enough but he'd as soon not spoil her looks.'

'So ho,' I mused. 'Even at that pass a wilful creature. It would be which bank the money was transferred to; the one thing she never told the woman Consuela. So Master Tristram must needs come here to find out. And by that time in London the wench had already escaped unbeknown to him. You're doing fair, my man. It's a pretty tangle. So what next?'

The wretch took a fresh pull at his bottle. 'Wasn't no next. Master Tristram come to give a heave to the door and tumble me into the chamber, then has me out again with his boot at my arse. So I go back to my pig's head and say be damned to both of 'em, and the end of it parson lets Master Tristram out himself. Then they was at the door and I up to my duty as I should and parson cries "As God will be my judge, Tristram, if any harm befalls that child I'll write a letter to the admirals." Master Tristram says something very soft as I couldn't catch and after that parson got the sinfuls on the Wednesday and took to his bottle. Her was always perplexed in her mind when her got the sinfuls.'

'You don't even have the wit to listen at a keyhole properly,' I observed, regarding the little toad with dislike. There were yet more questions I might have put to him, but I doubted he could tell me much which I might not perceive for myself or discover easier elsewhere. Time also was pressing and with a few last words of warning on his present and future I took my leave, scattering the gaggle of women in the hall like geese and thankful to be shot of the place.

But I was still beset for Gaffer Gudgeon was waiting to waylay me at the lych gate. With his billy goat bleat he hobbled along clutching at my sleeve and crying, 'There's a matter of a sovereign, master. That horrible boy, if it be a boy, promised a sovereign. It's a sovereign to anybody as'll let me out of this, he says.'

Feeling my breath come short again I started to tell him where to look for his sovereign but was taken by a better notion. You should never neglect a kindness to the poor however undeserving they may be and Providence ever chalks it up to your account. 'Gaffer Gudgeon,' I asked, 'would you say that Jabez Coffin's got a sovereign or two stowed away somewhere?'

'Oh by God yes,' he piped. 'A sharp man is Jabez Coffin.'

'Nor he wouldn't put it in a bank.' Regretting that I hadn't stopped to look for it myself—though awkward with Mr Ryde at my heels—I continued, 'Well then, if you was to go to the mill and search around for his hoard you might set yourself up in beer and baccy for the rest of your life. I don't fancy Jabez'll interfere with you, he ain't feeling just like it presently.' Cutting short his questions I finished, 'Do it quick now for the Coroner's Officers'll be here by noon and if they get their fingers on it you may whistle for his treasure.'

The old rascal went off at a gallop which surprised me, such is these countrymen's greed for gold, and well rid of him I returned to Mrs Matcham's, where surrounded by a court of village urchins Master Maggsy was sitting on the wall watching for my chaise. Here I added a post scriptum to my epistle to the coroner, advising him that owing to a further series of untoward events there were two more mortalities awaiting his attention, and adding my further compliments. One way and another they would remember my name in Ponder's End for many years to come.

By this time our gangling Parish Constable had presented himself and bidding him kindly not to exert himself, as his horse looked as if it might fall dead if pressed too hard, I sent him on his way just as the sound of wheels outside heralded my own conveyance. Then bidding Mrs Matcham an affectionate farewell, and even giving the dear soul a florin over and above what she asked for my entertainment I went out to my sturdy Jagger. The good fellow was all grins, with a knot of villagers at their doors to survey our turnout, and I even raised my cane to my hat myself as I said, 'Let's be off fast,' but then asked him softer, 'what of the young lady?'

'Very chippish as I've heard,' he answered, 'Mr Gedge had it from Mrs Tibbets who got it from Miss Silver, Lady Dorothea's maid. Whole gig full of clothes come for her yestereven, and then she took supper sitting up with Miss Harriet and the doctor, and ate enough for two. But that ain't the most of it,' he added. 'They reckon she's a wild 'un. Mr Gedge had this from Mrs Asher who got it from Mr Masters. Seems she sent for Mr Masters up to her chamber last night and as cool as you like asked him where she could lay hands on a pistol, or better still, a brace. Mr Masters declares he never took such a turn in his life, and most improper in a house like ours.'

'You're right, Jagger,' I said. 'She's a particular wild 'un and we'd best get back quick.'

He gave me another of his grins. 'Seems there's a gentleman of the same mind at The Brewers, sir, where I asked for you. Got a hired chaise and hosses, and seems he knows all about us. He gives a look at our cattle and says "Be damned" and then asks is it worth ten sovereigns to hold 'em a bit so's to see that he gets to London first.'

'Then I hope you took it,' I said.

'To be sure I did,' he replied. 'I'd never wish to offend a gentleman. Though I told'n I'd be bound to give you a bit of pace to start with so's you wouldn't take notice.'

'That's right,' I agreed kindly. 'You're a smart lad, Jagger, and I'll tell you something. When I find my own carriage, which won't be long now, I shall ask Lady Dorothea to let you come to me. Now how can we best oblige the gentleman?' I asked while Master Maggsy stood by with his ugly ears flapping and his eyes alight with mischief. I should have been warned by that, but continued, 'I'm bound to stop at The Bell in Edmonton, and I'll engage to have Mr Ryde wait there likewise. So while I'm about it you can make your arrangements.'

'Plain as daylight,' he answered. 'His boy'll go by the coach road by Tottenham so they'll meet the London press. Then I'll advise 'em through Paddington where they'll have a turnpike or two to halt 'em, whiles I reckons to take the country ways as we come.

There's nothing I likes better than a good straight sporting event,' he finished.

This concluded, within a minute or two more we were pulling up at The Two Brewers, where Mr Ryde was waiting with his chaise, some impatience, and the surliest post boy I ever saw in my life. He studied my horses afresh with a certain ill favour, but I announced, 'I hope you're in no great haste. My fellow seems unaccountable tender with his cattle today, and I must stop at Edmonton for a bit. There's fresh information to be had there and I fancy Miss Lydia'll wish to hear it.'

'Be hanged to that,' he answered. 'Will it take long?'

'Not as you'll notice,' I promised. 'But suit yourself. Though Miss Lydia won't thank you if you let it slip.'

'I'll wait then,' he said shortly. 'But be quick about it.'

We took the road at a fair clip, but nothing out of the way; and at The Bell it looked as if a coach had just gone through, for the landlord himself was standing in the doorway with one eye on his ostlers leading the spent horses to the stables. This was good fortune, and while Jagger and Maggsy edged across to Mr Ryde's chaise as if careful that I should not see them I acquainted myself, finding the fellow civil enough and made the more so by the sight of my turnout. 'Bow Street, eh?' he asked. 'About the Reverend Peregrine is it? By God that's a wicked business, a poor old gentleman like that. I heard of it but an hour ago. You Bow Street men come fast.'

'It's our trade,' I answered. 'Have you heard also that one Jabez Coffin took a lead breakfast off a pistol bullet and don't feel much the better of it?'

'What,' he cried, 'another one? Coffin you say? God help us, what's the world coming to?'

'Bad,' I said, 'and getting worse. Coffin was dealing in contraband. Brandy and French wines.' Master Landlord looked uncommon innocent on that and I continued, 'But that's no business of mine; or not unless I choose to make it so and pass a word to the Customs and Excise. I'm more concerned with a young lady travelling this way. Uncommon pretty looking, red hair, and a negro manservant.'

'Recollect that well enough,' he admitted. 'Shan't never forget the manservant. He put the chambermaids into fits; either the giggles or the vapours. Would have a mattress laid outside the lady's chamber door, and slept there if you please. And out of all order and decency if you ask me.'

'Americans,' I explained. 'They're born eccentric. Well now, the young lady came here last Thursday week and proposed to remain till Saturday. But she went off on Friday night and never came back. How was that, I wonder?'

'Here,' he started, 'I hope there's no trouble in it; I like to keep my nose clean. It was simple enough. They was off all day on the Friday and come back about supper which the lady took up in her chamber. Then about the middle of it a lad came from Ponder's End asking for her, and after that the negro came down to announce that his mistress has had a message to go to Coffin's Mill and they must call the post boy out. Which he wasn't best pleased over, at that time of night. But the lady offered him double his pay and a bit over and they had fresh horses put in the chaise and off they went.'

'And you didn't account that strange? Or did you fancy it was something to do with the contraband at the mill?'

He looked at me sideways. 'Mr Bow Street, when you've been as long on a coach road as I have there's nothing strange. To tell the truth I thought a young lady with looks like that had private business of her own best conducted at night. I was damn sure of it when the post boy came back grinning all over his face less than an hour later.'

'What did he say then?'

'Why that he found the mill and there was a fellow there with a lantern to guide the lady and servant across the meadow. He waited a bit and after a time the same fellow came back and paid him his hire and lodging; says the lady was remaining there the night and she'd make her own arrangements tomorrow. He was to carry her baggage back to London for deposit at the White Swan on Holborn Bridge and pay off her account here. He claimed the fellow told him he might keep what was left over for himself; and by his manner that was a good bit more than he commonly picked up.'

I looked across to my party. Jagger was in confabulation with Mr Ryde's post boy, and Mr Ryde was bending from his seat to talk to them and laughing while Maggsy was standing with his back against the nearside wheel, his hands behind him and a look of fearful innocence upon his face; and when Maggsy looks as innocent as that you should start to pray. There was little more time and I enquired, 'And you still didn't reckon it strange?'

'No, be damned I did not,' he cried, out of patience. 'I've told you, I thought it was a rattle on the flour sacks or a runaway elopement, and no affair of mine. Now, master, if there's any more let's have it quick. I've business to see to; the Nottingham Flyer's coming down any minute.'

I came then to the most important matter, for Miss Lydia's tale was now plain enough. I said, 'Look careful now and be sure. That gentleman in the post chaise. Have you ever seen him before?'

'I have not,' he replied. 'And I hope I may never see you again neither.'

With that dusty farewell I returned to my carriage, where Jagger gave me a grin and a wink, while Maggsy looked as if he was fit to join the Heavenly choir and Mr Ryde called, 'What now, Mr Sturrock?'

'No good of it,' I said, bundling Maggsy into the chaise and climbing after him, 'it was not as I expected.'

'Then be hanged to it,' he answered, 'let's go.'

God knows what had been said while I was engaged but seemingly the ostlers fancied there was a contest afoot and were holding our horses' heads like starters. 'Now then,' cried one, taking upon himself the office, 'whips when I give the word, gentlemen. But watch for the Nottingham Flyer to let her have the road. Now,' he bawled, 'give way!'

We were off with a rasp of gravel and clatter of hoofs, whips

cracking, the crowd raising a cheer, Jagger letting out a curse and
Maggsy howling; myself ramming my feet against the front boards
and my back into the leather, commending my soul to my Maker.
By some mischance, or some low post boy's trick, the others took
the lead from the start, thereafter swung wickedly across our horses,
and had not Jagger pulled them damned near on their haunches
we had been thrown over in the first half minute.

He joined his observations and canticles to mine and Maggsy's
in a fine chorus, and had the Lord listened to even the half of
them Mr Ryde and his post boy had gone on their way in a puff
of smoke each with a red hot thunderbolt up his arse. But there
was no such Divine Dispensation and after that dastardly shift
they took the crown of the road and held it, so there was daylight
on either side of them but no room to pass; while Jagger in a fine
rage and with plenty in hand kept close at their tail but to the off
side, seeking to drive the rogues over. Never did I hear such an
address on the manners, morals, parentage and hereafter of all post
boys, but was not backward with my own devotions, desiring the
Devil to snatch the rogues away by their privates or some similar
mischief, to which Maggsy added his own amen of screeches and
whoops of wicked laughter.

We rocked and clattered on to the thunder of hoofs, the horses
snorting, our wheels ringing on the road, and Mr Ryde yelling
Indian cries, with fowls squawking to the hedge-rows and one old
dame gathering sticks casting her bundle away and falling into the
ditch with her clouts over her head. But then by some chance Mr
Ryde's chaise caught a rut on its offside wheel and lurched, looking for an instant like oversetting altogether. The post boy recovered it fast enough but in so doing was forced to pull to the left,
and with a ringing yell of triumph Jagger drove up level. So for a
space we raced on hub to hub, post boy and Jagger lashing at each
other with their whips, Mr Ryde leaning out to bawl at me, 'By
God, sir, I thought you claimed your fellow was unwilling,' and
myself retorting with several observations of my own.

Then clear above the uproar came a dreadful sound. The note

of a horn; and there rounding a bend not a hundred yards before us the Nottingham coach. Four in hand, coming at a hard gallop every inch of twelve miles an hour, crowded with passengers on the roof, a fearsome Jehu with one hand to the ribbons and the other flourishing his whip, his guard winding blast after blast on the horn to clear their road, and bearing down upon us in a cloud of dust. Bouncing like a whore's tits and clutching my beaver to my head I did not merely commend my soul to my Maker, I gave it to Him with both hands, but at the same time roared, 'Jagger, you poxy, spavin hocked, blue arsed, stiff cocked baboon, give way!'

This did penetrate the madman's skull and he pulled the horses; so with another cheer from Mr Ryde the post chaise rattled ahead, but it was a damned close thing for the coach was near on us and that villain of a driver lashed out at the post boy with his whip as they rocked past wheel to wheel. Then it was our turn. Roaring all the vulgar blessings of the London stables and his passengers howling and yelling, the rogue flicked his whip at us too as they thundered by in a flash of red and blue and gold with flecks of foam from the snorting, monstrous horses. But now the road was open ahead and nothing to stop Mr Ryde getting clear; which he did with a wave of his beaver and a most ungenteel gesture, leaning from his chaise to give it to me. I had thought he was a gentleman.

For ourselves we fell to an easier pace and I spent the next minute or so describing Master Jagger with some fervour, as Master Maggsy went off into fits of laughter until I demanded, 'Well, you little monster, what have you been up to?'

'God's Tripes,' he crowed, 'I wonder it hadn't ha' come off already with the belting it took, I was awaiting for it as they scraped past that coach; I reckoned any instant we'd have Mr Ryde and that post boy flying arse over cobblers.' He went off again until I gave him a smart cuff and then he answered, 'Half loosed the axle pin out of their near side hub, that's what. And I never get no luck neither,' he added in aggrievement, 'I'd ha' thought to see 'em overtipped by now.'

'There they go,' cried Jagger on that, and on a further straight we perceived them now a quarter mile ahead and still going hell for lick, but now in some trouble for they was starting to wobble.

Maggsy let out another whoop, but our own turning to the right was approaching and I commanded, 'Keep on now, Jagger; I'll have no stopping to see what happens to 'em. We want no further discussion. Mr Ryde may not know the sporting customs of our country.'

So in another minute we were bowling along in sylvan solitudes and what further misadventures befell our friends was hidden from us by a Modest Providence; but from somewhere about a meadow's distance away I fancied I heard a crash and angry cries. I thought it proper to admonish Maggsy. 'That,' I said, 'was a most ungenteel stratagem, and we must pray the horses haven't come to any harm. I shall never bring you up to be a gentleman. And now,' I added, 'we'll have your report, and your explanation of how you came to be at Ponder's End.'

'Got catched,' he said briefly.

'You got catched,' I mused. 'Now there's a smart trick for such a clever little monster. But did you condescend to discover what I asked for? Which ship the wherryman put Miss Consuela and her gentleman aboard, and about Lieutenant Kemble, or any gleanings of Captains Lopez and Furlong?'

'Never had no time for them two,' he said. 'Was about asking Rosie of 'em when I got catched. But firstwise of that I goes after the whore, Meg; which she says the lootenant was took with the ague for better'n a week, and likewise wouldn't have no physician as he couldn't put up with 'em nohow, and fust time from his bed was the day he gets corpussed; which Meg reckons is bad luck.'

'It ain't of the best,' I agreed. 'So he did see Mr Colville for the first time that day; and a simple explanation for it. And on that same day he recognised Mr Midshipman Tristram Peregrine. You're doing very well, Master Maggsy, but it's no great matter now. What about the ship? Did you discover that?'

He gazed at me unkindly. 'Nothing's no great matter when I've found it out for you, is it? As to the ship, I reckon it's the one they took me on when I got catched. It's called the *Hester Ryde*.'

'What?' I demanded. 'The *Hester Ryde*? Are you sure of that? Be certain now for it tells us our man.'

'I got a pair of eyes on me, ain't I?' he asked.

Jagger was settling to a comfortable trot and I looked out at the bounteous fields, vegetations, and rustic cottages bowling past, while I reflected that we were getting near to the end of it now and Maggsy embarked on his elegant tale.

'Well then,' he started, 'being done with Meg I come next to the Prospect to seek for Rosie, as I conclude she's best to start on for Lopez and Furlong, and likewise I fancy she might be game for a rollick. But not so, as no sooner was I within the door'n this lady come up and says "Little boy, would you wish to earn yourself a crown piece?" and I answer as to that I don't take to being called a little boy, and moreover it's the same one as was in that chamber t'other night, Consooela, as I recollect her rum way of talking, but I reckon I'm as smart as she is so says "Try me and see." Next thing she led me outside and down to the water steps, and then I says to myself "God's Tripes, I'm a goner," for there was that mulatter and about four others.'

'You're simple,' I observed. 'But continue.'

'Simple enough to save you getting triped anyway,' he retorted. 'Anyway I reckons "What ho, I can't take this lot on, so might as well go easy and very likely find something out for old Sturrock, not as he'll be thankful." So they bundle me into a boat and set to rowing down the river and the mulatter says it's all the same to him whether he'll knock my head in or cut my throat, whichever I like least so I recollects that cabin boy and concludes to sit quiet. I'm particular obliged you corpussed that one. So we come to the ship and I see the name on the arse end done in gold letters. She was up against a wharf and we come to her on the river side and one of the villains says "Up you goes my darling," which wasn't near as sweet as it sounded as he lifted me on my way with his toe up my jacksy and I went flat on my chaps on the deck. It felt like

London Bridge had fell on me, and knowed no more till I come to and couldn't see nothing on account there was a bag over my head.'

To render the little wretch's account into politer language he now thought that by the stink he was in the ship's hold with a great noise of bumps and bangings, feet trampling above, and once somebody bawling 'Careful of that lantern when they're stowing powder, you God damned sea cook.' He fancied there were several rascals about him, but only one of them spoke; and by now you will know who this must have been as well as I did myself. Questioned none too gently, he was somewhat evasive on how much he had told and according to him it was this villain alone who hit on Ponder's End. 'So it's that damned button,' he had announced. 'The Peregrine coat of arms. Sturrock said it would lead him on a longish journey, and so it has; it's led him to old Matthew Peregrine. And he's very likely carried the girl there too.'

'Uncommon nasty tempered he was,' Maggsy complained. 'Worse'n you, and I reckons I've had enough of this, so gives a moan and lets on to be corpussed or in a swoon and after that they leave me be. But the woman Consooela says that's what his fancy notions does for 'em; to which he answers they'd have been all's well save for one mischance and give him but twenty-four hours and he'll have the whole lot of 'em out of it along of the money as well; once let him get out to sea and meet up the *Mary Carson* off the Niger Coast with fresh supplies and the whole damned British Navy might look for him for ever.'

'It's just as I thought,' I said. 'But you never saw any of 'em?'

'I told you,' he replied. 'I'd got a bag over my head all the time before I worked it off for myself at that mill. Anyways they all went off and left me for a time then till another lot come and dragged me up on deck, as I knowed by the fresh air. Then they heaves me over the side and I thinks, God A'mighty, this is where I get drownded only it wasn't that neither but dumped in the bottom of a boat with four or five others coming after.'

I shall not recount the little monster's tale of suffering in this boat, as the most part of it was indelicate, but he had the wit to listen to the men grumbling and cursing and complaining; a common practice of sailors. 'They was going on a barrelful,' he said, 'most as wishing they was well out of this, and one says it's all rare and dandy for the captain to be riding in a chaise with his fine friend while they was aheaving their guts out, and another tells 'em to stow their gab and pull. He says they was a poxy crew of lilywhites and rec'lect that if Captain Blackbird hangs they'll all hang with him, or contrariwise there's good money in it. I reckon he was the boss as he sat at the back and never done nothing but cuss 'em all, and I fancy it was that mulatter.'

They came to the mill at last in near darkness and Maggsy was left in the boat. There were men moving about and voices nearby but not close enough to make much of them above the rush of the water until one cried, 'Be damned to you I've got troubles of my own with this cove poking about; and I tell you there ain't no wench here for he was seen to come on his own and he's lodging at Mrs Matcham's.' On this they moved away, and after a further time Maggsy was dragged off once more to be flung down in some place which he declared stank of grain and liquor.

'And I reckon that's my tripes as good as gone,' he continued, 'and the sooner I'm out of this lot the better, so set about them ropes but don't have no good of 'em save I work the bag off my head. Then I see a crack of light under a door and roll across to it. Well then they was still colloguing beyond but it ain't much more'n a mumble till the same one cries, "God's Truth I've a mind to turn King's Evidence on you myself and save my own neck," and t'other who was at me on the ship answers "Come now, Jabez, you'll not do that to an old friend. It'd be the worse for you if you did." On that seemingly they all go out as a door slams and I hear no more.'

'You're doing very well,' I encouraged the brave child. 'What next?'

'Apissing myself to get loose of them ropes, that's what's next. Then come a flash of lightning, which I see there's a window and works over to that; couldn't get up to it but seems the men are out there as the same says "Stand by, you lot," goes on "I'm grieved for the parson but it's him or us," and another answers something but smothered by a clap of thunder. But the fust adds "I'll go back with the boat and you can beat it out of the boy where to find that damnation vixen. But for God's sake watch Coffin and remember we sail with the tide by two o'clock tomorrow. If you ain't aboard by then I'll heave to as long as I may abeam of Bow Creek." '

'Two o'clock is it?' I said. 'We've little time then.'

'No more did I,' Maggsy retorted. 'I'm acussing and praying, till of a sudden comes hosses snorting and harness ajingle, and I thinks God's Tripes, what's now? Sturrock's at work sure enough, there's nobody but him could've stirred up this lot. Well then a waggon door opens and in comes a carter and that old funnyguts carrying a lantern, and he cries "God's sake what's here?" so I says "What's it look like? You get me out of this lot quick and it's a sovereign for you." Which he done, and I fell flat on my chaps two or three times but got outside and says to take me to Sturrock, though he claims you're Mr Moxon; and God knows what tricks you'll get up to next. Anyhow we was on the road when we hear them pistol shots, and I says that's Sturrock for certain whatever he's calling himself. And so it happened.'

'You've done very fair,' I observed, 'though rash and impetuous. In the Art and Science of Detection you should never offer a sovereign till all else fails. Jagger,' I added, 'whip up those horses. Events are running ahead of us and I don't like the look of 'em.'

So indeed it proved when we came to Hanover Square. At this hour of the forenoon there was a number of carriages and chairs by the railings, but no sign of Mr Ryde yet nor likely to be for some time to come. Descending in haste, and taking it upon myself to order fresh horses put in the chaise with all speed, I mounted the steps to have the front door opened for me instantly. For the first occasion I recollect Masters the butler seemed pleased to see me; as well he might for behind him in the hall was a scene of lamentation. Miss Harriet looking like a parrot with a particular hard nut in her beak, the doctor marching to and fro as black as thunder, and a weeping maid.

'What's this?' I enquired and added, 'my respects, ma'am.'

'Why,' Miss Harriet snapped, 'she's gone. Walked out of the house by the servants' entrance; the servants' entrance if you please. Never did I know such ingratitude. Nor such forwardness.'

'Ma'am,' the doctor interposed, ever ready in defence of his darling, 'she left a message.'

'A message?' Miss Harriet asked as if cracking another nut. 'What's a message? Any hussy can write sweet words.'

The doctor himself passed me a scrap of paper and I read from it aloud, ' "Miss Harriet and dear Dr Ian. I beg you not to call me ingrate. I has family matters of urgent concern to settle. These there is no right to bring you and Dr Ian into, but this being done vow I shall return and throw myself upon your mercy. Lydia Palmer." '

'I'll give her Lydia Palmer when I see her again,' Miss Harriet announced.

'She'll be damned lucky if you ever do,' I observed, and addressed myself to the maid. 'When did this happen?'

'Half an hour since,' the wench wept. 'Miss says "Dear Mary, it's a great secret but I must go out; do you lend me a cloak and hood and I'll give you a guinea when I come back." Then she asks where she can find herself a hackney and I says it's not a step round to Prince's Street Mews where there's a respectable livery.'

'Did she have money with her?' I asked.

'A lady don't carry money,' Miss Harriet snapped.

'But how can she hire a hackney without?' the doctor demanded. 'And where's she going?'

I wasted no words asking how much or little she had told them of her tale but said to Miss Harriet, 'Ma'am, will you desire Mr Masters to have Mr Gedge saddle a riding horse for Dr McGrath. She's going to Coutt's Bank,' I continued. 'And there she'll find our villains have already been and gone and her inheritance with 'em; they've all the proofs of her identity. Then she'll turn to Mr Moxon the lawyer for money. With intent to buy herself a brace of pistols.'

'God A'mighty,' Miss Harriet cried, 'what's she want pistols for?'

'For their common use, ma'am. To make a point if your discussion starts to grow unfriendly.' I turned back to the physician and said, 'Dr McGrath, I want you to ride fast to the Admiralty and then come on to Captain Bolton's. There's no good in trying to take her at the bank or Mr Moxon's now. I shall go straight to try and cut her off from reaching a certain ship at Wapping.'

'The Admiralty?' he demanded. 'What the devil d'ye want there?'

'A record you might get quickest. I'm after an incident that took place aboard H.M.S. *Irresistible* off the Carolinas in 1777. It concerns Midshipmen Mark and Tristram Peregrine, and I fancy it was mutiny or some such thing. Tristram Peregrine murdered Lieutenant Kemble, or caused him to be murdered for no better reason than the poor fellow recognised him.' Miss Harriet let out a squawk on that and I finished, 'You may also advise their Lordships that Mr Midshipman Tristram Peregrine, now known as Captain Blackbird, may presently be found aboard the ship *Hester Ryde* lying by Wells' victualling yard on the river. But sailing at two o'clock today.'

'God's sake, man,' he cried, 'd'ye know the Admiralty? It might take me a week, waiting in the ante rooms and cooling my heels in the corridors.'

'It'd better take you less than minutes if you want to save the wench,' I told him. There was a fresh clatter of hoofs outside then and I moved quick to the window lest it was Mr Ryde; but it was only our own good fellows with the fresh cattle, and I continued to Miss Harriet, 'There's but one more thing, ma'am. I'm not sure of it, I'm not sure of anything concerning the gentleman; but any time now you might have a Mr Ryde of Charleston, Carolina, arriving here.' Turning a sidelong look on the doctor I added, 'Miss Lydia Palmer's intended husband.'

'Her what?' he demanded, dumbstruck. 'What's that ye say?'

'Her intended husband,' I repeated. 'Come to rescue the young lady and carry her back to America.' The man was stricken like a pole-axed ox, and I continued, 'I daresay if you're bashful about the Admiralty Mr Ryde'll go fast enough; by way of the American Ambassador at St James's. But that'll take time. She might be well on her way to Africa before they move.'

Dr McGrath regarded me with the worst of his lowering looks. 'Mr Sturrock,' he announced, 'ye'll permit me to obsairve that ye spend too much damned time havering.'

CHAPTER TEN

Once outside he was mounted and off in a cloud of dust; lost to him his wilful lady might be, but the poor soul was still game. Reflecting that love was a touching madness I instructed Jagger to make for Wapping at his best pace and in another minute, with Maggsy agog for fresh mischief, we were off once more; and too much traffic about to suit me, for I was in some anxiety. Nonetheless we made a spanking pace of it in Oxford Street, rattling through the press of carriages, phaetons and tradesmen's gigs, exchanging a compliment here and there and word for word with a soldier that fancied himself a cavalry man, and not above near killing a pestiferous street arab who bolted out under our horses' heads. Then we was held the best part of ten minutes by some rascally drayman blocking the narrow part of High Street by St Giles' Church, where it took our combined Creeds, Collects and Revelations, and all three of us offering to fight him before the contumacious rogue pulled his horses aside astounded. Holborn was better and we bowled along in a clatter, though nearly oversetting a chair with an ancient lady in it. But in New Bridge Street again it seemed as if the whole of London was out, buying, selling, and pilfering; and here Jagger had recourse to his whip, though not a wise thing, as the rascals at this end of the town have no respect for the nobility and it might have caused a riot.

By God's Mercy we escaped unmurdered and now pulled up Ludgate Hill, to find yet more idle crowds about the shops and stalls of St Paul's Yard. I had long since exhausted all that a patient man may say; even Maggsy was stricken hoarse, and calling up what philosophy I might I reflected that this cursed headstrong hussy must needs face the same hazards, or even worse with an obstinate rogue of a hackney driver, and we might yet head her off. But these wenches move fast, the more so when driven by their own devilments; and in the City the multitudinous signs of the bankers and merchants were already starting to swing in a rising breeze.

At length we came down to the forest of masts, our nostrils assailed by the stinks of the riverside, but held yet more by the slow moving warehouse waggons and doltish carters in these narrow wharfside streets. It was prayer and patience, curse and chorus, until at last we came to the Prospect with its everlasting knot of idlers; and even before Jagger had reined in I was out of the chaise with Maggsy after me, scattering them like chaff, into the tavern and up the stairs at a rush.

Captain Isaac was sitting there as calm as you please in the back bay window, surveying the crowded shipping through his spy glass and smoking a pipe, with a pot of rum by him. 'Now, Isaac,' I demanded, 'where's the *Hester Ryde*?'

'Her's warped out,' he answered. 'Were loading up to late last night, going on with flares. Her's in the stream now, anchored fore and aft, bows down river and ready to sail. But the tide's still flooding for an hour or so, though the wind's veering west. Her'll slip with the slack water. What's about then?'

'The wench's come back,' I said. 'Heading for that ship; and if she gets aboard it God help her. A damnation red headed jade as wants her clouts turning up and her arse slapping till her nose bleeds buttermilk.'

'Ain't no call to talk like that, Jer'my,' he remonstrated. 'She's a sweet pretty child.' I near enough gagged at the thought of her sweetness, but before I could find words he asked, 'Be you going after her?' and announced, 'then I'm acoming too.' He finished off his rum in a swallow, heaved himself up and commanded, 'Give way there.'

There was no stopping the old rascal for all his wooden leg and plain signs that he was more than a little drunk and with Maggsy scampering ahead, chuckling vastly at the prospect of a boarding party, he was already stumping down the stairs roaring, 'I wisht I had my old cutlass, but I'll make shift without it.'

Then as we turned out to the chaise there was a fresh clatter of hoofs and the physician came up riding like one damned, yet not without a light of triumph. But also by the look on his bony face there was mischief boding, and I cried, 'You've been quick about it. Did you get what I wanted?'

'Aye,' he cried back. 'And a gey fine tale it is. But be damned to that. Have ye found the lassie?'

'We have not,' I told him, 'and I don't like the shape of it.'

'Then be damned,' he answered, 'get on your way, will ye?'

What with the pangs of disappointed love, his natural evil temper and hot Scot's blood the fellow was plainly a madman. But in kindness I forgave his uncivil manner and retorted, 'I'm still in command, sir. We'll make for Limehouse Hole Stairs; that's where she came ashore and it's where she'll head for now. And if you're so hot, sir, do you clear the way.'

He was off on the instant with a fresh clatter, striking sparks from the cobbles; and I shall confess freely that he was of some small use, for even the rude carters were struck speechless and pulled aside in haste on the sight of this maniac riding down at them.

Once out of Wapping and towards the wilds of Poplar Marshes we got on faster and before long Captain Isaac roared, 'Steady as she goes; avast there.' Here we had our first sign of the wench for just at the dockyard was a hackney, its driver reclining like a lord within, and a bony flea bitten nag with its snout deep in a nosebag. The physician had already dismounted and was questioning the fellow as we ourselves tumbled out—leaving Jagger, voluble in disappointment, to guard our animals and carriage—and he caught up at a trot while we hastened over and around the tangle of ropes, moorings, sacks, and bales, with dockers bustling and shouting about us and the ships, masts and rigging on the river hard by.

'It's the lassie,' he cried. 'Quarter hour since. She bid the fellow wait for her.'

'And he might have to wait a long time,' I observed. 'Please God we have her before she reaches the ship.'

By now Isaac was stumping down a flight of steps to the water bawling at a wherryman, but this rogue proved obdurate at the size and number of our party and the sight of my pistols; not even my orders would move him until McGrath roared, 'By God, Jacob Miles, the next time your wife pups you can pull it out yourself; and you ain't paid me for the last yet. Be damned I'll take an oar with you.' So we clambered in, Maggsy at the nose like a wicked figurehead, and embarked on the perilous flood with Isaac returning to his younger days and bellowing, 'Pull now, you lubbers,' and beating on the boards with his wooden leg to keep the stroke. It was not an enterprise I relished, as I fancy boats little better than horses.

'What of the Admiralty?' I asked the physician.

'Time enough for that,' he grunted, pulling at his oar. 'By the maircy of God I came upon a staff captain I knew well.'

Mindful of the fellow's incivilities I said, 'As no doubt you'd performed some small service to him in the past.'

'If you call taking a leg off a service,' he panted.

The midstream was clear of shipping, this being the fairway, and we came out through the hulls and barges here on the Poplar side to perceive by the Rotherhithe bank across the grey billows such a profusion of ships, lighters, masts, spars, and sails as defies description. We were now in open weather, crossing the river and working downstream, the doctor and his companion heaving near enough to pull us clear out of the water at each stroke, and old Isaac for all the world as if he was walking his own decks again sniffing at the tide and wind. 'Near enough the flood,' he announced, 'and the wind westerly. Jer'my, we ain't got a lot of time.'

Then Master Maggsy himself let out a screech which split the sky. 'God's Tripes, there she is. Copperknob.'

From a small boat low in the flood it is not easy to pick out another just as low, and less so when you are pitching and jerking, but I could just make out a flash of blue with red atop of it against the heaving grey and browns and blacks of the waves, shipping and flying spray. It resolved into a wherry like our own, but with only one oarsman and a single passenger sitting upright and proud in the stern. It was that damned rash, wilful wench sure enough, and by now too far away to catch. Her boat was already drawing close under a square rigged black ship having a raking bowsprit and masts and long, fast build; even I as a landsman could see that she was built for speed and handling, and Captain Isaac was near weeping with rum and affection. 'Oh, by God,' he exclaimed, 'she's a beauty, she's a darling. I'd give the Widow Rooke to have command of her. Once she slips she'll show the legs of us.'

There was a fellow already by the wheel, another beside him with his hands cupped to shout orders, men running up the shrouds like monkeys and at the yards shaking out her canvas; and a figure in frock coat and beaver appearing on the poopdeck. 'She won't be long,' the captain cried. 'She'll slip the for'ard moorings, set rags enough to give her steerage way and lift the after hook. Pull, you cripples,' he bellowed, thumping his leg on the boards again, 'put your piss into it. A one titted lilywhite with a drunken sailor tucked atween her legs could throw a better heave with her arse.'

Despite the old gentleman's poetics our oarsmen were doing their best; the waterman grunting a curse with each stroke, the doctor dark faced and saving his breath. We were gaining, but not fast enough; and in the wench's boat the waterman was now but idling with the oars, bringing it about and holding it against the current while the girl herself was standing up and crying out something with the wind flapping her cloak and flying her red hair; a pretty picture if you had time for such things. Colville was coming to the rail with a man to each side of him but at the same time shouting some order back over his shoulder. Then it looked as if he and the wench were holding some parley.

It was too late to stop the rash creature. We needs must board the ship, and I commanded, 'Sheer off; come about the starboard side.'

'No, by God,' the doctor panted, losing a stroke by turning to look over his shoulder, 'we'll go straight in and get the lassie.'

'How?' I demanded. 'You damned fool, we're hid by the ship itself from Rotherhithe. He can have the wench aboard before anybody can stop him. And drop a shot and sink us too.'

So much struck the boatman for he announced, 'God rot and blast this, it's no concern of mine; starboard it is.'

We turned upstream to swing around the ship's counter, so close that I noted above us the cable crew standing ready but now themselves watching the scene on the port side. I heard Colville's voice giving orders, the wench crying out something, and the physician cursing. Then we were bumping, with Isaac grappling a boat hook at the rail, the doctor seizing a rope to heave himself over and Maggsy scrambling after chattering that he'd got a score of his own to settle and a fair notion how. I paid little notice to the rascal, being engaged in getting aboard myself though hampered by my pistols and stopping for the sake of peace to give a hand to Captain Isaac, who was bawling above the wherryman's frightful oaths, 'Here, I'm acoming too.'

Never was a man worse served by his lieutenants; the physician plainly fighting mad, Master Maggsy scuttling away very nearly on all fours to melt away seemingly unobserved behind a deck house, and Captain Isaac well past his prime. The ship was thronged with men, all about their nautical labours and a more piratical looking cut throat crew I have never seen. There was no sign of our mischievous wench and in all the bustle our own appearance went unnoticed until one fellow yelled, 'Hey there!' and a heavy built rascal swung about to survey us; by his blue coat and brass buttons the mate or sailing master. 'Hell's teeth,' he started, advancing on us with two others, but before they could come to quarters I cocked my weapons and said plainly, 'Bow Street. Take me to your captain.'

Whether he would or not I shall never know for on that instant from somewhere below came the crash of a shot and a woman's scream followed by the weaker spitting crack of a second pistol misfired. Here the physician lost his last wits. He turned like a viper to strike the nearest man a blow which lifted him clean off the deck, uttered a strange Scots howl, flung another aside like a sack, and made for an opening under the poop; and Captain Isaac stumped after him bellowing and doing his best to gut one more with his wooden leg. Damning the pair for impetuous fools there was nothing I could do but cover 'em, levelling my Wogdons at full cock and saying to the press of villains, 'Hold still now.'

That held them for long enough, though more were running along the decks with others swinging down from the shrouds, and moving slow but firm, keeping my pistols steady, I said, 'If you want a ball in your guts, Mr Mate, you're welcome. Or if not keep your men quiet.' So I backed off the way McGrath and Captain Isaac had gone, to the poop companionway and after cabin, and turned to survey the scene. And I hope I may never see another like it.

Miss Lydia was against the forward bulkhead with a useless little pistol in either hand, her face as white as a bed sheet thus throwing up the brilliant eyes and flame of her hair. Crouched on a settee under the stern window was a dark eyed and dark haired woman moaning and clutching at her right shoulder with blood on her fingers. And Mr Colville standing with a pair of cocked pistols held on that foolish girl. With it all the doctor rumbling like a mad bull but set to stone, Captain Isaac cursing and belching gusts of rum to add to the stink of gunpowder, and behind me the press of villains.

I could have killed Colville as he stood, but dare not chance the wench at a mere twitch of his finger. Nor could I expend one or both of my own shots with that gang of cut-throats crowded behind. They were stilled for the minute though a single word would set 'em off like a bombshell, and for all I'm as good a man as any in a mill I see no sense in suicide. 'Well now,' I observed, 'you've got us beat, Mr Colville. Yet you can't escape neither, nor your crew. Why don't we come to terms?'

'God's sake,' burst out the physician, 'is that the best you can do?'

'What else is there?' I asked.

The other woman moaned, but Miss Lydia said nothing—though from the look in her eyes it was not from lack of words—and behind me the men muttered and shuffled until Mr Colville commanded, 'Quiet there!' They were silenced on the instant, and with his pistols still held steady he seemed to be listening to the sounds of that beautiful ship as she came to life and strained to be free. 'Leave three men here, Mr Tuke,' he ordered, 'and get the rest back to their work. Give way when you're ready.'

The rest of them tramped off and three came into the cabin, ugly rascals who looked more than ready for anything; there were orders bawled above, feet running afresh on the decks, and while Captain Isaac muttered and grumbled I got myself a step closer to the girl. But Mr Colville was quick enough and his voice sharp. 'No, Mr Sturrock. Another inch and I'll take her with one shot and you with the other. You have no terms,' he added.

I looked down at my own pistols as if nonplussed. 'We might have. Doctor McGrath, tell Mr Colville what you learned at the Admiralty.'

The poor fellow's face was dark with blood. Never have I seen a young man closer to an apoplexy but he started, 'Aboard the *Irresistible* off the Carolinas, October '77. There was Midshipmen Mark and Tristram Peregrine and Senior Midshipman Robert Kemble under Captain James Dyke. And also a Lieutenant Wilkes, known to be a savage bully. Verra well then. There was some quarrel, Mark Peregrine struck this Wilkes in sight of the crew, at which some of 'em cheered, and Dyke ordered him flogged. It's not a verra common thing to flog a middy but Dyke was a strict master. All hands were mustered to witness punishment for all they were in enemy water and Yankee ships on patrol. Have ye ever witnessed a naval flogging, Mr Colville?' he asked.

'He did this one,' I said. 'Pray continue, doctor.'

'Tristram Peregrine seized an iron marlinspike and flung it at Dyke; it struck his left eye, penetrated the brain and the captain died of it soon following. Aye. Verra well; in the confusion of that, and as it's thought aided by some of the crew, Tristram Peregrine leapt overboard. And pretty well the same minute two Yankee frigates were sighted. It seems there was a running fight and the Peregrine they were flogging was himself killed. When the *Irresistible* limped back to the West Indies Station half of her officers and crew was either wounded or dead and it was concluded that Tristram Peregrine was either drowned or picked up by the Yankees.'

'And so he was,' I agreed, listening to blows of a mallet striking out a shackle overhead, the roar of a chain and a voice crying, 'Give way'. I felt the deck lift and tilt under our feet and continued, 'And no doubt made his way to the Ryde estates at Charleston. Or maybe to the other Rydes at Boston; where in the end he took command of the ship *Mary Carson*. And so became Captain Blackbird the slaver and sometimes Barbary pirate.' The wench caught her breath at this, and I said, 'That's right, Miss Lydia. I know the whole tale, or most of it. I daresay it's family history to you.'

The man was getting easier by the minute, and so long as the physician did not fall into another fit of madness I'd have him laying his pistols down before long. We were moving now; the woman in the stern window seemed to have fallen into a swoon for she had stopped her moans, and there was something fresh. A light stink at first; it might have been a whiff of tarry smoke from the shore. But if I was any judge it was more like Master Maggsy at his wicked tricks.

I went on, 'Mutiny, murder, desertion to the enemy, and piracy. The Navy'll hunt you for a lifetime once they know you're alive, Mr Colville. But that ain't the worst of it,' I added. 'You'd be better with the Navy than my wicked little devil of a clerk. He's running loose aboard your ship, and did you but know that imp of Satan as well as I do you'd have every man jack of your crew to look for him. The child's a monster. He's got some grudge against you for the way you mishandled him, and he's very like to blow your gunpowder up for revenge.'

He did not know whether to believe that or not, but he sniffed at the air himself. 'One man there,' he rapped out, 'report to Mr Tuke. Have the ship searched.'

Captain Isaac let out another great curse, the girl looking sideways at me as if asking what next, while the ship lifted again, riding faster. But the physician was calmer now starting to perceive my play and waiting for the next card. I moved to the table close by where the wench was standing and laid my pistols on it—but still close enough to get 'em fast—saying, 'Come, sir, set yours down likewise.' The two sailors remaining were watching me somewhat puzzled but ready enough for mischief, and I finished, 'I'll tell you something you must know if you're to save your neck and crew. We'll come to terms.'

'Terms?' he cried. 'There are no terms, you damned fool. You're aboard my ship now and bound for Africa.'

'Not yet we ain't,' I said. 'She's afire.'

Even as I spoke a wreath of smoke came in followed from somewhere forrard by the cry of fire and a chorus of shouts and orders. The two sailors turned towards the companionway, one of them asking, 'Cris'ake, what now, capt'n?' and he answered, 'Get and see, be damned,' making a step to the door himself and shouting for Mr Tuke.

It was the last chance we might have and I took it. I turned behind him like a boxer, awarded him a wicked kidney punch with my right and used my left to strike one pistol down. It exploded harmlessly into the deck; and not to be outdone, roaring with rage the physician flung himself under the other at Mr Colville's knees and brought him over with a crash which seemed to shake the ship. He was a rash fellow and might well have killed himself, for that weapon likewise went off with a roar, but his curses reassured me in what time I had to notice them as the two sailors now came back followed hard by Mr Tuke. Him Captain Isaac engaged, but the others flung themselves upon me; and all this while fresh cries of 'Fire!' came from the deck, running feet, thickening smoke, and a howl which could only have been Master Maggsy's melodious voice.

By now I was fully engaged with the other two fellows fighting my way back to my own weapons, only to perceive to my utmost horror that Miss Lydia had them one in either hand. I can face a dozen rogues with equanimity but the sight of a woman with pistols by Wogdon in her grasp chills my blood. Hard pressed as I was with the rogues I gave one a blow which flung him against the bulkhead, tossed the other atop of the woman on the settee and cried, 'God's sake, ma'am, have a care; you'll do a mischief.'

But she had neither ears nor eyes for me, watching breathless as the physician and Mr Colville fought like a pair of street dogs; one with a kind of dour Scots fury, the other sadly descended from his former elegance. What befell then it is not in my power to relate, as in any battle there are so many actions and counter actions, and I was taken up again by my own obstinate rogues. But Captain Isaac came roaring like a bull, wielding some nautical weapon he had seized to ward off two more rogues, and to make confusion yet more confused Master Maggsy now appeared screeching his own observations and brandishing a cutlass.

What with the struggling figures, curses and grunts, sounds of blows, Maggsy's inharmonious cries, furniture books, papers and charts flying every way, the smoke thickening and that damned wench standing there with the pistols it was an uncommon mixed business. A business only stilled by the crashing bark of one of my Wogdons; the physician falling back, our wench standing there yet whiter but her eyes flaring blue and the pistol still smoking in her hand, and Mr Colville thrown against the ship's side with his left arm hanging shattered. In the sudden silence he said, 'You damned vixen.'

'That was for my Geoffrey,' she announced, 'whatever you've done with him. Would you like the other; for myself?'

'Stop, ma'am,' I cried. There was but one instant to have command—as plainly none of those rogues liked having a woman loose with a pistol among them any more than I did—and I took the weapon away from her as fresh thundering footsteps brought the return of Mr Tuke, and four or five more after him.

'God A'mighty,' he cried, 'what's this, captain?'

It was a nice moment for we were outnumbered and had only the one shot left between us; but holding my pistol steady on the mate I answered, 'The end of it, my man. If you don't get blown to hell first you're bound for Execution Dock. Yet I'll save you and any of your men who behave themselves.'

That and the thickening smoke made some of them look at each other, while Mr Colville got himself across to a chair, leaning on it with his face like tallow under the tan and blood dripping on the deck. As if I was not there he asked, 'What's our position, Mr Tuke?'

'Well afire, sir,' he replied. 'The forrard hold and too damned close to the powder for my liking.' He turned no very friendly eye on Master Maggsy; the mischievous wretch standing there with his hair singed and face blackened like a veritable imp of the Devil. 'I'd limb that little bastard if I could. I've got the pumps working, but it's getting hot.'

'Then stop 'em,' Mr Colville said. 'Let her blow.'

Mr Tuke himself opened his mouth to protest, but as a fresh waft of smoke came billowing in the five or six men shifted and muttered among themselves again and one of them growled, 'That be hanged; there's ten kegs to go up.'

'So save yourselves,' I told them. 'Your captain's done for and so are you if you don't set about it fast.'

Two went, and then another after them, while Maggsy whispered one of his own choice observations, the physician turned towards his lady love and Captain Isaac cursed afresh. But still that determined rogue would not give up. Weakened as his voice was he demanded, 'Lily livered are you, Tuke? I thought you'd more bowels. You've thirty-two crew aboard and there's arms in the locker there. What're you waiting for?'

Mr Tuke made a move, but with his eyes on my pistol thought better of it, as did the three remaining rogues behind him. The smoke was thickening yet more and the physician cried to Colville,

'Losh, man, are ye mad? Give your men a chance to save themselves.'

'God's sake, sir,' Mr Tuke cried, 'we've but minutes left.'

'And I'll warn ye,' the physician added, 'ye'll be deid yourself verra soon if you don't have that shoulder looked at.'

It was indeed a pretty mess, and may God ever preserve me from the like attentions of that wench, but I interjected, 'We've no time for medicals. Now you men be off and set about that fire, and put your backs into it unless you fancy being blown to hell on your arses.' They lost no time in going and I finished, 'Doctor, if there's arms in that locker let's have 'em out.'

He needed no second bidding. Coughing in the smoke and even thrusting the wench aside to get at them he wrenched open a pair of doors in the bulkhead, and here was all we needed. Good, heavy ship's pistols; a brace for the doctor, two more for Captain Isaac—thereby stopping his curses—and a fresh pair for myself. But when the wench made to lay hands on a couple I said, 'No, ma'am; we're tempting the Devil to be on this ship at all, and I'll not tease him too far.' She flung back an angry retort, and none too ladylike, but I went on, 'Doctor, I'll ask you to order the fellows on the fire; and by the stink and smoke the sooner the better. Captain Isaac, you'll take command on deck; have Mr Tuke with you, and if he proves troublesome you know what to do. But remember particular to heave to by Bow Creek. We've got another gentleman to come aboard.'

They none of them thought to ask who that might be. The physician went off with one last sheep's look at Miss Lydia, the captain stumped away bellowing, 'Aye, aye,' and shepherding Mr Tuke with Maggsy behind, and only the wench was left to ask, 'Have you no orders for me, sir?'

'Why no,' I answered, 'save to get out of my sight.'

Once again I might have been fried by blue fire. 'Be damned to you,' she started, but stopped to ask, 'Where is my Geoffrey? What did they do to him?'

'Ma'am,' I told her somewhat more gently, 'you do well to mourn him. He was a good man. I'll have Dr McGrath tell you the whole tale in due time. It'll come better from him. And ma'am,' I added, 'you've one in a thousand there; save he's got a temper very near as bad as your own.' She so far forgot herself as to very near reward me with a smile, and I finished, 'Now for God's sake get up on deck. And in case that powder blows keep as far to the stern as you can.'

So left alone at last I turned to the final necessities; and wasting no time about it, for I had no wish myself to go flying arse backwards through that stern window—in particular at the wicked hands of Master Maggsy. I looked first to the woman, Consuela Smith, but she was well enough. A flesh wound in the upper arm and a considerable effusion of blood, but no more than in a deep swoon; she would live to tell her tale to a judge if we didn't all get blown up within a minute. Mr Colville was in a worse case with his shoulder quite shattered, though he might last if we could get him to the naval dockyard fast enough; to be plain I cared little one way or the other.

But he still had spirit. He opened his eyes at me and muttered, 'That red headed bitch; and you, Sturrock. If I could get a pistol I'd still shoot you.'

'You've left it too late,' I said. 'And you're a fool, Mr Colville, Mr Tristram Peregrine, or Captain Blackbird. I'll tell you the cream of the jest. You need not have killed Lieutenant Kemble, or had him killed. It was the mulatto, I suppose?' He nodded and I told him, 'Well then the poor man knew you but he'd never have split. He said so on his last breath. But for Kemble I might have concluded Miss Lydia Palmer's affairs was not worth my notice. And you shot the parson to stop him telling me what happened aboard the *Irresistible*?' He nodded once more and I asked, 'Was he in the plot? Was he at Coffin's Mill that night?'

He shook his head now, his chin down on his chest, but I pressed him. 'One last thing and I'll leave you in peace. Have Captains Lopez and Furlong any part of this?'

'Be damned, no,' he got out. 'They'd neither have the guts. They knew of Captain Blackbird and knew his livery button when they saw it but had more sense than to tell tales. I could outsail and outshoot them any day or anywhere.'

There was no time for more. The smoke was coming thicker yet, and I could hear the pumps clanking faster with Dr McGrath's voice shouting orders. Saying only, 'The best you can hope for is to die aboard your own ship,' I turned to the drawers of the table.

It was all here, as I knew it must be. A pistol by Simeon North of Middleton, and the fellow to that one I had taken from the mulatto. All the legal proofs of the wench's identity, together with a signet ring and locket, and a paper covered with copies of her signature; a letter of credit on Coutt's Bank made out in her name to the Banco di San Giorgio in Genoa. And another of the same in the sum of forty thousand to the order of the Reverend Matthew Peregrine, Lord Falconhurst, issued in favour of Tristram Peregrine Esq. So even that poor deluded parson had tried to buy the villains off, most likely the night Tristram had called upon him.

I made an observation which might have astonished even Master Maggsy, and was stowing these documents away when the physician returned; smoke grimed, bloodshot, his shabby coat made even worse by singeing and in looks yet more lowering than ever I'd seen him before. 'Well, sir,' I enquired, 'are you letting it burn?'

'It's more smoke than fire the noo. We've dowsed the powder with water. Aye. Ye'll permit me to obsairve that you'd do well to skelp that little keelie of yours.'

'Save that without him we might all be lying in the slave hold by now,' I said.

He did not answer but turned to examine Mr Colville and the woman. Neither took him long and when he had done I asked, 'Will they live?'

'The woman's well enough. I wouldna say the same for him. But I'll not patch a man up for the hangsman.' Nor did I answer that for I was of two minds myself, and he fell to another of his fits of rumphs and coughs before asking, 'Were you telling me that Miss Lydia's intended husband's come from America to take her back with him?'

'That's right,' I agreed with some malice. 'A fine gentleman. All the money in the world and the manner to go with it.'

'Aye,' he mused. 'Ah well, I should've known better.' He looked down at his cracked boots. 'I'd best get back to my work in Wapping. As ye say, Mr Sturrock, a fine young gentleman. He's just come aboard.'

'Has he, by God?' I demanded. 'And are we abeam of Bow Creek?'

'Ye're over fond of riddles, my man,' the physician replied. 'Will ye present my kindest compliments to Miss Lydia? I'll be away to make myself useful about the ship.'

'God's sake, man,' I told him, 'come down out of your love in a dignity. D'you want that wench or not?' He turned the colour of a nice cut of prime beef, and I continued, 'Well then, I'm not the man to see another rush upon his doom but I'll do my best for you. I want a word or two with Mr Ryde myself.'

I hastened to the poop deck with the poor fond fellow after me. Through the smoke there was a fine bustle below, men about the pumps, others at bucket chains, and a crowd of boats lying by on the river though keeping a cautious distance yet. There was little danger of our rogues escaping now; some would hang, no doubt, and more would be pressed from the convict hulks to the Navy when the war started again but they were safe enough presently.

It was quieter aft, where Captain Isaac stood with a pistol apiece on Tuke and the helmsman, running his eye over the ship and bellowing an order now and again for the pleasure of it. Likewise, as you might expect, Master Maggsy close by him, arms akimbo and fancying himself also a sea captain. But I had eyes most for Miss Lydia and Mr Ryde by the rail, noting that there seemed little intended about them; for with fresh colour in her cheeks, her hair blowing and eyes sparkling the wench was plainly telling him where he could take himself to. And by the look of her a place warmer even than this ship. The physician stopped, gazing dumbstruck on his goddess, but I said, 'Well now, Mr Ryde?'

If the fellow was dismayed to see me he gave no sign; I fancy even that he took me for a fool. 'By God,' he cried, 'so you're here, are you? I'll have a settlement now, you damned English rogue.'

'A settlement indeed,' I promised. 'But tell me first, did you go to Hanover Square? And who did you see there?'

'Why, be hanged,' he retorted hotly, 'some Lady Dorothea Dashwood, as you told me.'

'So she's returned from the country,' I mused. Miss Lydia seemed puzzled and the physician drew closer while I asked, 'A sharpish little grey lady?'

'Something like that,' he replied. 'I'd no time to study her. I came as fast as I could hire a fresh carriage.'

'And very proper,' I observed. 'Yet what foxes me is how you knew where to come. The name of the ship was never mentioned at Hanover Square.' That was one shot across his bows for a beginning, and I continued, 'But Bow Creek was spoken of; at Coffin's Mill last night. Mr Tristram Peregrine or Captain Blackbird then told some other person at present unknown that he'd heave to here to take him aboard. And I don't see anybody else but you, Mr Ryde.'

'Mr Sturrock,' the wench announced, 'I demand to know what this is.'

'All in good time, ma'am,' I told her. 'I understand the gentleman's your intended husband? Or so he told me. And I might have believed it save he added that you'd sailed away without a word to him. It wasn't the act of a dutiful and loving wife to be.'

The fellow was game enough, though casting his eyes over the ship and clearly wondering what was afoot. 'What the devil...?' he started but Miss Lydia interjected, 'You take too much upon yourself, Cousin Milton.'

'He does ma'am,' I agreed. 'He took it on himself this morning to shoot another rogue with whom I was engaged. Not to save me, Mr Ryde,' I said, 'but to stop Jabez Coffin turning King's Evidence if I'd have had the best of him. As I fancy you'd have shot me first had not my clerk been there and you saw little chance of silencing that monster.'

Before either he or Miss Lydia could say much to this Captain Isaac hailed, 'Two cutters closing on our bows, Jer'my; port and starboard. Six men in each and navals by the look of 'em.'

'Very good, Captain Isaac,' I replied, watching my man; but he was safe enough and the physician was closing up to him, a fresh dourness on his face. I told the whole tale; the gentleman with Consuela Smith at The Prospect of Whitby, what Maggsy had overheard at Coffin's Mill, and Mr Ryde's haste to reach London. It was all plain enough, and I concluded, 'So there you have him, ma'am. The chief and main instigator of the plot; aided and informed of all your actions by Consuela. And I fancy that when it was hatched this ship, the *Hester Ryde*, was already in Charleston and he sailed across in her. As I fancy also that they meant to put you aboard Peregrine's second vessel, the *Mary Carson*, to be taken to Algiers.'

'Why yes,' she answered, as if that were of little interest. She seemed to study the unhappy man curiously for a minute and at last asked, 'What will happen to him?'

'He'll hang,' I answered.

'God's sake, Lydia,' he cried, 'you'll not believe this tarradiddle? You'll give me leave to tell my side of it?'

'Be quiet, sir,' she ordered him, and continued to me, 'I do not wish it. Dr Ian,' she said, 'dear Ian, do me one more kindness. Be so good as to fling him overboard.'

And, be damned, before I could prevent the doting fool that is what he did; grinning like a jackass and even obstructing me as I rushed to the rail to stop this fearful miscarriage of justice. Not even Bow Street can stand before a wilful woman.

There is little more to add. Within the hour we were berthed in the Royal Naval Dockyard and our prisoners safely under hatches. Within an hour or so more, after our long recital of explanations and reports in the commander's office, we were returned to Limehouse and our carriages in a naval cutter; chiefly by the exercise of Miss Lydia's blue eyes and red hair, on that same grizzled old commander. He confided to me that he thought it best to get her out of the way quick for the sake of discipline and the younger officers; and he was no bad judge.

Nor did Mr Ryde escape justice for long, as he was taken at last when Mr Colville's second ship the *Mary Carson* was captured some few weeks later while still waiting for him off the Niger Coast; but before that I, and even Master Maggsy, were bidden to a wedding from Hanover Square. Dr McGrath, as I understand, now enjoys a thriving practice in Philadelphia and a thriving family; though what the poor man's end will be with that wild creature only God knows. Yet I shall not judge her too harshly for in the end she showed a nice appreciation; on the very day they sailed from England there came a special messenger bringing a package containing for me a banker's draft for five hundred guineas and for Master Maggsy—would you believe it?—a gold watch, the which he is never tired of flourishing to explain how he solved a confused mystery. So Providence rewards the upright; but He had done better to present that little monster with a bundle of kindling wood.